More Books by Marie-Nicole Ryan

THREATENED

Hill Country Lawmen, 2

Marie-Nicole Ryan

RYANDALE PUBLISHING

Copyright © 2019 by Mary Varble
Cover by Mary Varble
First Ryandale Print Publication: 2019

All rights reserved, Ryandale Publishing.

Library of Congress registration pending

Dedication

To my mother for a lifetime of love and joy.

Chapter One

Wednesday

"Ranger Rasmussen calling for Sheriff Tate." Ben waited, his fingers drumming the oak desktop.

"Sorry, Ranger. The Sheriff's in a town council meeting right now. Can Chief Deputy Rasmussen help?" Ben smiled at the dispatcher's formality. Must be new. The deputy was his younger brother Will. His smile deepened. "He'll do."

Will picked up, his cheerful tone in Ben's ear. "Hey, big bro. What's going on?"

He took a deep breath. Might as well just come right out with it. "The Houston Makarov gang is making serious inroads into the Hill Country."

His brother let out a ragged breath. "Shit. Not those fuckers, again."

Bad history there. One of the mom's enforcers had murdered his brother's girlfriend last year. "Yeah. Looks like protection rackets—to start with. Given there's going to be a casino opening in Los Marcos County in the near future, I need to shut the mob down before they get entrenched in the Valley *and* the Hill Country. Have Vince call me. I'll be in town all day tomorrow talking to business owners. I want Mayor Briggs and the town council involved before we're knee-deep in rattlers."

Where you had protection rackets, drugs, vice, and human trafficking followed. Plus, there'd been increasing chatter about *Los Malos Dias* drug cartel increasing their presence in the region. The last thing the Texas Hill Country needed was a mob war between the Russians and a drug cartel.

"You got it. Say, you gonna see the folks while you're in town?"

"Hell, yes. I've been craving some of mom's fried chicken." He chuckled. "Don't worry. I already gave her a call."

"Good deal. I happen to know she misses her favorite son."

Smiling, Ben let the good-natured jibe pass. Everybody in Kenton Valley knew Will was the baby of the family. And their mom's favorite, even though she hotly denied it whenever anyone brought up the subject. "See you then." He paused, "But—"

"Don't worry. I won't forget to give Vince your message."

His little brother could just about read his mind. "Yeah. Yeah."

Still, keeping the Valley clean of the mob and a drug cartel would be no easy task. It would take every resource the sheriff, town council, and the business owners could muster.

And courage. Live and let live didn't work with gangs like the Makarovs. As for Los Malos Dias cartel. Better to chop off the head of the snake before it could strike. And that snake went by the name of Reynaldo Reyes.

Beth adjusted the can of green peas so the label faced outward. Setting her hands on her hips, she surveyed the shelf and nodded. Everything just the way she liked it. Neat and orderly.

"Nice store you have here."

Startled, Beth spun around. "Sorry, I didn't hear you

come in." A new face. *Nice.* "How may I help you?"

The handsome stranger reached inside his coat pocket and produced a business card. *Matthew Freeman, District Vice-President, Helmsman Security. Your protection is our business. Our only business.*

She ran her thumb over the surface. Embossed. Expensive. "I haven't seen you in here before. Am I right?"

"Just call me Matt. Yes and no." His smug smile ruined the initial favorable impression.

"My business is new—in Kenton Valley, anyway—but I've been in the Mercantile before. A dark-haired woman waited on me. She mentioned I was just in time for lunch. Very nice Bistro, by the way."

"Thank you," Beth said with a curt nod. "That was my sister, Lola. We're the co-owners." She glanced around the store she'd worked so hard to make quaint as well as appealing to modern customers.

"Ever consider installing a more up-to-date security system?" His ever so slightly elevated brows indicated his disdain for her current arrangement.

"Really?" Very few merchants in the Valley bothered with fancy security systems. "The one we have has always been sufficient." Okay, so her system consisted of an old-fashioned bell over the door and fake cameras. He didn't need to know that.

"But will it meet your future needs?" His voice deepened; his dark eyes boring into hers. "Seems to me Kenton Valley is ripe for change."

Beth frowned. "You almost make that sound like a threat." Jerking her gaze from his, she brushed an infinitesimal speck of dust from the counter. "The Valley is fine the way it is. And so is my security system." True, she hadn't heard the bell when he'd entered, but she'd been distracted—right?

"Keep the card." Except for the barest trace of a Spanish accent, his voice reminded her of a TV newscaster's. "You never know when you might change your mind."

She set her hands on her hips and glared. "Now that *really* sounds like a threat."

"I didn't mean—" He held up his hands in a gesture of surrender. "We've gotten off on the wrong foot. Let me try again. Have dinner with me tonight. I'm sure there's somewhere in the Valley where even a newcomer like me can share a steak dinner and a bottle of wine with a potential client."

"There is. But—"

"Come on... give me another chance. I'm trying to find my feet here, so to speak."

His have-pity-on-a-stranger-in-town attitude—way more appealing than his self-satisfied security salesman pitch. What did she have to lose? Besides tall, dark, *and* handsome. What more was there to say? And the accent was sort of sexy.

"All right," she sighed. "Steak and Texas go together like white on rice. I suggest the country club. Best wine cellar in town."

His broad shoulders shrugged. "I haven't been here long enough to join."

"No problem. Make the reservation in my name." She hesitated. She'd been about to say, 'Pick me up at eight. I live over the store and use the rear entrance.' But what did she know about this man? Not a damned thing. "I'll meet you there at eight."

He flashed a smile. "It's a date then."

"Yes, it is." What the hell? Pickings were slim when it came to eligible men. Ben Rasmussen wasn't going to take up residence anytime soon. No, he was occupied with Ranger duties in Waco. Truth be told, she'd rather be having a nice dinner with him.

His purposeful stride from the store didn't help to calm her nerves. Hadn't mama always said, "A stranger is just a friend you haven't met yet"? Yes, she had. And mama was usually right, but the Valley was changing. Her daddy frequently added, "a little caution goes a long way." She missed having her folks nearby, but they were living their dream retirement fantasy in RV land.

Yet, there was something to be said for giving someone the benefit of a doubt. Besides, what harm could come to her at dinner, surrounded by the Valley's elite?

Walking to the front of the store, she watched him enter the hardware store next door. What was he up to? Drumming up more business?

"What on earth are you doing?" Lola elbowed Beth, interrupting her spying.

"Ouch." She rubbed her rib. "Just checking where that fine piece of manhood is headed."

"No. You made a date with that guy. You don't know a single thing about him."

"Honestly, there isn't a man in this town I don't know *something* about. Either I went to school with him and know him all too well, or he's married to someone I know. In case you haven't noticed, there's a dire shortage of available men in the Valley."

"Believe me, I've noticed." Lola's gaze traveled in the opposite direction toward the sheriff's office.

"Besides, I'm meeting him at the country club. Nothing—and I mean nothing's—going to happen there." Beth slipped her arm around her sister's waist. "Don't pull that hangdog expression on me. I know you're still pining over Will. Give him time to heal."

"It's already been a year." Lola gave a sniff. "I never know quite what to say. Whenever he's in the store or the

Bistro, I can tell from his expression he doesn't see me as anything more than a friend."

Beth sighed and squeezed her sister tighter. "Just our fate: the Wheaton sisters and the Rasmussen men. On one side, we have Deputy Will, pining over a dead girlfriend, and on the other Ranger Ben, definitely *not* pining over his ex and totally uninterested in dating another blonde, or so the rumor mill says." She fluffed her light unruly locks. "Maybe I should try dying my hair dark."

"No way." Lola reached over and tousled Beth's hair. "Go ahead. Have your date with the handsome stranger. And while you're gazing into his eyes and playing footsies under the table, ask if he has a *brother*."

"I can certainly do that for my baby sis." She returned the favor, but Lola's sleek dark bob was impossibly resistant to tousling.

Glancing at her watch, Lola scurried away. "Time to open the Bistro," she said over her shoulder.

Time to get ready for her date and panic had set in. Hands trembling, Beth yanked her hair back in a ponytail and let out a groan. "I really ought to have this mess straightened."

"You'll be sorry," Lola said from the doorway. "I'd give anything to have your hair. Besides, the way you've let it grow out, it's more wavy than curly."

"Agh!" She yanked the scrunchy from her hair and tossed it.

Lola bent over to pick up the red scrunchy.

"Don't bother. I'll get it later."

In the mirror, Beth caught Lola's disdainful gaze. "What *are* you wearing tonight?"

"My usual version of understated elegance? Black slacks. White silk blouse."

"Boring." Lola wrinkled her nose. "Don't you think that little black dress you bought in San Antonio would be better?"

"No. I don't want him to think I'm trying too hard." Beth sighed. "I don't know why I agreed to meet him in the first place."

"Frankly, I don't, either." Lola walked over to the ornate walnut jewelry box atop the low boy chest. "Jewelry?"

"The gold chain I always wear, and the gold hoops mom gave me for graduation."

"Simple, but nice. Not too much. Now for your hair. Let me see." Lola rooted around in Beth's jewelry organizer and produced two gold combs. "Slick your hair back from your face with these, and let the rest of it do what it always does."

Beth snorted. "No one will ever mistake me for Zoe Briggs Rasmussen Vayden, that's for sure," she said, referring to Ben's ex who seemed to find it necessary to wear every piece of jewelry she owned at the same time. Beth stood back from the mirror and shook her head. "You know I'm tempted to call and cancel." She nodded. "Yes, that's what I'll do."

Her sister's eyebrow rose. "After he made reservations in your name at the club? That's just tacky."

"Crap. You're right." She faced Lola. "Okay. Here's what we'll do. I'm meeting him at eight, so call me at twenty after and tell me there's a problem with the store. I should know by then if I want to stay for the entree. Deal?"

"Deal."

Finally dressed and perfumed—just a spritz mind you—

Beth strode to the front entrance of the Kenton Valley Country Club, familiarly known as the KVCC. She hesitated, then squared her shoulders. It was dinner. Nothing more. Nothing less. Dinner she could do.

Matt waited near the reception desk. "You look great."

Hm. Nice manners. "Thank you." She nodded to the maître d' and smiled. "Good evening, Dominic."

"Good evening Ms. Wheaton. Your table is ready. It's on the terrace overlooking the rose garden. I hope you and your guest have a lovely meal. James will be your server tonight."

"I'm sure we will. And thank you."

"You are definitely known here," Matt said.

"Mom and dad belonged. My sister and I have been coming here since we were kids."

"And your parents, are they still living?"

"Yes, they retired south of Houston and live in what I call RV land." Actually, her parents lived in an upscale gated community, but they frequently took the RV on the road for long trips.

Before she could give the server her wine order, her phone rang." Dang it. Lola wasn't supposed to call this early. "Sorry, I have to take this." She rose, walked away from the table, then answered, "Too soon. I haven't decided yet."

"No," Lola said. "You need to come to the store *now*. There's been a break-in."

"Very funny. Thanks. I'll be sure to *rush* right over."

"No really. I've already called the Sheriff's Department."

"Okay..." What was Lola going for? An Oscar? "So, you're *not* kidding. It's not funny—"

"*Seriously.* Get over here *now*."

The intensity of Lola's panic flooded through the phone. She wasn't kidding. The phone trembled in Beth's hand as she returned to the table. "I'm sorry. I have to go.

There's been a break-in at my store."

Matt stood. "I'll settle the bill and go with you."

She shook her head. "No, go ahead and have dinner. They can put it on my account."

"No." He stood. "I'm coming with you."

"Fine." Even as she said the words, her distrust of this man returned, stomping around in her brain.

Today, he came to my store, warning me I might need his services, and tonight my store's broken into. Coincidence. Maybe not.

"On second thought," she said. "We came in separate cars, I'll take mine, and if you still want to come, you should drive your own vehicle."

Heart racing, Beth sped to the Mercantile and parked. The street in front of her store was cordoned off by three Sheriff's Department vehicles. She jumped from the Maxima and ran to the nearest deputy. "What happened, Will? Is Lola all right."

"Your sister's fine, just a little shook up."

Shards of glass, remnants from the front store windows, crunched beneath her shoes. Bastards! "May I go in and see what other damage they did?"

"Sure." He raised the crime scene tape, and she ducked under it. "Just kid stuff. They made a heck of a mess. Watch your step though."

"What about our apartment upstairs? Did they break in there?"

"No. I think your sister surprised them."

"Where is she?"

"She's upstairs. Deputy Longworth is taking her statement."

"Good."

Gingerly, she entered the store, Will on her heels. What a mess. A quick scan showed cans and other goods had been knocked off the shelves, kicked hither and yon. "Pretty gutsy to this do right after closing. Did anyone catch a glimpse of who broke in?"

"A gang of four or five. Males. That's the best description Lola could come up with."

"The Valley doesn't have gangs. I don't understand." Or maybe she did. "My store cameras are fake, but what about the other stores along the street? What about the pharmacy? I'm pretty sure Abbie installed real cameras after the trouble last year." Other than the drug store, most of the stores probably had fake cameras like hers. A lot of good they would do.

Will's brows drew together. "*That's* on my list to check. I'll get in touch with the other owners as soon as I get back to the office."

"Sorry. Didn't mean to tell you your job." She turned around and sighed. "What a mess. I'll have to call Bob at the hardware store. I need to board up these windows with plywood."

Someone called her name. She spun around.

Matt stood on the far side of the crime scene tape. She'd forgotten all about him. Sort of. "Excuse me. I need to speak to someone. We were on—well, a date."

"Go ahead." Will nodded. "But he needs to stay on the other side of the tape."

"Sure thing, Deputy." She gave him a saucy salute which resulted in one of Will's rare smiles.

Beth picked her way through the broken glass, went outside, and joined Matt. "I'm sorry. You might as well go on home. I'll be here for quite a while with the deputy. All in all, it's a major mess. Except for the front windows, it's pretty minor."

"That's a relief. And your sister is okay?"

How thoughtful. "She's fine. Thanks for asking."

"I feel so bad." He sounded sincere. "Honestly, when I approached you earlier, I never expected anything like this. It's clear proof the area is changing. More rapidly than you might like."

And that should suit his business model just fine.

Up in the apartment she shared with her sister, Beth found Lola and Deputy Longworth sitting in the living room. The deputy scribbled notes on a pad while Lola pressed an icepack to her right cheek.

Beth's heart rate spiked. She rushed to her sister's side. "What happened? Will told me you were all right."

"I *am* all right. I did this to myself." She made a face.

"Tell me—" She stopped short when the tall blonde deputy stopped writing and raised a single brow. "Sorry, Darby, I didn't mean to interrupt." Deputy Longworth was one of only two female deputies in Los Marcos County, as well as a friend from school.

Darby smiled. "That's all right." She closed the notepad. "We're through. Mainly, this is the hand-holding and reassurance phase of the interview."

Beth nodded, redirecting her attention to her sister. "Okay, tell me everything—start to finish."

Lola set the icepack aside. "After you left, I came downstairs to double-check everything was locked up. I was afraid we'd forgotten something in the flurry of getting you ready for your first date in *over a year*."

Beth gave an eye roll. "Really, do you have to tell everyone about the sad state of my love life."

Darby gave a quick bark of laughter. "Don't worry about me. I know too well this town is decidedly short on available men."

"Did you see them—the gang?"

"I was on my way down from the apartment when I heard a noise—actually, a *lot* of noise. The back door was open, and I saw one of them acting as the lookout. He was wearing a black ski mask. He saw me and started up the steps, so I turned around and ran back upstairs. That's when I missed my footing and bumped into the open door. I managed to get inside and lock it. Then I called 911. The gang wasn't inside more'n three or four minutes."

"Long enough to make a hell of a mess."

"What about damage in the Bistro?" The café was her sister's pride and joy. She shook her head.

"I didn't notice any damage. I guess they didn't take time."

"Thank heavens for small favors." Lola picked up the ice pack, shook her head, then set the ice pack aside.

After Beth retrieved her phone, she called Bob Cherry at home. He agreed to come right over and board up the front windows. "You're the third business vandals have hit in the last two weeks."

"What?"

"The Tidy-Kleen on Oak got broken into earlier this week. And a week before that, the Sleepytime Motel just off the Interstate."

"Actually, I'd heard about the cleaners, something about clothes strewn all over the place."

"That's right. *And* they removed all the tickets from the clothes waiting to be picked up. Owners had a heck of a time figuring out what belonged to who. And before the vandals left, they busted out the store window. Guess that was just for pure damn meanness 'cause Sheriff Tate said they broke in from the back of the store."

"What about the motel? Isn't someone always on duty?"

"Yeah, scared the life out of the clerk. Barricaded him in a closet and took the money from the register and the reservations computer. Anyway, guess I'd better quit jawing and get busy."

"Appreciate it, Bob." And she did. More than that, she appreciated the way everyone cooperated in the Valley. It was a fact she'd always counted on. And losing the comfortable hometown feel wasn't a good thing in her book.

After hanging up, Beth turned to the deputy. "Do you think we'll be safe here tonight, Darby?"

"Lock your doors. I'm guessing you have a weapon or two handy?"

"You'd be right." Jerry Wheaton had taught both his girls how to handle a weapon. Even now, she and Lola met once a week at the shooting range. Lola was the better shot of the two, but Beth was still a damn fine shot.

"You should be all right then. You'd have a strategic advantage over anyone trying to come up the back stairs." Darby leaned forward and lowered her voice. "One thing you might want to do, get some *real* cameras for the store, and a couple in the back alley wouldn't hurt."

"That's on my to-do list for tomorrow." Now would she call one Matthew Freeman or not? Maybe she would. What better way to keep an eye on the new man in town? "Are they through downstairs? I need to get a start on clearing up the damage."

"I'll check. If they're through, we'll leave a deputy out front until you get those windows boarded up."

"Thanks, Darby."

The deputy rose from the sofa. "I have to get back and write this up, but I'll tell them to let you know when you can get to work."

Feeling considerably less than her five-feet, four-inches tall, Beth watched Darby leave and sighed. If a woman who looked more like a supermodel than a deputy sheriff had trouble finding a date, what hope was there for the Wheaton gals?

Chapter Two

Thursday

The next day Ben drove into his old hometown, noting the changes since his last visit. He shook his head. Kenton Valley was already showing signs of rapid growth. A new retirement community of condos going up. An industrial park on the approach to town. Construction had already begun on the new casino. Several large bulldozers and backhoes were hard at work moving earth. And one damn big sign: Briggs Construction—hmph, should've known his ex-father-in-law would have a hand in any project that would make him richer than he already was.

As much as the town needed new business to survive, he hated the negative influences that progress often brought with it.

He drove to the city office park, adjacent to the courthouse, parked, and entered the two-year-old structure.

Striding to the Sheriff's Department located on the first floor, he nodded to the receptionist. An attractive blonde. Right. Easy to see why she was hired. "Ranger Rasmussen to see Sheriff Tate."

The blonde smiled prettily. "He's expecting you. Go right in. Down the hall—"

"Thanks. I know the way." He strode to Vince Tate's office door and knocked.

"Come on in."

Vince rose and extended his hand. "Good timing. Town Council is all excited about the new casino."

"And you're not."

"Hell, no, I'm not." Tate sat and leaned back. "Crime is up. We've already had three attacks on local businesses. From the one witness statement, they're only in the business four minutes or less. Very organized. Efficient. And they create a nuisance. They enter from the rear but break out the front windows before they leave. According to the motel clerk, they worked with military precision. Four young males. Armed. Never spoke a word."

"Hm." Taking a seat, Ben rubbed his chin. "Knew about the first two break-ins. Heard about last night's right before I left Waco. That kind of precision doesn't sound like teenage gang activity."

Vince nodded. "Not to me, either. Now, the Mercantile received the most damage. Store was closed. No one hurt. But it's a trend, and I don't cotton to those kinds of trends."

"I agree. Here's what I want to do. Call a meeting. All the business owners, the town council, merchants' association, what have you. We've got to work together. I've seen this before. First minor stuff. Then attacks escalate. Next thing you know, someone is telling owners they have to pay for protection."

"A protection racket? That's what you think we're looking at here in the Valley."

"Yep."

"Houston mob?"

"Or Los Malos Dias."

"The cartel?" Vince frowned. "We've never had much of a drug problem around here. Some weed. A little meth once in a while."

"Opioids. That's Los Malos Dias's specialty. Heroin, too."

"Are you sure?" Vince shook his head. "We can't afford to let that crap get a foothold in Kenton Valley."

"What do you think having a casino is going to bring

with it? On the way into town, I saw where they've already cleared land and started construction. A year from now, you won't recognize this town."

Tate's face reddened; he averted his gaze.

Might as well go for the jugular. "Why on earth did your wife donate that parcel of land to the Bureau of Indian Affairs?"

Vince bristled but then took a deep breath. "Abby thought she was doing something good for the tribe who used to live around here. Believe me, I did my best to talk her out of it."

"She could've donated that land to anyone. Or just held on to it."

"What she wanted was to right a wrong. She didn't want the land. It was a daily reminder of her father's mistake, one that, however indirectly, ended the life of an innocent young woman."

Ben shook his head. "What's done is done." He stood. "Call that meeting. Let me know when you set the time. I'll be out at my folk's place tonight. Right now, I'm headed over to the Mercantile to talk to the Wheatons."

"Will do."

Walking back to his pickup, he regretted challenging the sheriff so directly. Vince Tate was an old friend. So was Abby. To Ben's way of thinking, she'd screwed up. Or to put it another, maybe kinder, way: no good deed goes unpunished.

From the moment Ben walked into the Mercantile, he spotted Beth Wheaton, her nicely-rounded butt in the air. He smiled, appreciating the heat that sizzled up his spine. He leaned against the counter and narrowed his gaze as she bent up and down, picking up cans of corn and tomatoes, replacing them on the store shelves.

Stop it. You're here to do a job, not admire the scenery. Very nice scenery it is too.

"Ahem." He cleared his throat to catch her attention.

She straightened. On turning, her cheeks flushed a pretty pink. A riot of blond waves tumbled about her shoulders. Beth wasn't one of those bottle-dyed blondes, like his ex, Zoe. Instead, natural highlights streaked her tresses in deep golden tones of honey. His hands fisted as he fought back the urge to bury his fingers deep. He took a deep breath and banished the image of those silken strands spread across his pillow.

"Well, Ranger..." She set her hands on her curvy hips. "Do you have a reason for being here? Or did your pony run out of oats."

Snarky, too. He smiled.

"I was stunned by..." What in hell had he meant to say? "...the damage. Impressive."

"Yes. In the few minutes they were here, they managed to make a real mess."

"Efficient. Organized."

"Pfft." She gave an eye roll. "I don't know about that."

"Um," he hesitated, remaining off-kilter. "More nuisance than true damage, except for your front windows." He nodded toward the sheets of plywood. With the front of the store boarded up, the interior was dark, even with lighting. "How long before you can get 'em replaced?"

She gestured with her thumb. "Let's go back to the office. I'm ready for a break."

He followed, admiring the gentle sway of her hips as she strode through the store. His mouth dried. He swallowed.

In the small office, papers were stacked in precise piles upon a heavy oaken desk or on shelves that appeared a century, or more, old. His gaze swept the tidy room. *Nice place.* On one wall, a bulletin board contained notices and sales receipts arranged in an orderly fashion. His attention settled back on Beth, now sitting behind her desk. She gave him a tight smile. "I've called a glazier in Austin. With the double glazing, it'll take them a couple of weeks to fabricate."

He eased into the closest chair and sat. *Wouldn't mind having all day to while away, right here.* "I understand you don't have an alarm system or cameras." He stretched out his legs and relaxed back into the soft leather chair.

She shot him an impatient frown. "Never saw the need till now. But I will have soon. I've already contacted someone."

The shape of her lips. Lush. Kissable.

Focus.

"Good answer," he drawled.

"In the meantime," she continued, "Will said he would check on camera footage from surrounding stores."

Getting way too comfortable in her presence and the coziness of her office, he squared his shoulders and straightened. "No use. The culprits entered from the rear, and none of the other businesses had the foresight to place cameras in the alley. That might change."

"That's definitely going to change," she said with an emphatic nod. "I plan on having a couple set up back there since that's where Lola and I park and enter our apartment. We'll both feel safer with additional security."

"I'm sure you will."

Keep on track. Damn good thing Beth was so straightforward and business-like. That way he could keep his mind on the job instead of her.

A shuffling sound over his shoulder drew his attention. Lola entered the office carrying a broom and a long-handled dustpan.

"Oh," she said, startled. "I didn't realize you were in here." Tall, slender, and as tan as a California beach babe, her blue eyes lit up a room when she smiled. Beth, on the other hand, was shorter. And when she stood, the top of her pretty head barely reached his shoulder. His gaze returned to the older of the two, noting again Beth's rounded curves and big brown eyes the color of milk chocolate.

"I'm headed over to the Bistro," Lola said, setting aside the cleaning implements. "Coffee anyone?"

He glanced back, startled. "What?"

"Coffee?"

Jeez. He'd already forgotten she was there. His cheeks grew warm. "That would be good. Black. Thanks."

"Make it two, sis," Beth said.

"On it." With a wink, Lola left the room.

Clearing his throat, Ben said, "I came by to let you know Sheriff Tate will be calling a meeting for all the business owners. You and Lola really ought to attend. The town will have to band together to fight what's coming."

"*What* do you think is coming?" Her expression grew worried. "Surely last night was a one-off kind of thing."

"No way. Crime. Drugs. The cartel. The Mob. That damn casino will attract 'em all."

She took a deep breath, her breasts rising and falling. "I was afraid you were going to say something like that."

"We have to stop it before it starts." *Get out of here before you make a fool of yourself.* "The Texas Rangers will support all your efforts." He stood, ready to make his getaway.

"You're making this sound like an invasion."

"It is."

Beth combed her fingers through her curls, then leaned back and heaved a sigh. "Mom and dad were right to retire.

Sometimes, I wish I could."

"You can't give up. This town wouldn't be the same without you...and Lola."

"We'll definitely be at the meeting," she said with a brisk nod.

Lora entered and set two steaming cups of hot coffee on the desk. "Here you go."

Ben nodded his thanks and grabbed the cup. "I've—uh, got to move on and talk to the others who've already been hit. I'll be talking to everyone when Sheriff Tate gets the town together."

Steeling his nerve, he strode from her office. No good could come from getting involved with another blonde—not even a smart, sexy, snarky one like Beth Wheaton.

Beth waited until she heard the front door close, then let out a sigh. Was she mistaken or had she detected a note of warmth from the usually taciturn Ranger? Damn her blond curls. No. Damn Zoe Briggs for breaking his heart, in the first place. His turning up was so unexpected. At first sight, of him, her throat had closed. Her mouth dried. Her face blazed. The image of him lingered. Tall. Long legs encased in crisp jeans. Slim hips and wide shoulders. The rest of him wasn't bad either. Piercing blue eyes bore into her soul and a thick head of chestnut-colored hair topped off a handsome face, marred only by his usual stern expression. Now, they could make some beautiful babies.

Stop it.

"Oh no. He's gone, the man of your dreams." Lola's teasing brought Beth back to reality.

"Taking up mind reading, are you?" she scoffed. "Besides, you're more his type than I am." She lifted her lip in a sneer.

"As if." Her sister let out a burst of throaty laughter. "Honey, he only looked at me long enough to nod thanks for the cup of coffee I brought him. He couldn't take his *eyes* off you."

"Don't be silly. We were discussing all the crime he thinks the casino is going to bring. It was a serious conversation, so of course, we had eye contact." Beth clenched her fists to keep them from shaking. She scanned the desk. That stack of papers could be neater. She rearranged them, once more. "I'm definitely calling Matt Freeman to install a security system. Up-to-date, high-res cameras, the whole nine yards."

"Having two men after you isn't fair."

"Hah," Beth scoffed. "Don't act like you're interested in either of them. Besides, Ben Rasmussen doesn't know I'm alive." In spite of her casual words, deep inside, a glimmer of hope flickered that someday soon, Ben would get over his heartbreak and appreciate the woman before him.

As for Matt Freeman, she could care less. No comparison.

"You're right about one thing. I could care less about either one of them, but you are so wrong about Ben's not knowing you're alive." Lola plopped into the chair the ranger had just vacated, then leaned forward. "So, what about our apartment? Are we going to get an alarm for that too?"

Beth twisted around to the file cabinet behind her and began rummaging through the folders. "I'll see what Matt recommends, but I think door and window alarms should be sufficient for the apartment. Plus, the two cameras in the alley."

"Hmm, this is really starting to sound expensive. Don't forget about those front windows. An arm and a leg come to mind."

"I know," Beth said with a quick nod. "I'm pretty sure our insurance will cover most of the cost of replacing the windows." She pulled the insurance folder from the file drawer. Scanning the policy, she jammed her finger at the third clause. "See. There it is. I was right. Vandalism is covered."

"You're right...as usual. Are we going to open today? The Bistro is untouched."

"I thought we'd open the Merc at eleven. I should have everything in order by then, and the Bistro can open at eleven-thirty as usual."

Lola popped up from her seat. "Then I'd better get busy. Sandwiches and salads don't magically make themselves, you know." She turned to leave.

Beth stared down at the insurance document with hope swelling inside her. Maybe she hadn't imagined the warmth in Ben's baby blues, after all. Even Lola had noticed. Was he getting over his aversion to blondes? Only time would tell.

Ben spent the rest of the morning talking to the other business owners on Main Street. As a group, they were evenly divided over the coming of the casino. Half of them were excited about the increase in business. The rest dreaded the negative results of increased crime.

Shortly after one, a hunger pang rumbled through him. Might as well grab lunch at the Bistro. He hadn't eaten since hoovering a sausage biscuit early that morning. Besides, he wouldn't mind running into Beth again.

Great. The Merc was open for business. Crossing the threshold, he stopped short. His hand tightened on the doorknob as his gaze narrowed on Beth and a tall stranger discussing the proper placement of cameras. Even worse, she smiled prettily and nodded as he talked. Too damn comfortable with the salesman or whoever the hell he was.

He walked over to the pair. "Sorry to interrupt." Not at all. "Ranger Ben Rasmussen," he said, offering his hand to the stranger.

"Matt Freeman." Freeman shook Matt's hand and shook it. "How may I help you?" he asked, with just a trace of an accent.

Mexican?

"What about a couple of hidden cameras? Thieves tend to spray paint cameras if they're obvious."

An expression of annoyance flickered across Freeman's face. "We were discussing that very topic."

Before I interrupted. "Good. You know what you're doing then. We don't want a repeat of last night's business."

Matt nodded. "We certainly don't." He smiled down at Beth.

"No, we don't," she replied with a smile that brought out her dimples.

Damn. Why was she awarding Freeman with her smiles? Who was he to her? Were they involved? A flash of fury hit his gut.

Freeman handed Ben a business card. "Helmsman Security," he said. "I've been contacted by several business owners since last night's event."

A few nuisance break-ins and his business takes off. The first thing he'd do after lunch would be to check out this asshole's record and business. Whether he didn't like the man because he was just too right-time, right-place, or if he really resented the free and easy way Beth acted around him, he wasn't sure.

Not sure? Hell, yes, he was. Jealous. And no right to be.

He gave Freeman his own card. "Excuse me. I'll grab

some lunch."

Nodding, he shoved open the door and strode into the Bistro. Most of the late lunch crowd had already left. Red-checked tablecloths along with fresh daisies in pots made the Bistro an inviting spot to chow down.

Lola stood behind the counter, smiling. "Hey, there Ranger. Nice to see you in my little café."

"Can a man get it real meal here, or is it all salads and green stuff?"

Lola chuckled, leaned forward, and assumed a conspiratorial expression. "Just for you, I'll rustle up a grilled ham and cheese."

"Easy on the cheese and heavy on the ham, and you'll have a customer for life."

"Will do. And how about a bowl of *healthy* vegetable soup?" Lola's blue eyes sparkled with mischief.

"Sounds great." He settled onto the red vinyl-covered stool, then glanced over his shoulder at Beth and the slick sonofabitch who blocked his view. At least one sister was glad to see him. Just the wrong sister.

A cup of coffee slid across the counter and he grabbed it, a lopsided smile kicking up his lips. His hand curled around the handle. Black, just like he liked it. Still, he couldn't keep his damn mouth shut. "How long have y'all known that Freeman dude?"

Lola glanced toward the store. "Him?" She wrung out a wet cloth and wiped the counter. "Beth met him yesterday. In fact, they had gone out to *dinner* when the break-in happened."

His gut twisted with rage. He gripped his coffee cup to keep from throwing it. He sucked in a deep breath. "She's dating that clown?" Dammit. He'd waited too long to ask her out. Living in Waco kept him out in left field when it came to Beth's social life.

She patted his forearm. "Don't worry, Ranger. It wasn't much of a date." She leaned her elbows on the counter and lowered her voice to a stage whisper. "They didn't even get to order their entrees." Why shouldn't she go out with someone since he'd made no prior claim? And why hadn't he made a claim? The knife in his heart twisted deeper.

Once burned, twice shy?

Yeah.

But Beth was different. Nothing like Zoe.

He bit into the grilled ham and cheese, then chewed and swallowed. The glob of food thickened in his throat as he heard Beth and Freeman enter the Bistro.

"We need to do the same in here," Beth said, "but on a smaller scale."

Freeman passed behind Ben. "Two cameras should be sufficient, as well as another panic button in case of any problems that might arise. The man stopped behind Ben's stool, then clapped him on the shoulder. "That suit you, Ranger Rasmussen?"

"Fine by me." Only by focusing on the buttered slabs of French bread he gripped could he avoid shrugging off Freeman's hand. Ben straightened, turning to look at Beth. "No. You need a third panic button for your office, easy to get to and unobtrusive. Gotta keep you safe, Beth."

The flush that crested her high cheekbones likely matched the one that heated his. His gaze slid to Freeman's hand still on his shoulder.

A moment later, the bastard dropped his hold and smiled.

And he'd better get out of here before I bury my fist in this asshole's smug face.

Freeman nodded. "Will do."

Ben polished off his soup and sandwich, wiped across his mouth with a napkin, then turned around and stood.

"Thanks, Lola. Great food."

"Come back anytime, Ben. You know Beth and I *always* enjoy your company," she added with a cheeky smile.

Beth was over in the far corner debating about the placement of the hidden cameras. Dammit. The woman was a mystery, and now she had this Freeman dude hanging onto her every word.

She placed her hand on Freeman's arm and said something too low for Ben to hear. Dammit. She was flirting with him. She was.

He swallowed the knot in his throat. "Ahem. Don't forget. Town meeting, Beth. It's important."

Her coffee-brown eyes were level with his and narrowed as she tipped her head sideways. "Of course, we'll be there."

"I'll let you know as soon as the sheriff sets a time and place." He gave an emphatic nod. He strode from the Bistro, ready to chew nails. If Beth would just give him a sign she saw him as more than a friend...

Women.

Peering over Matt's shoulder, Beth watched the hunky ranger stride away, his long legs taking him farther from her.

"Something the matter?" Matt asked.

"Oh—uh, not at all." She picked up a stack of papers and rearranged them, then set them back down. "Sorry. Since the break-in, I've had so much to deal with. I hope I can fit the sheriff's meeting into my schedule." *Oh, for Pete's sake, what drivel.* Could she sound anymore lame? Not likely.

"I'll place the order," Matt said, "as soon as I get back to the office. I'll order priority shipping and should have them tomorrow."

"And the alarms?"

"I can install them this evening if it's convenient."

Beth nodded. "Yes. That's much more convenient than a break-in. "I'll close the store early at seven. Any time after that work for you?"

"After seven will be fine." He gazed down at her. "You know, I still owe you a dinner."

She dismissed his offer with a shake of her head. "Time enough for that once we get the store alarmed and secured."

A flicker of displeasure darkened his eyes. "Of course. That has to be your priority." He closed his notebook. "I'll go back to the office and I'll see you at seven." His handsome face pulled into a slow smile. "Pleasure doing business with you, Ms. Wheaton."

Why the switch to formality? Had she offended him by refusing his dinner offer? "Beth," she said. "Just Beth."

"See you later, Beth."

She watched him leave and shrugged. "Oh, well..."

"So not the man of your dreams then," Lola said into Beth's ear.

She let out a huff. "I barely know him. It's true he's good looking, speaks well. Obviously well educated, but—" She lifted her shoulders in a shrug.

Lola filled in the blunt truth. "He's not Ben."

Beth looped her arm around her sister's shoulder. "Maybe... But I'm not the one for him. Vince told me that after Zoe took off with her Houston Astros ballplayer, Ben said he'd never get involved with another blonde."

"I don't think Ben sees you as a blonde, per se." Lola emitted an evil chuckle. "No, darlin', he sees *you* as the woman whose bones he'd really like to jump."

"Honestly, *you're* the one who needs to get laid and leave me the hell alone. Ben does *not* look at me that way."

"And you're blind as a bat."

"Pfft." As much as she wanted to believe her sister was right, she really couldn't. "I refuse to discuss this anymore. I need to get busy and place a call to our insurance company."

"Fine. I give up trying to talk sense to you. It's nearly two o'clock. Eva left an hour ago, so I'm going to close the Bistro. Is there anything else I need to do over in the Merc?"

"Yes. You could check the par levels in the storeroom and reorder anything we're short on. After that, would you run to the hardware store and pick up a new microwave. Those bastards broke the one in the snack area."

"Got it." Lola turned and started clearing the counter where Ben had eaten his sandwich.

Beth headed back to the office and sat. She couldn't help but compare the two men. Both handsome. Both intelligent. What was it that drew her thoughts primarily to Ben? She'd known him longer. In some ways, he was very much a known quantity. He'd always occupied a corner of her heart ever since he chased off an eighth-grade bully on her first day of middle school. Ben's roots grew deep in the Texas Hill Country. The Rasmussen family had lived here for over a century. Many of the Rasmussen men had served and protected the area residents for over a hundred years. There was deep satisfying comfort in knowing his history.

As for Matt, he was definitely an unknown quantity. She'd known him less than twenty-four hours. Why had she even accepted his dinner invitation in the first place? Was it her pathetically dull, boring life that made her crave a little excitement? Going to dinner with a stranger. Not something she'd ever done in her staid and ordered life. Given that their dinner date had been cut short, there'd been no chance for that oh-so-necessary kind of small talk where she could begin to find some answers. Matt Freeman was the opposite of comfortable.

But *comfortable*, as in Ben, hit all the right spots.

Her sister was wrong. Ben might not be the man of her dreams. But that didn't mean Matt was.

A loud buzzing shattered the quiet/stillness at the dispatcher's desk at the Sheriff's Department. The cop on duty swirled around to locate the source on his business locator board. His eyes widened, and he hollered over his shoulder. "Hey, Sheriff. The silent duress alarm from the pharmacy's going off."

Abby. Vince's heart nearly burst in his chest. His wife was due to deliver their son in another month. "On it." Heart racing, Vince grabbed his hat and sprang from his chair. "Longworth, with me. Dispatch, let the Chief Deputy know. Send backup. No sirens or lights."

He ran for the door with Longworth on his heels. The drug store was only four blocks away. "No siren. No lights. What's this town coming to?" He jumped into his vehicle. Squealing from the parking lot, he turned toward Main. He parked the Durango half a block away from the drug store.

"Let's do this." Hunkered down and weapons drawn, he and Longworth approached the rest of the way to the drug store on foot.

Upon reaching the drug store, Vince motioned for Darby to take the far exit. Carefully, he peeked through the front window.

Only lights showing were in the far reaches of the store. Movement. Two individuals. One had to be Abby. Only she could've entered the duress code. The other—bulky, tall male. Signaling the deputy, he held up two fingers, then pointed at the store interior.

Without warning, Longworth stripped off her gun belt and ripped off her uniform shirt leaving her wearing only a skimpy halter top. Tossing her belt and shirt aside, she started banging on the door. "Abby! Someone! Anyone! My baby's sick. I need you to fill his prescription. I can *see* you, Abby. *Please* help me."

What the hell! Darby was going to get his wife killed!

Chapter Three

After he'd talked with the majority of business owners on Main Street, Ben drove the ten miles from town to his family's small ranch, small by Texas standards, that is. When the sprawling log- framed house came into view, Ben smiled. The home where he'd grown up had begun its life as a sharecropper's cabin, but time and good fortune had allowed for add-ons until it reached its current state. Originally, his great-great-great-great-grandmother had taken in washing to support her family when her husband had taken off and gotten himself killed in Apache country. Influenced by her industry, her sons had worked hard and prospered, and one of them, Billy, had begun the family tradition of being lawmen.

He parked behind his father's Ford pickup and bounded up the steps to the front porch where his mother Adela waited. A tall, Texas-bred woman, who looked nothing like her fanciful name. "Mom." He grabbed her in a bear hug and swung her around.

"My Ben." She gave him a loving smile once he set her down. "How you've grown."

He snorted. "You always say that. I'm a man full grown and have been for the last fifteen years."

"I know, but the one you see the least is the one you want to see the most."

He ruffled her iron-gray bobbed hair. "I'm sure your other three sons don't appreciate that sentiment."

"But I tell them all the same thing." She gave a hearty chuckle. "Come on in. Your dad's anxious to see you too."

Ben strode into the den, now duly christened the man cave. The years had been kind to his father. In his mid-fifties, Byron Rasmussen still put in full days on horseback overseeing his ranch.

His once flaming red hair was now a soft gold, but his eyes still sparkled with a blue fire and a ready wit.

His father stood. "'Bout time you rolled in here. Your mom's been cooking all afternoon, and the smells coming outta that kitchen are driving me plum crazy."

"Come on and eat," his mother said from the doorway. "Your brothers are starving, too, or so they tell me."

Ben followed his dad into the dining room and sat at the table. His brothers Jack and Brock had spent ten years each in the Marines before coming home to help run the ranch. Noting the empty spot, he said, "Will working tonight?"

"He's on his way," his mom said. Everyone knew Will was her favorite. Accepted and not resented since Ben, Jack, and Brock all agreed Will was the best of the bunch. And he was the baby.

Platters of fried chicken, bowls of gravy, mounds of fluffy mashed potatoes, string beans, and homemade biscuits covered the old pine table. Mom had used her best tablecloth, and a feeling of guilt swept over him. Visiting his parents shouldn't be a special event, but given the rarity of his visits, it was.

"Mom, it looks wonderful. You've fixed all my favorites. And you're the best damn cook I know."

"Language," she warned, more from habit than anything. She passed the platter of chicken to his dad.

"Yes, ma'am. Beg pardon."

"And thank you, son." She gave him a self-satisfied smile.

His father winked. "What brings you home, son?" He forked a chicken leg and the gizzard onto his plate then passed the platter to Ben.

Ben took the heavily-laden platter "There's a lot of concern about what negative influences the casino will bring. I'm here to talk to the business owners and get ahead of it. But it's already started. Break-ins mainly. Vandalism of a sort that means there's more to come." He grabbed the other chicken leg and thigh for himself.

"Break-ins." Adela shook her head while passing the potatoes. "I don't like the sound of that. Not at all."

"Wouldn't hurt to lock your doors, mom, when Dad and the boys are out working the ranch."

She set the bowl down with a thump. "You think I don't know how to use a shotgun?"

"Just sayin', mom. Best to err on the side of caution." He took a bite of fried-to-perfection chicken and groaned his approval.

His cell phone rang. Dang it. He swallowed with a gulp. "Gotta take this." He rose from the table and walked into the living room. "Ranger Rasmussen."

He listened while the Dispatcher told him of the active scene taking place at the drug store. "I'm on my way."

He walked back into the dining room. "I'm sorry. I have to go."

"Oh, dear." She nodded. "That's the way it goes when you're a lawman. Never fear. I'll keep you a plate. We can nuke it when you get back. You *are* coming back, aren't you?"

Her hopeful expression got him in the gut. "Sometime. Too soon to say." He walked over to his disappointed mom and hugged her. "My old room ready?"

"You know it is." She caressed his cheek. "Stay safe, son."

"Do my best." He nodded, ran out and jumped into his SUV, revved the engine, and threw it into gear.

Up ahead the night sky was just starting to darken as he sped through the grove of cottonwoods that led to his parents' ranch. The moon was just starting to rise in the northeast.

Damn, he'd waited too late to get ahead of the crime wave. Now it was more a matter of playing catch up. Have to do better.

His heart racing, Vince listened as Longworth continued calling Abby's name. "I need my baby's prescription filled. Bring it to me now. He needs it. Abby, he's sick. What the hell's the matter with you? I'm not going away. Please, help me. Baby Johnny is really sick."

Abby must've unlocked the door. He heard her tell Darby, "Sorry, but I'm already closed. Just hand me the prescription. I'll bring it to your house."

From his position, he couldn't see or hear enough. But Longworth deserved a freaking Oscar for her performance. "Please. Please. Don't put me off," she begged. "Please."

"I will. I promise. Go on home, Mrs. Longworth. This won't take long. I'll see you in a very few minutes."

He heard the door shut. Now what? He poked his head around and saw Darby motion for him to come quickly. He ducked low and ran for the far exit. When he reached Darby's position, he peered inside. There was only one, but he was armed. At least his wife was all right, for the moment.

Inside he heard a high-pitched shriek and his gut clenched. "We've got to get her out of there."
But then he saw the perp running for the door with a stash of drugs.

The perp blasted through the door then stopped still, dismay and disbelief spread across his face at the sight of

Vince and Longworth's raised weapons.

"You're done, asshole."

While his deputies took the assailant into custody, Vince ran to the back of the drug store. Panicked at finding his wife crouching on the floor, he knelt and scooped her into his arms. "Doll, are you all right. Did he hurt you?" He scanned her face for marks. Clear. Thank God.

She gazed at him, the love apparent in her sparkling emerald gaze. "No. I thought he was going to shoot me, but my water broke, or I peed. I was so scared it might be the latter."

The heat of a thousand suns raged through him. He clenched his fists. "I oughta kill that SOB. You're trembling. Are you sure you're all right?" Why his eight-months-pregnant wife wanted to work the night shift was a mystery? Maybe now she'd see sense.

"I *think* so. Maybe we ought to stop at the clinic. No, wait. I have some test strips."

"Test strips?" he asked, bewildered.

"They test fluids for acidity or alkalinity. Amniotic fluid is alkaline. Urine is acidic."

"Okay, doll." He gave her a smile. "I always knew you were smarter than me."

"Everybody knows that, darlin'." She patted his cheek. "Now help me up. I'm very wet."

He helped her up, then chuckled. "You may be smarter than I am, but I smell pee."

She gave him an eye roll. "You're probably right, but it won't hurt to double-check."

***

By the time Ben arrived at the scene, Deputy Longworth had already cuffed the culprit who'd had balls enough to think he'd just take the sheriff's wife prisoner while he stole a bag of drugs.

He nodded at Longworth. "Good job. I want to question him. Where's the sheriff?"

The deputy jerked her head toward the drug store. "Inside with Abby."

"She all right?"

"Shook up. But all right."

He strode into the drug store and met the sheriff and his wife coming out. "Longworth said Abby was all right."

"I *am*."

Vince had his arm around her waist, what there was left of it. "I'm taking her to the ER just in case."

"Mind if I follow?"

"Not at all," Vince said, gazing lovingly at his pregnant wife.

A pang of remorse hit Ben. His old friend had remarried and was expecting his first child. He and the sheriff had one thing in common. Vince's first marriage hadn't worked out, either. For a while, everyone in town figured she'd run on with the bank VP, but their bodies had been found on Vince's ranch. While it made for a touchy situation, Ben's investigation had proved Vince's innocence.

"I'm really all right. I don't want to make a fuss."

"Good grief, woman," Vince said. "You were held up, held hostage, and you could've been killed."

"Since you put it like that." She gave an eye roll.

That settled it. Abby was all right. Her spunky attitude was back to normal.

"Go on ahead. I'll be there before you know it." Spying Beth and the security dude standing on the sidewalk across the street, Ben said. "I need to speak with Beth. See if she saw anything."

He strode across the street to the Merc where Beth and Freeman were watching the action. "What did you see?" he asked Beth directly.

She heaved a sigh, causing her breasts to rise and fall...and his heart rate to spike.

"I didn't see anything. I was back in the office doing paperwork." She glanced up at Freeman. "What about you?"

"Nothing." He gave a casual shrug. "I was busy installing the security system."

"You saw nothing. Are you sure? Was this guy alone? What about his vehicle?"

"I didn't see another vehicle or anyone else. My attention was on my work. An accomplice could've already left before Vince and Deputy Longworth arrived. As far as I could tell, he acted alone."

"Thanks." *For nothing.* "She needs that alarm system fully operational before you leave tonight. Is that going to happen or not?"

"I'll do my best. Now if you'll let me get back to work..."

Ben grunted his approval. Something about that guy really got his goat. Too smooth by half. But Abby seemed to like him. Guess that was what really got his goat.

Abby liked Freeman a little too much.

After leaving Beth alone with her security guy, Ben followed Vince to the Los Marcos County General Hospital. He waited while Abby was safely bedded down in a cubicle before pulling Vince aside. "I'd like to interrogate this guy. Maybe we can find out who he's working for."

Vince nodded. "Appreciate all the help you can give me. I'm sort of distracted."

"Understood. Would you mind if I ask Abby a few, very few questions?"

"As long as she agrees, fine by me."

Ben pulled aside the curtain to Abby's cubicle. "Doing okay?"

She gave him a reassuring smile. "Nothing's changed."

"I have a couple of questions."

She shot him a wide grin. "Fire when ready, Ranger."

"Was he alone the entire time? Did you get the impression he had an accomplice somewhere out of sight, maybe?"

"As far as I could tell, he was alone. He grabbed me out front right as I was locking up. Made me go back inside."

"He spoke English?"

"Definitely, but with a heavy accent. Believe you me, we understood each other perfectly."

"And he was after drugs?"

"That's it."

"Did he make threats?"

"Oh, yeah. He made plenty of those. I tried to tell him only the sheriff had the override code, but he *knew* Vince was my husband, so I had no choice but to enter the duress code. In the end, though, he raised his gun. I really thought I was going to die. That's when my *water* broke."

"Are you in labor?"

She shook her head and chuckled. "It wasn't amniotic fluid. I peed. That's how scared I was."

"Can't say as I blame you," he said, trying hard to hide a smile. "Thank you, Abby. I'm so glad this turned out all right."

Giving her a quick nod, he left the ER. Time to interrogate that son of a bitch.

x x x

The thief who'd held Abby Tate captive sat sprawled in the interrogation room. "Been read his rights?" Ben asked his brother, as they stood outside in the hallway.

"You know how it goes. Says he *no hablo Ingles*."

"And that's a problem?"

"Hell, no. Just softening him up for you. At least four of us in the office are fluent in Spanish. We Mirandized him in Spanish and English. He waived his rights."

Ben smiled. "Abby said he communicated well enough with her in English."

"There you go then. Have at it, bro."

Ben opened the door and entered the so-called interview room. Interrogation was the room's real purpose but calling it an interview room held fewer negative connotations.

"What's your name, *amigo*?"

"*No hablo Ingles*." Slack-jawed, he shrugged.

"That won't wash. That pregnant woman you terrorized tonight says you speak *Inglis* well enough." He leaned across the table. "Your name? So, I don't have to call you Juan Doe."

Juan Doe scowled, then spit on the floor. "Fuck you."

"Now that's some good old Anglo-Saxon English you've got there. But we hate when you spit on the floor. Kinda disgusting. You've heard about germs?"

"Fuck you."

"No matter. Your prints will tell us who you are. And probably who you work for. Who do you work for, Juan? Who put you up to breaking into the drug store?"

"Fuck you."

"You're beginning to bore me, Juan, old buddy. Why did you bother waiving your rights if you're not going to talk to me?" Ben sat. Going to be one helluva long night. "Want some coffee? Water?"

Juan shook his head.

"Now I could be wrong, but you don't look like a druggie, so I have to assume you wanted those drugs for resale."

No response.

"Come on now. I missed a really good supper, one my mom cooked especially for me. Are you hungry? Looks like we're going to be a while until you decide you want to talk to me. Want something to eat?"

Juan raised his head. "Yeah. Tamales. *Real* tamales. And Mexican beer."

"Can't serve alcohol in here, but I know where we can rustle up some great tamales."

He walked to the door, opened it. "Hey! I need some tamales from Rosa's Cantina. If she's not open, tell her it's for me." For the last twenty-five years, Rosarita Hernandez had served the best Mexican food this side of the border. As a teenager, he'd eaten many a meal at her cantina, while teasing Rosa that he'd marry her when he got old enough.

Will met him in the hall. "What the hell are you up to? You're kissing this guy's ass. I'd like to stomp him. Terrorizing Abby that way."

"I understand why you feel that way but bear with me. There's method in my madness."

"I hope you know what you're doing."

"I do."

Muttering to himself and shaking his head, Will turned and walked down the hall.

Back in the interrogation room, Ben sat and leaned back. "It might be a while. Rosa's Cantina might be closed, but she'll fix you a nice meal since I asked her to."

At the mention of Rosa's Cantina, Juan's eyes brightened. Maybe he knew Rosa. Maybe this guy was more local than Ben thought.

"Jose," he said. "Jose Gonzalez.

"Thanks, Jose. Wanna tell me why you picked tonight to grab a pregnant woman off the street and break into her store."

"Drugs, man. I needed the money. Dude told me, 'Only a couple of women in there. Help yourself.' Didn't know she was expecting. I saw her let the first one go home. When she came out, I grabbed her. I wouldn't have hurt her."

"She didn't know that." He kept digging. "Who told you *only a couple of women*?

"No one. I knew."

"No, you said, 'man said only two women.'"

Jose shook his head.

"Now then, I thought we were getting along so well. Do you want me to send those tamales back after Rosa had to reopen the cantina."

"I don't want to die. Can't tell you. He'll kill me."

"Help us, Jose. We can protect you. "

"Protect me? No way. I have a family."

"If you go to prison, who's going to take care of your family then?"

"At least I know they be safe. If I tell you who put me up to this, he or his people kill me *and* my family."

"Not if you help us. We can put him and his people behind bars."

"No. No way, man. They already in danger. I needed those drugs to pay a debt. I owe him." He buried his face in his hands and sobbed.

A knock on the door stopped Jose's sobbing. Deputy Powell stuck his head inside. "You ordered tamales. Rosa sent you a huge dinner." Powell was a tall Anglo, with sandy hair and an acne-scarred complexion.

"Bring it in."

Ben took the dinner and set it before the prisoner. "I

kept my word, Jose." Ben rose. "Keep an eye on him," he said to the deputy. "I need to confer with my brother."

He walked down the hall to the outer office, then stopped at his brother's desk.

Will glanced up at Ben's arrival. "Any luck?"

"He's scared out of his mind. He owes someone. Someone who has men to do his bidding. Who's the likely candidate? You know the Valley better than I do."

"If it's a gambling debt, we're talking about one real low-down guy going by the name of Ace, real name Raphael Aceveda. He's smalltime, but he surrounds himself with four thugs. If he's into debt with a loan shark, then we have Alonzo Griggs who has reputed ties to the Houston mob. There are several thugs on his payroll who act as collectors when a payment is late."

"Either of those sound like someone who could've driven this guy to break into the pharmacy and steal drugs to sell. Our guy here's a family man. Afraid what will happen to his family. Someone out there is definitely pulling his strings. Someone right here in this town."

Will tapped his fist on his desktop. "My money's on Aceveda. We've had him and his thugs in here on numerous occasions, but can't prosecute because witnesses refuse to testify."

"Have any threats been followed up on?"

"Difficult to say. Witnesses either leave town or refuse to testify."

"Leave town or disappear?"

"Difficult to know. Let's just say no bodies have been recovered."

"What are you going to do if our Juan Doe won't talk?"

"His name's Jose Gonzalez. At least, he told me that much. Let 'im eat and see if that loosens his tongue. He's going to be in trouble with someone if he doesn't make good on his debt."

"Not our problem."

"Check on his family."

"Now that we have a name, Deputy Garcia might know them. He's off duty, but I'll give him a call."

Ben waited while his brother spoke with his fellow deputy.

"Not good. As far as Luis knows, Jose works for Briggs Construction, and his family is still in Mexico."

"Meaning Aceveda could have cartel connections."

"Los Malos Dias."

Ben frowned. "Is Gonzalez legal?"

Will reached for the phone. "I'll check with Briggs, our duly-elected mayor. His company should have his employment documentation on file."

According to the foreman for Briggs Construction, Gonzalez was in the country legally, but his work visa would expire soon. Ben headed back to the interview room to relieve Deputy Powell. "Thanks."

The deputy nodded. "Sure."

Ben shut the door, sat and leaned back. "So,how was it?"

Gonzalez gave Ben a grateful smile. "Good. Real good. *Muchas gracias.*"

"I really need a name, Jose." He leaned forward, resting his forearms on the table. "Who do you owe this money to?"

"Appreciate the food." Gonzales shook his head. "I can't help you. Too much trouble already."

"Ace the one holding your marker?"

Gonzalez's eyes widened. He scooted back from the table. "No! Not him."

"I can't let you go without a name. Well, hell, I can't let you go no matter what. The sheriff has something to say about that. I'm a Texas Ranger. You know what that means?"

"*Si*. I know about Rangers."

"We can do a lot more to protect you than—say, the sheriff can."

"My family, man." Sweat glistened on Gonzalez's forehead.

"Your family is still in Mexico, right?"

"*Si*. They in danger."

"Aceveda. Is he connected to the cartel?"

"No. No. No. Don't make me tell you." Gonzalez stood and started pacing.

Shaking his head, Ben stood. "Since you can't help me, I hope you enjoyed that meal. It's the last one like that you'll see for a long time."

He walked to the door and opened it. "Deputy Powell, holding cell for this one."

Ben glanced at the car clock. After ten. He swung by the Merc. Lights off. Good. Apparently, Freeman had finished installing the alarm system. It wouldn't hurt to check on Abby, see if she was safely settled for the night. No reason why he shouldn't, given the previous evening's break-in.

He drove around the block and entered the alley that served the Main Street businesses for deliveries and owner parking. He gazed up at Abby and her sister's apartment. Lights on. Good. Might as well see if everything's okay.

He parked, then climbed to the second-floor apartment. He knocked.

Freeman, dammit, opened the door. "Ranger."

Ben nodded. "Freeman."

Beth, now casually dressed in jeans and a pink Lynyrd Skynyrd T-shirt came up behind Freeman. "Matt's just finishing up placing alarms up here on our door and windows. Lola and I were both a little leery of staying here after the break-in."

"Understandable and smart," Ben said with a quick nod. "I wanted to double-check and see you were all right."

"That's so nice of you. Come on in," Beth said, giving him a smile.

Freeman moved aside, pretty damn slow, too.

From a beige leather sofa, Lola gave a cheeky wave. "Matt has the store's security system all set up, and he's almost through here." A smile played about her mouth. "The cameras will be here tomorrow or the next day."

"Sounds like it's all under control," he said, grudging every word that Freeman could interpret as praise.

"Coffee," Lola suggested with an impish smile. "You've had a long day, I'm sure."

As much as he would've preferred to stay, he wouldn't be pulled into whatever game Lola had decided to play. "No, I'd better be going. He gave Beth his card. "Call if you have any further concerns."

"I will." A quizzical expression crossed her face. "Are you sure you won't stay?"

"Best be going. I'm glad you're taking your security matters seriously." Now that sounded as if he had a stick up his ass. No. Just being polite, as was his nature. No way could he relax around Beth when Freeman was hanging onto her every word. And it didn't look like he was leaving anytime soon.

So be it.

Something about that dude...

A background check. Next on the agenda.

***

After Matt drank one last cup of coffee and finally left, Beth shut the door, then whirled on Lola who was lounging on the sofa. "What kind of silly game were you playing with Ben? Honestly, he couldn't get out of here quick enough."

"And *Matt* almost had to be kicked out the door. What's wrong with you? Ben's the one you've always been crazy about. So why on earth are you shoving someone you barely know in his face? Are you trying to make him jealous? He doesn't strike me as the kind of man who plays games."

Beth shrugged. "No one asked Ben to come by here." She picked up a stack of interior design magazines, straightened them, then set the magazines on the coffee table.

Lola sat cross-legged on the sofa. "No. He stopped by because he was worried about you."

"About *us*. He's a lawman." Honestly, her sister could be such a pain at times. "That's where his interest lies. Not in me." She walked over to the kitchen island, collected the dirty cups, opened the dishwasher and set the cups in the upper rack.

"No. *You*." Lola made as if to pull out her hair. "You drive me crazy. Do you honestly think a Texas Ranger doesn't have anything more important to do than check to see if we're all right?"

Beth shut the dishwasher with a slam. "He was being *polite*," she said patiently. "I doubt we'll see hide nor hair of him for another month or two."

"Agh! You need your vision checked." Lola gave an exasperated sigh. "Because you can't see what's right in front of you. Ben is clearly jealous of Matt, and you're too blind to see it."

"What I don't need is my *darling* sister interfering. Ben

isn't interested. As you said, he couldn't get out of here quickly enough." She started wiping the countertop with a wet wipe. Now if Lola would spend more time helping clean the kitchen instead of trying to run her life...

Lola hopped from the sofa and leaned on the island. "That's because you were fawning over Matt, whom, I might add, you've known for less than twenty-four hours."

"Ben Rasmussen has had plenty of time to get over his ex and make a move *if* he were interested. Damn it. He's not." She jabbed the start button on the dishwasher. It hummed to life.

"Well, at least you know you're not his transition girlfriend. Zoe remarried five years ago."

"No," she said with a casual shrug. "That role was taken by any one of four or five girls in Waco, none of whom was a blonde."

"How do you *know* that?" Lola asked, her eyebrows arched almost to her hairline.

Beth's neck grew warm, then her cheeks. *Fair skin blushes. Dammit.* "Will sort of keeps me up to date on Ben's social life."

Lola let out a whoop. "Stalker!"

"No such thing!" She huffed then tossed the wet wipe into the trash. Enough cleaning. She strode into the living room and plopped on the sofa. "I'll have you know I've never asked Will one single thing about Ben's life in Waco. He just volunteers the information. I only listen to be polite."

"OMG! You're so full of it." Lola headed to the hall, stopped, turned, and said, "I'm going to bed. You need to do some hard thinking about what you're playing at. Ben is here. He's available, and if you don't take advantage of the situation, you're *crazy.*"

"Go to bed and leave me the heck alone." She watched her sister walk down the hall. *Finally, some peace and quiet.*

"And you'll be sorry."

Startled, Beth looked up. Lola was standing in the living room making a childish face. "I thought you were going to bed." Beth picked up a pillow and tossed it at her sister who nimbly dodged. "Go away. Leave me alone."

"Crazy. Sorry. And alone," Lola added then dashed down the hall and escaped into her bedroom.

Honestly, if Lola weren't her sister, she wouldn't put up with her antics. Lola was no better, pining over Will, waiting for him to get over Darla.

Beth pulled her feet up and hugged her legs, resting her head on her knees. But maybe—just maybe—there was some truth to what Lola had said. Matt was new. Attractive. Who wouldn't flirt a bit, even if his presence in town was suspect? But if she admitted the truth, Lola was right. Ben had always been the one Beth wanted. What was wrong with going after what she wanted? Not a damn thing. If he rejected her, then she was no worse off than before.

Still crazy. Still alone. But not sorry. Sorry would only apply if she didn't try.

On the way to his parent's ranch, Ben received a call from Will. "Found a message on Vince's desk. Figured you'd want to know that meeting for the business owners is tomorrow at nine-thirty. City Council meeting room."

"Thanks. Just so you know, Mom's keeping you a plate of leftovers. I might eat 'em myself if you don't show up."

"I'm heading out. Won't be far behind ya." His brother clicked off.

Good. The meeting was set. Another chance to see Beth without Freeman in tow. No way could he get a read on her. Her body language was all over the place, and if she was playing some kind of game.... Tough. He didn't play games. She'd never struck him as the type who would, though.

True, his job with the Rangers kept him busy with little time for a social life, but seeing her again made him realize there was a real lack. This realization, dammit, had come a little late.

He turned into the lane leading to the ranch and drove through the dark cover of cottonwoods until he reached the ranch. *Porchlight still on.* He smiled. Just like when he'd been a teenager. Mom wouldn't turn it off until Will showed up for his dinner.

Mom was predictable. Beth was anything but.

After inhaling the plate of food his mom had left for him, Ben accessed the Ranger database and ran a background check on Matthew Freeman and his business, Helmsman Security.

Everything seemed aboveboard with the business, no evidence of shell companies. The business started in 2016, owner Matthew Freeman. Cut and dried.

Matthew Freeman, MBA, 2008 graduated MIT Sloan School of Business Management—impressive. Undergrad at the Clarkson University, Reh School of Business. Majored in Business Intelligence and Data Analytics. 2006— interesting.

Too clean. Not even a traffic ticket.

So, what was he doing between receiving his graduate degree and creating his business? Where was the rest of his background?

Chapter Four

Friday

Beth quickly dressed in a powder blue pantsuit, a white top, and navy heels, then rushed down to open the Merc. The sheriff had sent out a town alert text about the meeting and location. Entering the rear door, she flipped the light switch, but with plywood over the front windows, the store remained darker than usual. She'd always taken pride in her window displays and felt they drew customers into the store. But two weeks was two weeks. No point in fretting over what she couldn't change.

Lola emerged from the Bistro, looking radiant in a ruffled yellow off-the-shoulder top and white jeans. Once in a while, Beth envied her sister's tall, slim good looks. But only once in a while. "Do you think the meeting will be over in time to open the Bistro?"

"Who knows?" Lola shrugged. "Eva and I have done all the food prep. I think she can handle the rest. If I don't make it back, customers can just order and pick-up their food at the counter. Shouldn't be a problem," she said with a smile.

"Kayla will be fine manning the register in the store. Darren will be stocking the shelves, so she won't be alone." Only too recently, she'd come to feel a responsibility for her employees' safety. Granted, the store had a new security system, but the cameras hadn't arrived yet.

***

From Ben's spot on the dais, he could see the meeting room was packed, and people were still coming through the door. Even Ben's dad and several of the nearby ranchers had shown up. Good. Vince was smart to have invited them. Running a ranch was a business as much as running a store like the Merc.

He scanned the crowd, hoping to catch a glimpse of Beth and Lola. While they'd both been invited, whether they'd both leave the store and Bistro was uncertain.

Ah. His heart lightened a bit. There they were. Beth was the epitome of a businesswoman in a light blue pantsuit, while her sister Lola was dressed more casually in a yellow top and jeans.

Vince stood and spoke into the mic. "If everyone would take a seat and settle down, we have a lot of territory to cover this morning. And I know you're all busy, so I'll get right to it. I want to introduce Ranger Ben Rasmussen. Most of you know him. For those few who don't, he grew up here in the Valley. He's stationed in Waco. Kenton Valley and most of the Hill Country is in his jurisdiction. "Ben."

Ben rose and nodded. "Thank you, Sheriff Tate. I'll get straight to the point. This town—no, this area—is changing fast. The casino, now under construction, is going to bring increased opportunities for all sorts of criminal endeavors. We've already seen an increase in vandalism, just this week. For those of you who don't know. The Tidy-Kleen and the Sleepytime Motel were broken into last week. Last night, vandals hit the Mercantile, and in addition, Abby Tate was grabbed as she closed the drug store and was forced back inside. This individual wanted drugs. And while we have that perpetrator in custody, I'm afraid this is only the beginning."

The noise level rose to a buzz.

"Now hold on." He tapped the mic to get their attention.

"Texas Rangers are facing this same situation all over the state. Drug cartels want to expand their territory. And whether there's ever a wall built or not, we need increased border security. Being in the middle of the state, we haven't had an enormous amount of incursion, as yet, but the advent of a casino makes this area ripe for increased crime and drug trafficking, as well as human trafficking. The Rangers will lend all the support we can, but you, the business owners, need to be vigilant. Upgrade your security. Don't leave your workers alone in your businesses at night."

Bob Cherry from the hardware store stood, his face red with anger. "What's the sheriff going to do to protect us?"

Vince got to his feet. "My deputies and I are working around the clock. This may be a small county as counties go, but I'm doubling the ratio of deputies to residents. I'm in the process of hiring more deputies to do just that. The city council, while I know you're happy with an influx of new business, need to realize that it takes time to train these new hires, and that takes additional funding."

"Where's that money going to come from?" Cherry asked.

"The state and from you, the taxpayers," Vince said.

The buzz evolved into a roar.

Ben waited until the roar began to subside. "All right," Ben began, "these break-ins were well organized. It seems to be a team. According to one witness report, they don't speak. They just go about their business. There's no way to know if they're local. The incident at the drug store seems to be a separate incident, but could still be related to cartel activity, however remotely."

Beth raised her hand raised to get his attention. As if she didn't already have it. "Miss Wheaton?"

"I want to say, as one of the business owners who's unfortunately been the recipient of one of these break-ins, that it's up to each of us to do what we can to protect our businesses. I know I was very lax on security. Frankly, I never saw the need. I was wrong. I'm already taking steps to secure my property, and I advise all of you to do the same. It's the cost of doing business. If we don't, our insurance premiums will go up with each claim. I expect mine will as a result of yesterday's break-in. In the future—no, from now on—we have to work with law enforcement and each other to keep our town safe." With a quick nod, she sat.

Admiration flooded through him. Beth's willingness to commit to security and cooperation was a bonus. "Thank you, Miss Wheaton. Appreciate you sharing your thoughts on the matter, and your cooperation is even more appreciated."

The meeting continued for another hour, but Beth's words had changed the meeting's tone from outrage to consensus.

Talking with the business owners on either side of the Merc, Beth waited until the crowd dwindled. From the corner of her eye, she watched Ben speaking with the sheriff and two of the city council members. When it appeared Ben was free, she excused herself. "I need to speak to the Ranger."

Hoping her cheeks weren't beet red, she walked over to Ben with a smile. "What do you think? Was the meeting as successful as you hoped?"

He gave her a slow smile that made her knees weaken. "Turned out that way. Sharing your perspective the way you did, helped a lot." He chuckled. "Matter of fact, you changed what was turning out to be a lynching party into a Sunday afternoon tea."

Whoee! There went the hot flush to her cheeks. She resisted fanning like some kind of demented southern belle. "Thank you, Ben. I'm glad you thought I helped."

Crap. Now what. Ask him to dinner. Ask him to father your children.

Instead, she swallowed the lump in her throat. No way would she ask him out. As for anything else....

While she was struggling to form coherent sentences, the mayor walked up. "Beg pardon, Miss Wheaton. I need to speak with Ben about this casino business." He walked to the far side of the dais, clearly expecting his former son-in-law to follow.

Ben followed, but he cast what she hoped was a regretful look over his shoulder.

Upstaged by Mayor Briggs, none other than the father of Ben's ex, what else could she do but go back and tend to her business.

She turned to leave and bumped into her sister.

"You and our handsome Texas Ranger were looking mighty chummy before the mayor dragged him away."

Beth headed toward the door, her heels clicking on the tiles. "I was just checking how the meeting went—if he thought it went well."

"And did he think it went well?" Lola asked, rushing to keep up.

Might as well say as little as possible. Maybe Lola would drop it. "He did."

"You were talking for quite a bit. What else did he say?"

Beth opened the door and blinked as she emerged into the blinding Texas sun. "That's all." She dug in her shoulder bag for her sunglasses.

"Oh, more than that." Lola grabbed Beth's elbow, slowing her forward progress. "You turned the meeting around. Surely he mentioned it."

Having located her shades, Beth put them on, sighing. Dammit her cheeks blazed with heat—and not from the sun. "He might've said something along those lines."

Lola smiled. "I knew it."

Ignore her. She'll drop it eventually. At least she'd made her mark on the meeting. Zoe Briggs Whatever-her-name-was-now wouldn't have made any contribution at all.

Dammit. Just as he was warming up to asking Beth to dinner, his ex-father-in-law had to interrupt. "Mayor, what can I do for you?" He kept his tone civil. Carlton Briggs wasn't his favorite person, just as Ben wasn't high on old Carlton's list of ten faves, either.

Briggs puffed out his barrel chest. "I'd appreciate if you'd go easy on badmouthing the casino. It'll do a lot for this town."

Anger rising like a red tide, Ben squared his shoulders. "I wasn't aware you had censorship powers over the Texas Rangers. I'll say what I damn well please about the casino. It's the worst thing that could happen to this county."

"It's talk like that—" Briggs broke off, his face flushed red. "I just wish you'd soft-pedal it a bit. Think about the business owners who'll prosper from the tourists who come to town."

"It's because I'm thinking about the business owners who are already suffering because of it. We're talking about crime, drugs, human trafficking. I know you have a vested interest in seeing the casino go ahead. Saw your big sign."

Briggs sniffed, then straightened his tie. "I guess we're not ever going to agree."

"We're not." Anxious to catch up with Beth, he glanced around. Gone. Dammit. "Are we done?"

Carlton seemed to hesitate.

Ben tamped down the urge to throttle his ex's father. "Something else you wanted to say?"

"Zoe's back." Briggs's voice grew raspy. "She and that ballplayer have split up."

So, she was back. "Not my problem."

"She wants to see you, Ben."

How like his ex to send her daddy to sound him out. "*Not* my problem."

"Call her. Talk to her. She's really down."

"Get her a shrink."

"Son, you've grown hard."

"Hard, am I? That's rich." Anger welled in his gut. Hard was a woman who blithely went from one man to another because he had better prospects and could support her lavish lifestyle. "Let's say I had a good teacher. One of the best. *Your* daughter. Now excuse the hell out of me. I have better things to do than counsel your spoiled brat of a daughter."

Briggs's jaw dropped.

"Nothing else to say? Good." Ben spun on his heel and left the mayor standing alone.

Had he made a mistake in coming back to Kenton Valley, even though on Ranger business? Why did Zoe have to come back now? Just when he was on the verge of starting over. Seemed like someone up there had a sadistic sense of humor.

After the confrontation with his ex-father-in-law, Ben sat across from the sheriff while Vince took an urgent call. All Ben could think about was Beth. And, dammit, Zoe.

Dammit. He was over his ex, but having her back in

town was a complication. Sending her daddy to do a preliminary end run was only her first move. What she'd do next was anybody's guess. But it wouldn't be pretty.

Focus. This was not the time to sit around mooning over a woman, not even Beth Wheaton.

Vince ended his call. "Now that was interesting. Suann Hausman, one of the owners of the Tidy-Kleen, says she's discovered her husband Frank has been paying protection money to one of Aceveda's thugs."

Leaning forward, Ben said, "You have my attention. Is she reliable?"

Vince smiled and leaned back. "She does the bookkeeping for their business and right away noted some missing money. She actually checked their CCTV camera and has the transaction with Aceveda's man on tape."

"Damn! Maybe we ought to recruit her for the Rangers," Ben said. Protection rackets already. Somehow they had to get ahead instead of playing catch-up.

"She's damn mad. I'll say that."

"So, Aceveda's not just involved in gambling. He's branching out into protection."

"We need to go softly. Her husband still doesn't know she figured out what he's up to."

Ben rubbed his chin as he considered what this meant for the business owners in the Valley, especially Beth. "He's scared and trying to protect his wife." And now he'd have to protect Beth, too. She was no pushover, but Aceveda and his thugs didn't scare easy.

"Have to wonder if the motel owners have been approached," Vince said.

"Why don't I check into the motel and do some quiet digging?"

"They'll be afraid to talk. And they might be watched."

"I can get an undercover operative to work in the motel.

But first I'll get someone placed in the Merc as well. Beth will be the next target if they're true to form. I'm sure of it."

"Uh, Beth?" Leaning back, Vince raised a questioning brow.

"What?"

"Beth—you're protective."

"She—uh, needs protection. They both do." He cleared his throat. "I don't have a good feeling about that Freeman guy."

"Really?"

"One thing struck me this morning. Why didn't Freeman bother to show up for the meeting? He has a business. Shouldn't he be concerned enough to show up?"

"What do we know about him?" Vince asked with a frown.

Ben gave Vince the quick and dirty resume on Freeman. "Basically, Freeman has no record, not even a damn traffic ticket. He's too clean."

"And what was he up to between graduation and starting his business?"

"That's what's bugging me. There's no enlistment record. Just a big fat zero."

"Some kind of Fed?"

"Beginning to wonder about that myself. DEA is my bet. Or FBI."

Vince frowned. "Don't like it when other agencies get involved in my county, especially when they don't announce themselves."

"Undercover is usually need-to-know, but given the Rangers' interest in this area, someone in Waco needs to know about Freeman's presence."

"I guess you don't know someone who'd notify them."

"Damn right I do!" He stood. "Right after I go to the Bistro for some lunch. Get you anything?"

Vince shook his head. "Thanks, but I'm meeting Abby."

"How's she doing after last night?"

"Can't keep her down. Believe me, I tried."

"Something about Texas women. They're strong and stubborn."

"You don't have to tell me." Vince ended with a wide grin.

Beth and Lola parked Lola's Jeep Renegade behind the Merc next to a Helmsman Security van. "Great." Matt certainly wasn't wasting any time. "He must be installing the CCTV cameras."

"That's quick." Lola turned off the motor.

"He said it might be today or tomorrow at the latest. Truthfully, it's a relief to see them installed today."

Lola opened the driver's door, got out, and slammed it shut. "I agree."

Beth got out of the Jeep. "I've always felt safe in our little apartment above the store. I really hate losing the home town feel. Knowing everyone. And the loss of trust—" She shook her head. "That's what I hate the most." She opened the back door and walked inside the Merc.

She found Matt at the top of a ladder installing one of the hidden cameras. "I wondered why you weren't at the town meeting. Now I know."

"You needed these cameras installed more than I needed to attend a meeting." He smiled down at her. "You *could* give me an update. Just hit the high points?"

"Certainly. I didn't expect to see those cameras before tomorrow."

"I put a rush on the order. I'm a good customer so they expedited it."

She walked over to Kayla at the cash register. The petite cashier was fresh out of junior college and had great people skills. "Any problems?"

"No, ma'am. Several customers came in and said they were surprised to see us open."

"Well, I'm not about to close down for two weeks. Besides, the Bistro wasn't damaged. As for the uncertainty about our being open." She gave a quick nod. "I'll fix that. "

Back in the office, she fashioned a small notice board with *Open* on one side and *Closed* on the opposite. She attached a cheerful red ribbon left over from last Christmas. Carrying her quickie craft project to the front door, she attached it with a thumbtack to the outside of the door. "There'll be no doubt now. We're definitely open."

Walking back to the register, she stopped long enough to align the labels on the cans of pinto beans. There. Much better.

Instead of an over-the-door bell which normally dinged when someone entered the store, there was a high-pitched beep. The new security system. But she missed the sound of the old-fashioned bell.

She turned. And wished she hadn't.

Zoe Briggs Whatever in all her Houston–bought finery waltzed into the Merc. "I see you still have your little store. How's business? Such a shame about the break-in. That can't help, now can it?"

Pasting on a smile to mask her irritation, Beth asked, "How may I help you, Zoe?"

"Oh, I doubt you have anything here I'd want. But I thought I might as well have a look. It's so dark though. I guess you're going to have your windows replaced sooner or later." She gestured dramatically, her gold and diamond jewelry flashing and setting her gold charm bracelet to jingling.

"Yes, they're already on order. A couple of weeks to fabricate and they'll be good as new."

Zoe brushed by wafting a heavy dose of musky perfume. "Oh, I see you have a little lunch counter."

Condescend much? "Yes, the Bistro is a very popular spot for lunch. We have free Wi-Fi too."

"How quaint."

Zoe sashayed over to the ladder and made a show of eyeing Matt's firm butt. "Oh my, you have some very fine help."

"Yes. He's very handy." Beth clenched her jaw. So, Zoe was back in town. How special. Well, Zoe could just take her over-permed hair and over-perfumed body back to Houston. And be quick about it.

"This where you want it, ma'am," Matt asked, playing along with an amused smile.

"Yes. That'll do just fine."

He dismounted the ladder and turned to Zoe. "Matt Freeman, Helmsman Security, owner."

"Oh, my. I misunderstood. I thought you were one of Bethany's employees." She batted her mascaraed lashes furiously.

"If I can do anything to help, Zoe, let me know. I've been in a meeting all morning, and I believe Kayla is in need of a break."

The door opened and again the security system beeped. Her gaze went automatically to the door.

Ben.

Oh, crap. Why now?

Removing his hat, Ben walked into the Merc. It took his eyes a second to adjust to the lower level of light.

"Ben. My darling Ben." Zoe rushed and threw her arms around his shoulders, her onslaught catching him off-guard. He staggered and dropped his hat. His neck and face heated. Gingerly, he untangled himself from her cobra-like hold.

"Damnation, Zoe. What the hell!" He bent down and picked up his hat, then slapped it against his thigh to dislodge any dust.

"I missed you so much." This time, her arms went around his neck. "Aren't you glad to see me, darlin'?"

Firmly taking hold of her wrists, once again, he extricated himself. "For Pete's sake, Zoe. Control yourself."

"That's just it. I can't control myself when I see you. It's been so long."

"This isn't the time or place. You're making a spectacle of yourself."

"Running into you here was so unexpected." She glanced around as if enjoying being center stage, but then centerstage was where she lived her life. Everything and everybody served a purpose in her life or they were of no use to her. Drama queen. The phrase was coined for women like his ex. And she was his ex. Make no bones about it.

"I'm here on business." Forget lunch. "If you'll excuse me."

"Pick a time and place."

He shook his head. Never.

"Dinner tonight at the country club." She added a whiney, "Please."

Why did women have to whine? The sound set his teeth on edge. "No."

Her eyes widened in disbelief. "No?"

"Beth," he called to get her attention. "In your private office, please." Ignoring Zoe, he nodded at Freeman who shot him a knowing grin. So, Freeman was here during the meeting, installing security cameras. Good to know.

A frown crossed Beth's pretty face. "All right. As soon as Kayla gets back from her break."

He strode over to the cash register. "Sorry for the disturbance. I don't know what she was thinking. I certainly never encouraged it. I didn't even know she was back in town until her father told me, after the meeting."

"You don't owe me any explanations, Ben."

"I do. Sort of. When he interrupted us, I was about to ask you out to dinner."

"You were?" Her hands went to her head. "Has my hair gone dark without my knowing?"

"Huh?"

She shot him a cheeky smile. "I've heard it said around town that you said no more blondes."

He smiled. "I don't consider you a blonde. Not in the pejorative sense, anyway." Not in any sense. Beth Wheaton was the total opposite of Zoe.

"Thank you, I guess."

"You and my ex... " And he said *ex* because to say Zoe's name only gave her power. "...are nothing alike. For one, you're not a drama queen. For another, you're intelligent."

A loud clatter of cans falling from the shelves caught his attention along with the clicking of heels as Zoe ran from the store. "You should charge her for malicious mischief."

Beth laughed, a lovely appealing sound that rippled with merriment. "Oh, honestly. Why would I bother?"

Beth—definitely *not* a drama queen. He lowered his gaze to hers. "She doesn't deserve to get away with petty vandalism."

"They're just cans. Darren can put them back on the shelves." She lifted her shoulders in a casual shrug. "No big deal."

"If you say so." Here was a woman who kept matters in perspective.

At that moment, the cashier emerged from the back of the store. "I'm back," she said with a smile.

"Great. If you don't mind, help Darren with the cleanup on one of the aisles," Beth said. "The Ranger and I have something we need to discuss in my office."

Kayla nodded. "Sure thing."

He watched Beth's cashier head down the aisle, then he followed Beth to her office. The gentle back and forth sway of her hips mesmerized him. Her natural walk, not an exaggerated, 'Look at me' show like his ex's.

Beth sat and motioned for him to sit across from her. "Wow, so much excitement."

He cleared his throat. "I'm here on business, too. Something has happened that gives me cause for concern. I want to place someone undercover inside the store."

"Really why?" Her dark eyes widened in surprise. "You think they'll come back?"

"If they do, it'll be more serious than a break-in." He gazed into her earnest brown eyes. "It's possible you'll be approached to pay protection in order to prevent more incidents like Wednesday's from happening again."

Her eyes widened with alarm. "Protection...really?"

He nodded. "One of the owners at the cleaners has already been approached and made at least one payment."

"The caveat being if I don't pay, they'll come back, and it'll be much worse. Someone could get hurt." Beth clenched her fists until the knuckles were white.

He reached forward, covering her small hands with his, hoping to reassure her. "Right."

"Tell me what you want me to do? I'll do it." Unflinching, she met his gaze.

"When you're approached, refuse." Even as he said the words, he doubted the wisdom. Using a young woman as bait was never a good plan, especially a civilian who wasn't trained to deal with a physical attack.

"But what about my employees? I don't want to endanger Kayla. She's not much more than a kid. My stock boy is off to college in the fall. Lola and Eva are next door in the Bistro. "

"That's why I want to place an undercover ranger in here."

"I have to talk this over with Lola. She owns half the store. We're partners."

"Of course. But do it today. There are signs they're picking up momentum. It won't take long for events to escalate."

"You said something about dinner?" she asked, reminding him of the real reason he'd come to the Merc. Funny how Zoe and crime always seemed to get in the way.

"With all this going on?" he asked as seriously as he could manage. Dinner with Beth Wheaton—high on his agenda. But was this the right time?

"Oh..." She chewed her full bottom lip, making him wish he could do the same. "You're right. Better to wait until things have settled down."

Ruefully, he stood. She certainly hadn't jumped at the chance of dinner and had given up too easily, to suit him. "Let me know what you decide after you talk to your sister."

"Of course."

"You have my card. It has my cell number."

"Right."

Hat in hand and basically inarticulate, he stood there, not wanting to leave. Not at all. "Later." Turning, he strode from the office, nodded at Freeman, and walked out through the store. Had he noted a trace of disappointment in her expression and tone? Possibly.

He set his hat on his head. Hell, disappointment was all too present in his life. Why would he expect anything else?

If he admitted the truth, seeing Zoe had affected him more than it should've. No denying her sensual allure, but at this late date, it'd palled. She'd become a caricature of herself. Too blond. Too much makeup. Basically, too much everything.

Being around Beth smoothed the edges of his life. He'd resisted a real relationship ever since he and Zoe had split. The Rangers kept him busy. Only now...

He shook the longing away. Still too busy.

After Ben left the office, Beth worried her bottom lip. So, he'd been on the verge of asking her out to dinner then faltered at the first hurdle. Well, that was more than enough time spent mooning over Ben Rasmussen. More important that they live to see another day.

She sent Lola a quick text. **Need to talk ASAP.** Drumming her fingers on the desktop, she waited. Beth looked up as Lola walked into their shared office.

"What's so urgent?" Lola paced. "Make it quick. The Bistro is hopping. Do we have to do this now?"

"Yes. Now." Beth quickly filled Lola in on Ben's plan to place an undercover operative in the Merc."

"A protection racket?" Lola's jaw dropped. She stopped pacing and leaned on the desk. "Has he confused us with Houston?"

"No. He's deadly serious. We need to decide today. He thinks we'll be approached soon."

"Having a new employee lurking around, isn't that going to look kind of weird or suspicious even?"

"Weird, suspicious, or not, Ben's right. We're taking a big chance on our employees' safety. I don't feel comfortable risking Kayla or Darren's lives if the Merc is going to be a target, and Ben is certain we will be. Don't forget what happened to Darla Murray."

"How could I?" Lola's expression turned sorrowful.

"Sorry. I shouldn't have brought her up. Darla's a painful memory for all of us." But her death last summer at the hands of a mob hitman/serial killer was a powerful reminder of what kind of evil could actually happen. "Anyway, I'm thinking maybe Kayla and Darren could take some vacation time, paid of course." She reached for the phone. "I'm calling Ben now to let him know we're on board with his plan."

"Fine." Lola headed for the door but stopped. "Just so you know, I'll be armed from now on. I'll see if Eva has a license to carry as well. Looks like the Wild West is coming back to the valley."

Lola sounded entirely too energized by the situation. Cautiously Beth said, "I don't plan on carrying, but I will have the 12 gauge under the counter at the cash register."

"Now that sounds like a plan," Lola said with a nod then darted from the office.

Lola pushed open the door to the kitchen and found Eva cleaning the stove, as usual, since she kept the kitchen spotless. "Eva, I know this sounds like off-the-wall, but do you have a carry permit?"

"I do." She set the spray cleaner and paper towels aside with a nod. "You think with all that's going on, we need to start carrying?" At sixty, Eva was wiry and strong, and in spite of being a wonderful cook, didn't carry an ounce of fat.

Lola nodded. "Until things are settled, maybe we both should."

"I'll start tomorrow." Eva picked up her cleaning tools

headed for the refrigerator. "I have a .45 at home and keep it locked up, away from the grandkids."

Wonder how sharp Eva's aim is? "Beth and I go to the range once a week. Want to start going with us?"

Eva chuckled, her dark brown eyes twinkling. "Wouldn't hurt none. Been a while since I felt the need to— uh, pack heat, as they say on TV."

Holding back a grin, Lola said, "It's a date then. Our usual time is on Tuesday at five."

"Tuesday at five it is."

Arming the cook, a grandmother. Was she going too far? Was it enough to keep them all from harm's way?

After Lola left Beth alone, she leaned back. A plan? Omigod. What kind of plan called for arming the Merc and Bistro's employees for a shootout? A modern-day gunfight at the Bistro Corral?

Matt poked his head in the door. "I wasn't eavesdropping, but I heard a lot of what the Ranger said."

"Are you finished with installing the cameras?"

"Two hidden cameras in the store, one in the Bistro. Four others are obvious. All wireless and connected to the monitors."

Beth nodded. She'd had to clear out nearly half the office and move it all to the stockroom to make room for the monitors. "I feel like I'm in a heist movie or something."

"Hopefully, there won't be any heists. You and your employees will be a lot safer."

"Thank you." Holding her breath, she signed off on the bill. "Security costs a lot."

"So, do doctors and hospitals," he said with a grin. "Chances are now you won't need either of those." He hesitated. "About dinner?"

"Sorry, Matt. I'm just not feeling it. There's entirely too much going on," she said with a smile. "Speaking of my employees, I need to call them in."

"I'll leave you to it, then." He left the office, but she could still hear him moving about. Packing his equipment probably.

Once Kayla and Darren were in the office, she said, "There are some things going on—the break-in for one, but there may be more to come. I want the two of you to take off for two weeks. Paid vacation. You can check out now."

"This is just a vacation, right?" Kayla asked. "Are you sure you're not firing us?"

"No, not at all."

"But if we go on vacation, that'll leave you here alone," Darren objected.

What a sweetheart. "Tonight, I'm closing early. We're wired up the yin-yang now, and that should make a big difference."

"What about tomorrow?"

"Arrangements are in place for coverage."

"Undercover?" Darren's gaze widened. "Cool."

"Sh," She held a finger to her lips. "It's a secret."

Darren and Kayla scurried to clock out, leaving Beth alone, once more. She let out a sigh. Whatever came, she was ready. Was she really? Her hands trembled. No way was she ready for a gunfight at the Merc.

Matt stuck his head in the door. "I'm all packed up and ready to leave. Are you sure you wouldn't prefer to have someone here?"

"I'm closing early. Lola and Eva should be finished with clean up in the Bistro. I'm headed upstairs to the apartment. Our home which is duly alarmed and secured. Thank you."

"My pleasure." He gave a nod. "If you have any

questions or concerns, please don't hesitate to call."

"I'm sure everything will be fine. The alarm system seems very straightforward. You're going to have a lot of new business if this trend keeps up."

"Yes," he said. "The town's misfortune is my good fortune. Have a good evening."

His tone was rueful. But his words were too true. "Goodnight, Matt."

Even as she used his expertise to secure their business and home, she didn't like the coincidental nature of it all.

Ben walked into the office of the Sleepytime Motel. He showed his identification. "I'd like to speak to the manager."

"I'm the manager, Hank McKennitt." McKennitt was balding with a ginger beard and bloodshot eyes. "What can I do for you, Ranger?"

"This motel was vandalized recently."

"Damn straight." McKennitt smacked the counter with his fist. "What're you gonna do about it?"

When faced with not an uncommon response to law enforcement, Ben held back an angry retort. Patience was the key. "I have reason to believe you could be approached by someone demanding you pay protection."

McKennitt's eyes narrowed to slits. "What makes you think that?"

Something, the edge in his tone alerted Ben. "One of the others has already been threatened. Have you already been approached?"

"Nah." McKennitt shook his head, averting his gaze.

"And if someone did approach you, what would be your response?"

McKennitt gave a crafty smile. "I'd refer them to the

owner."

The manager used the plural, so he'd been approached by more than one. "Who owns the Sleepytime?"

"Betsy and I do."

"Betsy?"

McKennitt pulled out a twelve-gauge shotgun from underneath the counter. "Meet Betsy."

"I see." Ben swallowed. "You need to warn your employees."

"I'm it, for now. The clerk who was here when they tore up the place up and quit."

Ben pointed to the security cameras. "Those work?"

"They do now. Hadn't bothered with tapes, but they're fully loaded now with brand new tapes."

"You will contact me." He placed his card on the desk. "If you're approached." He still didn't quite trust McKennitt. The motel owner was definitely holding something back.

Chapter Five

Friday evening

Ben strode into the Sheriff's Department and headed for Vince's office where he found the sheriff packing his briefcase. "Looks like you're getting ready to head home."

"I am." Vince added his tablet and shut the case. "I'm taking Abby home after she closes. I finally convinced her to reduce her hours and call in a temp for additional evening coverage."

"I won't keep you, but I wanted you to know I checked out the Sleepytime Motel."

"Yeah, Hank McKennitt owns that place now. Remember him from school?"

"*That* Hank? We called him Mac back then. He's changed a bit. I didn't connect him with the guy I met today. I wouldn't be surprised if he hasn't already been approached. Something about him is off. I've arranged for an operative to apply for a job there first thing in the morning. His last clerk quit after the place was vandalized."

"What about the Wheatons?"

"Beth called. She and Lola have agreed to an undercover there too. She's giving her two regular employees a paid vacation for a couple of weeks. Get this: Lola and the cook will both be armed. Not sure I'm too happy about that. Beth wanted Eva to take time off as well, but Lola said they might as well close the Bistro if Eva wasn't cooking."

Vince grinned. "Good point."

"I'm heading over to the Tidy-Kleen. I want to hear

what Frank Hausman has to say."

"Any plans after that? You're welcome to come to supper. I have it on good authority from Ms. Mills that roast beef is on the menu."

The Tate's cook, known by one and all as Marti, was reputed to be a great cook and rivaled his mom. Regretfully, he shook his head. "Thanks, but mom and dad are expecting me sometime tonight. Another time maybe."

"Sure thing. Tell them I'm looking forward to their next barbecue."

"Will do." The Rasmussen Ranch Barbecue was a local countywide picnic his parents had thrown ever since he was a kid. Sides of beef, barbeque beans, potato salad and a plethora of other side dishes drew folks from far and wide.

After driving the short distance from the center of town to the Tidy-Kleen, Ben discovered he'd hit rush hour at the dry cleaners. On his arrival, there were at least seven customers waiting to pick up their cleaning and laundry. He took the time to observe Frank Hausman's easy way with his customers. In his early sixties, Frank's weathered face still retained the vestiges of his former good looks. Iron gray hair, cut close, clear gray eyes, and a physique and posture that hinted of a career in the military. By no means, did Hausman appear to be someone who could be easily intimidated into paying protection money... of course, if his wife were threatened.

When the last customer had left, Hausman smiled. "Sorry, Ranger, what can I do for you. I'm sure you're not here for your shirts."

"No, Mr. Hausman." He glanced around and spied another customer about to enter. "Is there somewhere we can talk privately?"

"Sure." Hausman called over his shoulder, "Sue! Need you upfront."

Suann Hausman caught Ben's eye as she emerged from the back. She ducked her head and avoided his gaze. Guess she figured her secret investigation would soon be revealed.

"This way, "Hausman said.

Ben followed him into the back office where he gestured for Ben to have a seat. "What can I do for you?"

Ben cleared his throat. "It has come to our attention that various business owners here in the Valley have been approached to pay protection money."

"Really?" Hausman ran a finger around his collar, attempting to loosen it.

"It has also come to my attention that you are one of those who was approached." He leveled his gaze on the business owner.

Hausman squared his shoulders. "Not me. No, sir. I'm not that easily intimidated."

"And if your wife were threatened or perhaps further damage to your business?"

He shook his head. "Nah. You're mistaken."

Sorry, Mrs. Hausman. "I've seen the recording from your own cameras."

"My cameras? Then..." Hausman sighed. He seemed to shrink before Ben's eyes. "What else could I do? He showed me photos of my wife shopping and picking up our grandson from school. One on one, I'm not afraid of anyone, Ranger. I'm a marine. But I won't put my family in harm's way."

"What I suggest is that you continue to cooperate with them a while longer. Provide me with the recordings of those transactions so we can identify them and put them under surveillance."

Hausman nodded. "That's reasonable, I guess."

"How much are they demanding? And how often?"

"A thousand a week. Every week."

"Paying them may seem the easiest thing to do, but their demands tend to escalate as time goes on."

"They're not happy with an extra 52K a year from my business alone? Fuckers!" Hausman's fists clenched. "I was crazy to have made that first payment. I should've sold out when I had the chance, but I just wasn't ready to retire—not yet." His stricken expression said maybe now was the time.

"You were protecting your family. It's understandable." Ben rose to leave, then stopped. "Who offered to buy you out?"

"The mayor. It wasn't a serious offer, nowhere near what the business is worth." Hausman's meaty fists clenched and unclenched. "Wrap it up soon, Ranger, or I might have to take matters into my own hands."

"Hold on, Frank. We're trying to get ahead of this, but give us time. I don't want any more businesses broken into or people threatened. The sheriff and I are on this. Let us do our job."

Hausman nodded. "Whatever you say."

"Appreciate it." No matter that Hausman had agreed to let the law handle it, holding the retired marine to his word might prove difficult if he thought his family endangered.

While Ben drove through town, he checked in with his superior in Waco and filled him in on the newest developments and verified the addition of two undercover rangers who would be in place the following morning. After disconnecting, he noted that the Merc had closed early.

Good. She'd taken his advice.

Almost of its own accord, his SUV drove around the block and entered the alley behind the Main Street stores. A final welfare check was in order.

***

After having set the table, Beth watched the six o'clock news while Lola banged around in the kitchen. She sniffed. Something new. Something spicy. "What's for dinner?"

"Leftovers from the Bistro."

Big surprise. Their dinner always included the Bistro's leftovers. Waste not, want not was Lola's motto. Beth groaned. "Just once, I'd love to have a pizza."

"Then you're in luck, Eva created a Mexican pan pizza for today's menu and made an extra one just for us. And salad, of course."

"You're kidding!" Beth's spirits lifted. "Then Eva gets a bonus in her paycheck next week."

"What would we do without her?"

Indeed, what *would* they do without her? Eva Johnson was the best all-around cook in a hundred miles. Tex-Mex, stews, soups, salads, rolls, desserts—oh, her desserts were to die for—she could do it all. Tall and big-boned, a redhead with the sweetest disposition. All she lived for was to cook and to spoil her grandkids.

The sharp *rap-rap* on the door startled Beth from her food daydreams.

"I'll get it." She ran to the door, then stopped. *Ah, yes. Careful.* She checked the screen on the new door camera.

Ben. Her breath caught in her throat. Matt had installed an excellent wireless door camera, high-res and with night vision. Not that it was dark yet, but the option was still good to have.

She jerked open the door. "Hi," she said breathlessly. "I didn't expect to see you tonight. Has something else happened?"

Ben's dark brows drew together in a scowl. "You shouldn't open the door without knowing who's there."

Removing his hat, he stepped inside.

"Oh, but I *did* know." She demonstrated with an expansive gesture that would've done Vanna White proud. "Voila! Handy door surveillance camera installed."

A warm smile wreathed his face, erasing the scowl, the lines crinkling at the corners of his bright blue eyes. "Freeman gave you the works then. Good. I feel a lot better knowing you—you and Lola are safe."

Excited by his sudden appearance, she smiled. "Come on. Have a seat. We're just about to try one of Eva's new recipes."

"That's a tempting offer, but mom knows I'm in town, and she sort of expects her eldest son to show up for dinner, not necessarily on time, but some time." He gave her a wry smile.

Even a wry smile warmed the pit of her stomach. Anxious to keep him talking, she added, "Your mom must miss you, given you're stationed in Waco."

"She doesn't complain." His smile widened. "She's familiar with a Texas Ranger's duties. Both my grandfathers were in the Rangers." He gave a dry chuckle. "That might be why she married a rancher."

"Might be." The spicy aroma of the pizza was getting stronger by the minute. "Are you sure you won't have a beer or a bite of Tex-Mex pan pizza?"

"Not tonight." He shook his head. "I'd like for us to have dinner soon," he said, lowering his voice, "once we get a handle on stuff."

She nodded. "Stuff meaning break-ins, extortion, and crime in general—that kind of thing?"

"Right."

All business. All righty. "We won't keep you then. As you can see we're well-alarmed and secured. Be sure to tell your mom we're looking forward to the barbecue next weekend. We'll be there with bells on." She yelled to the kitchen, "Won't we, Lola?"

Lola poked her head into the living room. "With bells on."

"Thank you," Beth said. "We appreciate your stopping by."

He turned, then stopped. "Also, you'll have a new employee in the morning. She'll be there at seven."

"That's all you're going to tell me about her?"

"She'll tell you all she wants you to know. She's young, one of the best and brightest of a new crop of Rangers."

Business. All business. Surely he was off duty some time.

He remained standing in the doorway, shifting from one foot to the other. "I'll say goodnight, then."

"Goodnight, Ben." Oh, how she wished he wasn't always so focused on his duty. Of course, she couldn't begrudge his seeing his parents when he was so seldom in town. Still...

"Well..." Still hesitating for some unknown—to her, at least—reason.

"Is there something else?" Her heart gave a leap, maybe...

"Just wondering if y'all are staying in the rest of the night?"

She gave a chuckle. "It may be Friday night, but the Valley isn't exactly big on nightlife." She gave a theatrical sigh. "Bars and honky-tonks lead to hangovers. And hangovers aren't much fun when you have to get up early to open the store."

"True." He settled his hat on his head. "I'll say g'night."

"Night, Ben."

Beth shut the door behind him, then turned to her sister. "What the hell was that about?"

Lola gave her an eye roll. "*That* was about seeing if you

were nice and safe, all tucked up at home."

"No way!" Beth shook her head. "You're fantasizing again, but you're all mixed up. You're supposed to be focusing on Will." Truth be told, maybe her sister was right. Ben did seem interested. Again, he'd mentioned having dinner, but there were too many obstacles—like the increase in crime. Who could think about starting a relationship when danger threatened from every corner? As for getting laid, it'd been so long she'd probably forgotten the basics. Casual hookups were never her style.

His stomach growling, Ben headed out of town. He wouldn't have minded trying some of that Tex-Mex pizza. Why did he feel like he had a dang proverbial stick up his ass whenever he was around Beth Wheaton? Matters never seem to work out when he was around her due to his inability to relax. If he wasn't reading Beth wrong, then she was interested...somewhat.

In the rearview mirror, he spotted the headlights of a big truck coming up behind him and fast. He moved to the side to let the asshole pass.

The impact jarred through his body, ripping the steering wheel from his hands. He latched onto the wheel and fought to keep the SUV on the road.

No such luck.

The right tires dipped off the side of the road and lost their grip. The truck rolled. Sky and ground topsy-turvy.

Chapter Six

Beth had finished eating her salad and was reaching for that first piece of pizza when a chill slid up her spine. She rubbed the chill bumps on her upper arms. "Wow," she said with a shiver. "That's weird. Is the AC on too high?"

Lola frowned, snatched a piece of pizza, and set it on her plate. "Not for August in Texas. Maybe you're catching a cold or something. You know they say summer colds are the worst."

"No." Beth shook her head. "My nose isn't running. I'm not feverish. I just had a sudden chill."

"Maybe that's what they mean when they say, 'Someone just walked over my grave.'"

"Ew. That's creepy." Beth rose from the table and walked over to the window. The alley was in shadow. Again, she shivered. "Something's not right. I can feel it."

"So now, you're going all woo-woo on me. Sit down and eat your pizza before it gets cold."

Unable to tear her gaze away from the alley, she said, "I like cold pizza." She walked over to the door camera. The camera display was clearer than her actual vision. Nothing moved. Still, something wasn't right.

Ben blinked. Shook his head. He was hanging upside down. Chest and ribs hurt. He took a deep breath, as deep as he could without extreme pain. Dusk was gathering and the sun was low on the horizon except in reverse order. He batted away the four airbags that had deployed during the crash. The seatbelt cut into his chest. Crap. He fumbled for the belt release and held on to control the fall.

He listened. Had the SOB who'd crashed into him stopped? More important, was he coming back to finish the job?

No sound, other than crickets and the whine of a pesky mosquito. He slapped at the offending critter.

He brushed fragments of glass from his shirt and jacket. Driver side window open. Cool nighttime air wafted across his face.

Gingerly he moved his legs. Working okay. He eased his way across the roof of the SUV. "Unh." Ribs definitely bruised.

He crawled from the vehicle, resting on his knees for a minute or two to catch his breath.

Must be making progress if whoever was behind everything felt it necessary to send him a message. Someone had followed him from town. Someone who knew he was staying with his parents. And someone who knew what road he'd be taking to get there.

Unsteadily, he got to his feet, leaned back against the SUV, and shook his head to clear the cobwebs. He eased his arms from his jacket and shook off more splinters of glass. Bending over he gave his head a shake. More glass.

"Argh!" He blew out a sharp breath. Only a couple of miles from the ranch. Might as well get moving.

The evening sky was dark by the time Ben reached the ranch. Will's truck was parked in its usual spot, so he'd made it home before Ben had had his accident. He opened the door and walked inside, easing the door shut. Maybe he could make himself presentable before his mom got a look at him. Adela might be used to Ranger duties, but like most mothers, she tended toward the excitable end of the spectrum when one of her brood was injured.

She emerged from the kitchen, wiping her hands on her apron. "I thought I heard someone on the porch. I didn't hear a car, though." Then she caught sight of him and threw up her hands. "Omigod! Your face is bloody. What's happened?" She rushed toward him.

He waved her away. "I'm fine, mom. Had a little fender bender. I just need to clean up a bit. What's for dinner?" Never, ever his intention to scare the woman who brought him into the world.

"Whew!" She let out a sigh of relief. "If you're asking about food, I know you're okay."

He let out a chuckle. True to form, his mom, if anything, was pragmatic. "Let me get washed up. I'm starving."

After dinner, Ben walked outside to sit on the porch. Will followed.

"Correct me if I'm wrong, bro, but your fender bender was a little more involved than you let on." Will sat in one of a pair of rocking chairs.

"You'd be right. Someone ran me off the damn road about two miles from here. Damn truck rolled a couple of times."

"You don't look much the worse for wear."

Ben let out a chuckle. "I'm sore as hell. Ribs, chest mainly. I'm lucky. Airbags worked."

"So, you've been in town for about five minutes. Who've you already pissed off?"

"Beats me. I haven't done that much. Just some

interviews, talked to some business owners, and interrogated the guy who tried to hold up Abby Tate."

"I hear Zoe's back in town."

"Yeah." Ben shook his head. "Saw her. She hasn't changed much. Still same spoiled Mayor's daughter."

"Heard she and that ballplayer split up."

"Yeah. Mayor said as much."

Will stood. "I'm heading back inside for a piece of apple pie. Want some?"

"Nah." He stared into a star-filled night sky. "I gotta report to Waco."

The screen door slammed as Will went back into the house.

Reporting the attack to Waco might mean he'd be taken off the case. And that would suck, big time. The last thing he wanted was to leave Beth Wheaton to the mercy of whoever the hell was behind the break-ins and extortion racket.

Yes, he'd placed Ranger Donovan in the Merc, and he hadn't exaggerated her skills, but no one had Beth's best interests at heart the way he did.

Early Saturday morning

Beth walked down the long dark alleyway. The farther she walked, the darker the night grew until she could no longer see beyond the end of her nose. The night mist thickened, grew warm, then hot. She sucked in the hot air trying to catch her breath. No use.

"Wake up, Beth! You're dreaming."

Beth opened her eyes. Her sister stood hovering over her. Shaking her. "What?"

"I heard you all the way into my room. You were crying that you couldn't breathe."

"A nightmare." Beth sat up and shook her head. "I was having a nightmare. Walking down the alley. This black mist enveloped me, and I was smothering." She brushed the curls back from her damp forehead.

Lola sat on the corner of the bed. "Maybe it was the pizza. Too spicy?"

She shook her head. "No way. It was just a bad dream. I'm all right. Go back to bed."

"Earlier you had a chill. Now you're sweaty. Maybe you *are* sick."

"Go back to bed." Beth swung her feet to the floor. "I'm going to take a shower. That'll help me get back to sleep."

"If you say so." Her sister stood, watching, then sighed. "You're the boss."

After Lola went back to her bedroom, Beth showered and changed into a fresh nightshirt. But still, she tossed and turned. She beat her pillow into submission, then flipped it to the cool side. No, it wasn't that she *couldn't* sleep. She didn't want to. No way could she risk going back to that dream. If she shut her eyes, that was what would happen.

At six forty-five, Beth went down to open the store. Two cups of strong coffee had been the panacea for her restless night. As soon as she turned the notice board to *Open*, a young woman on the sidewalk waved to get her attention. Beth opened the door. "May I help you?"

The young woman held out her hand. A strong handshake, Beth noted. Was this her undercover ranger?

"I'm Kelly Donovan," she said. "A friend of mine told me you might have a temporary position open."

The young woman was attractive, in her late twenties or early thirties, tall and muscular. Straight dark hair and brown eyes. A penetrating no-nonsense gaze. Clad in a cambric shirt and a denim jacket, boot-cut jeans, if she was the undercover ranger Ben had promised, she was perfect.

"Your friend's name would be...?"

"Ben. He recommended me."

So, the undercover ranger was playing it cool. Good enough. "Come on in, Kelly. It so happens both my cashier and stock boy are on vacation, so I'm glad to meet you." Kelly entered behind Beth. Together they walked toward the cash register. "What's your work experience?" she asked, continuing in the same employer/prospective employee mode.

Kelly flashed a ready smile. "My parents run a grocery store in Waco. I worked there all through high school. I can stock shelves and run the cash register. In college, I did a lot of waitressing, so I can wait tables in the Bistro if need be."

"You certainly seem qualified." Beth nodded toward the rear of the Merc. "Let's go back to the office, and we'll take care of the paperwork."

Kelly followed Beth into the office. "Nice setup," she said eyeing the monitors.

"Brand new. Just installed yesterday." Beth hesitated then came right out with it. "Are you armed?"

Grinning, Kelly hiked one long leg. Patted her ankle. One here. One mid-back. I thought a hip holster would be too obvious. Knife on my other ankle. And I have a black belt in karate."

Before she could hold it back, a nervous giggle erupted from Beth. "Well then, I'd say you're sufficiently armed. All righty, you need to know there's a loaded twelve-gauge under the counter at the register. My sister is carrying, as is the cook in the Bistro."

Kelly flashed a wide smile. "Fine. As long as none of you shoot me or each other, we'll get along just fine."

"We *are* firearm trained."

"You're trained," she said, narrowing her gaze as if talking to a schoolchild, "to shoot at stationary targets that don't shoot back. There's a difference."

"Of course, I understand that." A flush crept up Beth's neck. "I don't have a stock delivery until the middle of next week, so mainly I'll need you at the register. My sister Lola handles the Bistro. Eva is our cook. Lunch is furnished, anything you want that Eva is cooking that day. There's no set menu. Eva cooks whatever she's in the mood to cook, and our customers like it that way."

"Appreciate that." Kelly nodded. "However, your safety is my main concern. We're hoping you will be approached. It's logical you will be."

"Meaning the others who've had break-ins have been extorted."

As if considering whether or not how much to reveal, Kelly simply nodded. "That's all I can say.

"Then let's get to work. Other than the Bistro, which doesn't open until eleven." Beth gestured over her shoulder. "Two aisles over, we have a coffee and pastry counter. The pastry delivery should be here any minute, so fire up the coffee pots. We'll see an influx of customers who should start rolling in here, any time."

After a quick breakfast and a cup of coffee, Ben called a wrecker service to tow his truck to Steve's Body Shop. After notifying his insurance company of the wreck, he borrowed one of the ranch's trucks to drive into town.

Still moving slowly from the seatbelt injuries, he eased his way into the Sheriff's Department. "Sheriff Tate in?" he asked the dispatcher.

The dispatcher smiled, showing her dimples. "Yes, Ranger. Go right in. He's expecting you."

Vince looked up, his expression full of concern. "Will told me about your accident last night."

"Yeah. Appears I've made someone nervous." He took a seat, trying not to wince.

A crooked smile "You don't look *too* much the worse for wear."

"Nah. I'm okay." Less time spent on his physical condition the better. "Let's get down to business. Ranger Donovan is in place at the Merc. She called me before I left the ranch. Ditto, Ranger Ocala has been hired at the Sleepytyme."

"So, now we wait?"

"I don't like it. But yeah, we wait for their next move. If we've put our people in the right place at the right time, we'll grab 'em." Waiting for someone to make another move on Beth just didn't sit right with him. But Donovan was the perfect choice to keep an eye on Beth while he intensified his investigation.

Around ten, Beth cleared away the snack counter and carried the trash bag out back to the Dumpster. She walked back into the office and sat at her desk, ready to go over yesterday's accounts receivable. Inexplicably, the hair rose on the nape of her neck. She looked up. Two men stood in the hallway outside her office. Had they entered from the rear of the store, right behind her? One short. One at least six feet. She tried to catalog their appearance. Swarthy complexions. Both mustached. One full-faced. One slim, the taller one.

"We're here to help you," the taller of the two men said.

He stood with his feet apart, hands in his pockets.

"Really? I'm not looking for any new employees." This was it. It was going down now. Heart rate spiking, hands trembling, she reached for the phone.

"I don't think you want to do that, *chica*."

"So, *how* are you going to help me? And *why* shouldn't I use the phone?" Okay, that was pretty snarky. Dammit. Just who did these bozos think they were fooling with?

"We'll protect your store so it doesn't get broken into anymore. Such a mess," the shorter one said. "Someone broke your nice, big window. Not very nice."

Her mouth dried. She tried to swallow. "I have security cameras," she managed to say. Difficult to keep the fear from her tone. Not sure she succeeded. "I don't intend to get broken into anymore. If I do, we'll have them on camera."

"Two thousand dollars a week, and you'll be protected. From break-ins. From fire."

"Floods too? Hell no!" she said loudly enough she hoped Ranger Donovan would hear. I don't clear that much a week." Getting more angry than scared, she smacked the desktop with her fist. "My sister and I have worked too hard to fork over our profits to creeps like you. She nudged the panic button with her knee. Kelly had a similar one at the register, as did the Bistro at theirs.

Not only would it alert the others in the store, but it would notify the Sheriff's Department as well. All she had to do was keep talking.

And stay alive.

The shorter of the two men advanced, his face drawn into a permanent scowl. He pulled a knife and ran a finger gingerly over the edge. His lips formed the word 'ew'. "You wouldn't want something bad to happen to you or your sister or your employees, now would you?" He leaned forward, placing his hands on her desk. His breath reeked of garlic.

She averted her face. "Of course not. But if you think I'm afraid of you, you're barking up the wrong tree." Totally scared to death was more like it. But she wouldn't give in to their strong-arm tactics.

The unmistakable sound of a shotgun being racked made the two men jump. The shorter one tried to grab Beth, but she scooted out of his reach.

"Hold it right there." Ranger Donovan stood in the hall outside the office. "You're under arrest. Drop the knife."

The knife clattered on the floor tiles.

By this time, Lola showed up, also armed. The sound of sirens. And the heavy tread of the authorities entering the store, the sound reassuring as they tromped down the hallway to her office.

Ben entered first, followed by the sheriff and Deputy Will. They made quick work of disarming the two men and handcuffing them. The sheriff and Will led them away so quickly, all Beth could do was lean back and try to catch her breath. She let out a loud sigh of relief. "Whew! What a rush. It's over."

Ben, who had remained behind, leaned over her. He caressed her cheek. "Beth, it's not over. "This is just the beginning."

"But they've been arrested." At the same time, she tried to process her feelings. Ben had touched her so gently. So, lovingly, even.

Her face warming, she gazed into his eyes and noted a cut over his eyebrow. When had that happened? Unbidden her hand reached forward. He captured it in his strong hands. "It's nothing," he said. "These two—they're low men on the totem pole. Taking them out of play is just the first step. We'll try to turn them in order to lead us to their boss."

"You mean there'll be more to come?" Her voice

quavered. Her stomach plummeted to her knees. How much more of this could she take?

"Yes."

"So what'll they pull next, I mean whoever's next? Those guys mentioned they could protect the store from break-in and fire. Is fire the next step? Will someone try to set our store on fire?"

Panic, true blind panic set in. Fire. The thought of burning to death terrified her. Her breathing grew rapid. Her heart hammered. She gasped for air. "B-ben, I—"

"Calm down," Ben said gently, stroking her hand. "We don't know what they'll pull next. It might not even be here at the Merc."

"We live right over the store." Her voice rose. "If they set fire to the store, Lola and I—we'll be goners." She tamped down the panic, forcing herself to relax. She took a deep breath. "Sorry. I don't usually panic, but it hit me all of a sudden. Overwhelmed me."

Ben's cool gaze was kind as he hovered near. Releasing her hand, he asked, "Want something to drink? Coffee, cold drink?"

"Water, a bottle of water. Just bring me one from the store fridge." Her mouth was as dry as the Chihuahuan Desert.

Jeez. Had she just had a near panic attack right in front of Ben? What a ninny he must think her.

He returned with the bottle and held it out. Gratefully, she took the cold bottle and held it to her forehead for a moment before opening it. "I don't think I've ever considered just selling the place and getting the hell out of Dodge."

Pulling a chair around the desk, he straddled it. "Is that what you're thinking now?"

"No." She set the bottle cap aside and took a long

refreshing swig. "Well... maybe, for a second. We Wheatons don't cut and run. Our family has owned this store for nearly a century and a half. I'm not about to throw in the towel. Not now. You think my ancestors didn't have problems. They stuck it out. We will too." She set the bottle down, making sure it didn't tip. *Cheap plastic bottles.*

"You're sounding stronger. Calmer." Ben gave her a warm smile.

"Sorry, it was a moment of weakness. You must think I'm a real baby."

"No, I think you're brave. Braver than you know."

His gaze remained calm and warm. His calm steadied her. And his warmth sent her emotions eddying into unknown territory. She covered his hand with hers. Being with him felt right. Felt good. More than good, wonderful.

Vince looked up when his chief deputy entered the office. "Okay, what've we got on these dudes?"

"As I figured, they're two of Aceveda's thugs, brothers Roberto and Ramon Diaz. Born here." Reading from his note pad, Will stood with his feet wide apart. "Luis is checking with his contacts across the border to check if there are any cartel connections. One interesting thing, though: there's a third Diaz brother—Julio. He just happens to work for Briggs Construction."

Vince frowned. Another connection with the mayor's construction company. "We pretty sure Aceveda has those cartel connections?"

Will nodded. "Yep. Aceveda has a family link to the cartel. His wife, Rosario, has cousins in the cartel. And—get this—she has a brother and an uncle on the Nuevo Loredo police force." Will placed photo IDs on the board.

Vince nodded, as he eyeballed the persons of interest. Los Malos Dias cartel was based in Nuevo Loredo, Mexico, right across the border from Loredo, Texas. Its circle of influence was extensive, and now it appeared, they were preparing to extend it further into the Hill County. Reynaldo Reyes, the reputed head of the cartel, was a successful businessman. Known for his charm as well as his ruthlessness, he moved freely between the two countries.

"All right." Vince stood. He nodded at Will. "Let's see what we can get these two to tell us." The main reason Reyes remained free was that no one could or would provide evidence against him.

A tap at the door brought Beth back to reality. She straightened, her cheeks heating up like a Fourth of July fireworks display.

Ranger Donovan shot Beth a quizzical expression. "I'm to continue as before?" she asked Ben.

"Right." He squared his shoulders and stood. "This is just the beginning."

Kelly nodded and headed back to the front of the store.

Knees still a little weak, Beth rose from her seat. "Thank you, Ben. I don't know what I would've done if Kelly hadn't been here."

"We cut it damn close. I hate to think what would've happened if she hadn't been here, too."

"I think they were just trying to scare me. But, my Lord, they wanted two thousand a week. That's what made me so freaking mad."

He gazed down at her, his brows drawn together in a frown. "You have to keep your cool the next time a situation develops *if* it does. Those men would just as soon gut you, as they would a fish."

Beth swallowed. "Nice imagery."

Walking behind her, he leaned over her shoulder. She resisted the urge to let her head fall back onto his chest. It would be so easy to do. "Let's see what your new surveillance cameras picked up," he said.

She centered the keyboard in front of her. "I think they came from the rear. I had just carried out the trash. Obviously, I didn't close the door properly. I know I didn't lock it." Beth backed up the recording to the time in question. "Here we go. See the rear cameras picked them up. A really clear view of their faces. The resolution quality of these cameras is great."

His hands rested on her shoulders, easing the tension. Entirely too comfortable. "That third panic button came in handy, didn't it?"

Beth looked up and shot him a wide smile. "It's worth its weight in gold. I'm so glad you suggested it. Located where it is, all I had to do was nudge it with my knee."

"Easy to bump into accidentally, though." He let out a chuckle. "Careful or you'll have the entire Sheriff's Department in here."

"Like I did today?" Thank God, they'd come running.

"Exactly."

She worried her bottom lip. Should she...? Heck why not. "I was really happy to see your face."

"Glad I'm not wearing out my welcome."

"Wear out your welcome—not likely." Damn her cheeks for heating up like a neon sign. "You know you and your brother are always welcome at the Merc." Oh crap, why had she phrased it that way? While her words were true, they in no way expressed how she really felt. Still, better not to scare the man off. Or remind him why he hated blondes.

His hands tensed on her shoulders. Damn. Not her

intention.

"Good to know," he said dryly, backing away. "I'm heading back to the sheriff's office. By now, He should have the scoop on your intruders."

"Don't let me keep you. Kelly will man the front. I feel quite safe having her here."

He nodded, but instead of walking out the front he walked to the back door. She heard him try the lock. She smiled. As he walked by her door he gave her a casual nod. "Just checking."

"Thank you," she called after him, then sighed. Why couldn't she control her runaway tongue? Why jabber on just to fill the silence and cover her discomfort. No, the truth was she wasn't uncomfortable around Ben. It was more a case of hiding her true feelings.

She stood. Might as well check out the store and see how Kelly was getting along.

Walking around to the front of the store, she found Matt Freeman chatting up Kelly. Gone was the businesslike ranger. Her body appeared to have been inhabited by a flirtatious, giddy, almost teenage persona.

Matt turned and favored Beth with a smile. "I see you've hired a new cashier. Did the break-in scare off your previous one?"

"Not at all. She's on vacation."

"That's right. I'm a temp, but if I'm really good, Beth might keep me on permanently." Kelly batted her dark lashes at Matt. "I just love meeting people. You could say I'm just a people person."

Okay, so she'd undergone this personality metamorphosis as part of her undercover assignment. Whoa. Freeman had no clue, and if Beth hadn't already seen Kelly's true personality, she'd have been fooled as well.

"I understand you've had more trouble," Matt said.

"Yes, a couple of thugs attempt to extort me."

"I was so scared." Kelly threw her hands up. "I didn't know what to do when that buzzer went off. And then the sheriff and his men showed up. It was so exciting. I thought we were being robbed."

Amazing performance. "More or less, that was their intention," Beth said. "Back to work, Kelly. I need to talk to Mr. Freeman."

She led him back to the office. "The cameras worked great. Would you like to see? The high-res is truly wonderful. Not grainy at all."

"They entered from the rear?"

Beth nodded. "I guess I didn't shut the door properly. *And* I forgot to lock it. It's locked now though. Ranger Rasmussen checked it before he left."

"The Ranger is still in town?"

"Oh, yes, I think he's going to be here for a while until things settle down or are hopefully resolved with all the bad guys arrested."

"I can't stress enough how cautious you need to be," he said.

"I know." Here was another man who thought she was a ditzy blonde. "It was a moment's carelessness. I can assure you it won't be repeated."

"So, the panic button worked and law enforcement arrived in time. Good to know." Matt nodded. "I have another appointment. I'll see you soon, I hope?"

"Of course. But instead of you owing me dinner, perhaps, I owe you one. Your system saved my life."

"I'm looking forward to it."

"Me too." She gave him her brightest smile. It was the least she could do. Right?

As soon as he'd left the store, Kelly appeared, no-nonsense Kelly. Not the giddy teenager. "Well, so that's your security alarm guy? He's totally hot, but he's up to something. I got a really weird vibe off the guy."

"Really?" Beth remembered her initial misgivings. "I did too, at first. But he grows on you. He did a bang-up installation, the works."

"Yeah, he did." Kelly paused, a frown appearing on her pretty face. "You need to change your wi-fi password, now that the system is installed. Did he install anything in your apartment?"

"Yes, an alarm system, including a door camera."

"Mind if I give it a once over after we close?"

"Have at it. But why?"

"Just a gut feeling. And I trust my gut."

Beth remembered reading how baby monitors and all sorts of devices could be hacked. "Okay, sure. I'll trust your gut too. After seeing your performance a few minutes ago, I'm in awe."

Kelly chuckled. "Yeah, that was Kelly from about ten years ago. She's fun to bring out to play."

"I didn't know what was going on for a second."

"But you caught on immediately and played right along." Kelly nodded as if approving. "None of my business, but are you really going out to dinner with the alarm guy?"

"I think so." *Maybe I really should pay attention to Kelly's gut. My own?*

"Ranger Rasmussen won't mind?" the ranger asked, arching a perfectly shaped brow.

"Why should he?" Had she given herself away so obviously that any outside observer could tell where her heart lay? Geez. "We're not a couple or anything near it."

"Really?" The ranger shrugged. "Like I said before, none of my business."

"What made you think...?" How had she given her feelings away?

"We're taught to observe body language, micro-expressions." Kelly smiled. "Maybe I was mistaken, but the two of you seem awfully comfortable together."

Beth waved away the suggestion. "We've known each other for—oh, ages."

"Like I said, none of my business." Kelly raised her hands in a gesture of surrender.

At that moment the front door alarm beeped. Saved by the *beep*. "Customer," Beth reminded her undercover employee. She heaved a sigh of relief after Kelly left the office. Something had to be done, or everyone in town would know she was carrying a torch for one handsome Texas Ranger.

All the way over to the Sheriff's Department, images of Beth's curvy body and kissable mouth flooded his mind. He could not figure her out. One minute, he thought she was ready to fall into his arms. The next, she was all cut-and-dried businesswoman. He'd gone so far as to place his hands on her shoulders. He'd felt her almost surrender as surely as he'd felt his own desire to touch more than her pretty shoulders.

Dammit. He'd been burned once by a blonde. Not anxious to repeat the experience.

But Beth was nothing like Zoe. While Zoe was voluptuous and seemingly all the woman a man could want, she gave so little of herself. Making love had quickly become mechanical after they married. Unfaithful. And on the make. Ready to move up to someone who could provide her with whatever her withered little heart desired.

She'd thought to find it with a pro ballplayer. What was she after now? Not that he cared, as long as she left him alone.

On the other hand, Beth was all woman, not blatantly, but sweetly. At least, that was the impression he'd formed in the last few days. He'd known her since she was a skinny kid with gold ringlets and warm brown eyes. No longer skinny, she'd matured into a woman he had to get to know better. Lord knew, he wanted to take her to bed, but she wasn't the type of woman who'd be up for a casual fling.

The bigger question: was he ready for a real relationship?

Ben entered Vince's office. "This is sort of getting to be a habit." He removed his hat.

Vince looked up and grinned. "Should I find you some desk space? Doesn't appear like you're heading back to Waco any time soon."

"I'm not. My boss figures I need to hang out here a while. I agree, especially, with two undercover agents in play. They're young. Eager. I don't want anything to happen to either one." He took a seat. "So, what've you found out about our two thugs?"

Vince spent the next few minutes giving Ben an update. "And they're familiar with the justice system. Too familiar. They lawyered up as soon as we read 'em their rights. Harold Deacon, Esq. is in there with them now."

"Deacon. Hmph."

"That's right. Lawyer to every lowlife in town. Aceveda has him on a permanent retainer. Ditto Alonzo Griggs."

"Deacon's originally from Houston, right?"

"Mobbed up there too. Equal opportunity lawyer. Mob and cartel—all welcome." Vince picked up the phone and made a call. "Need to set up some desk space for Ranger Rasmussen. Phone. Computer. The works. " He frowned. "Monday it'll have to be then. But early."

He replaced the receiver. "Monday morning is the best

we can do. Something about they'll have to rejig the office space a bit. But it'll get worked out."

"Appreciate it. Don't worry about the computer. As long as I have access to the internet and a printer, I have a secure laptop." He turned to leave.

"You staying at your parents'?" Vince asked.

"Another night or two. For the time being. I'm using one of their trucks, which reminds me I need to get a rental. Anything useful found at the wreck scene?"

"Nothing forensic, other than glass from a somewhat recent model Ford truck, 2009 forward. Any idea what color it was?"

Ben shook his head. "It came up behind me, fast. Dark is the best I could tell as I was flipping."

"We've notified body shops in the surrounding counties to be on the lookout. In this county alone, we have nearly fifty trucks registered that could fit the bill."

"And when you find the owner, it'll have been reported stolen that morning. I know how that works." Yeah, chasing down the truck was a dead end, unless there happened to be a handy security camera nearby. Talk about a long shot.

Ben set his hat onto his head and nodded. "See you Monday...that is if we have a quiet Sunday."

"We can always hope."

Not that it did much good. Whoever was behind the spate of break-ins and attempted extortion was just getting started. A quiet Sunday? Chances were slim to none.

Saturday evening

The rest of the day passed without incident. Beth closed the Merc and breathed a sigh of relief. Still, waiting for something—anything—to happen was draining. "What do we do first?"

Kelly stretched and smiled. "We have a glass of wine?" Not waiting for Beth's response, she chuckled. "Oh, you mean after we have a glass of wine, maybe we should change those Wi-Fi passwords."

"Something like that, but a glass of wine would be great."

Kelly rubbed her hands together. "Let's do the store's system first, then the wine." She sat in front of the computer. "Now give me the password Freeman gave you."

Beth opened one of the desk drawers and pulled out a piece of paper. "It's so complicated. I could never remember it."

"Here's what I do. Think of a line in your favorite song. Use the first letter of each word. Substitute a couple of the letters with a number, and all you have to remember is which two or three letters you made upper case."

"Hm." Beth worried her bottom lip. "I'll still need to write it down."

Kelly smiled. "Then save it as a document with an innocuous title, then store it in a file that's labeled something like miscellaneous taxes. You'll know what it is whenever you need to refer to it, but no one else will."

"Wow." Impressed by the ranger's simple solutions, Beth came up with her favorite song, *The Yellow Rose of Texas* by Bobby Horton. "Now for my favorite line." She wrote down the words, then followed the rest of Kelly's easy instructions.

"Ta-dah!" Kelly changed the password. "Now for that wine and the rest of the evening's entertainment."

Upstairs in the apartment, Beth brought Kelly a glass of

white zinfandel, then sat on the sofa.

"Thanks," Kelly said, glancing around. "I really like what you've done with the apartment. It has a very homey and comfortable vibe."

"Thanks. That's just the vibe we were going for." Beth took a sip of her wine. "Mm. I love this stuff."

Kelly leaned forward, her expression growing intense. "Now for the reason, I'm really here. Were you here while Freeman did the installation?"

"Mostly. Not all the time."

"My main concern is whether he installed a little something extra."

"Whoa!" Beth straightened. "You mean like hidden cameras?"

"It's been known to happen." Kelly took a slow sip of her wine.

Beth glanced around at the walls and ceiling. She got up from the comfy sofa and walked over to a bookshelf, but couldn't spot anything out of place or extra. "How can you tell?"

"First turn off everything that's connected. Phone, TV cable box, laptops." Kelly pulled a small black rectangular device from her tote bag. "I'll use an RF indicator to sweep the bedrooms and bathroom."

"Surely not." The idea that anyone would be sick enough to bug the bathroom.

"I'm sure Mr. Freeman did everything according to guidelines, but it never hurts to check. We'll be changing passwords on your home Wi-Fi, using another line of your favorite song. It wouldn't hurt to change your passwords on everything. Computers, phones, and tablets. I know it's a hassle."

"It may be time-consuming, but doing so will make me feel a lot more secure." Beth shivered. "I hate the thought of being watched."

"It's possible he has a backdoor entry to the store's Wi-Fi, but your home Wi-Fi is separate." Kelly set her glass of wine aside. "This won't take long."

After checking all the other rooms, Kelly emerged with a smile. "Nothing in the rest of the apartment." Slowly she walked around the living and dining areas.

After a few minutes, a shrill beep startled Beth. "What's that?"

"*That* is the sound this thingamajig makes when there's an RFI source." She pulled a chair over beneath an AC vent. She dug around in her bag, pulling out a small screwdriver and her cell phone. She climbed onto the chair. "Someone left you a present." She unscrewed the vent cover and photographed the device with the cell phone. "I don't know if Freeman installed this or not, but someone did. *Very* illegal." She removed the device and replaced the vent cover. "Wonder how he'll like that?"

"You think Matt did it, don't you?"

"Unless your sister is spying on you..." Kelly gave Beth an eye roll. "Yes, I think he installed it. Why he installed it—who knows? I have the model and serial number, and I can trace where it was bought and who bought it. It appears to have both visual and audio capacity. It's high-end, no doubt about it.

"One more thing, your door camera works both ways. Whoever is at the door can see inside, but their field of vision is limited. Even so, I don't recommend you check the door camera wearing your undies."

Beth clapped her hand over her mouth, stifling a giggle. "I'll have to remember that."

The front door opened. Startled, Beth jumped. Discovering their apartment had been bugged had her on pins and needles.

Lola came inside, her eyebrows arched. "I see I'm late for the wine tasting."

Beth quickly brought her sister up to date on the hidden camera.

"Sonofagun. I'd like to..." Lola drew her hands into fists. "I knew there was something a little too smug about that guy."

"You too?" Beth and Kelly said in unison.

Lola walked into the kitchen and poured herself a glass of wine.

"Why are you so late?" Beth asked. "I closed a while ago."

"Eva was showing me new pix of her grandkids. They are really growing up. The oldest one is almost ten. I remember when he was born."

"I didn't know the Bistro had been open that long," Kelly said.

Beth nodded. "It hasn't. Eva was our cook before mom and dad retired to RV land."

"Have you always lived over the store?"

"No, our family home is over on Spring Street. That's where we grew up. It's leased now, but Lola and I prefer living over the store. It's so convenient."

"Yeah, once we converted it from an attic to a *livable* apartment," Lola added with a wry grin.

Beth took a sip of wine, then asked, "Where are you staying, Kelly?"

Kelly wrinkled her nose. "Y'know I meant to find a B&B. I guess I've left it a little late. I saw a motel on the edge of town. I really ought to be going." She stood and picked up her bag.

The ranger had only drunk a single glass of wine, but why take the chance on an accident when there was an easy solution. "If you can hack a fold-out, you can stay here,"

Beth offered.

Kelly's expression brightened. "Just the one night, then I *will* find a place."

Lola leaned forward. "Beth, why don't we call Karen McAfee. She's a friend of ours and runs the Yellow Rose Inn over on Elm."

Beth nodded and made a quick call. "Okay, it's settled. She had a cancellation, a honeymoon couple who one of them was left at the altar. She didn't say whether it was a runaway bride or groom. You can check in tomorrow after ten. We don't open the store on Sunday until after twelve, and the Bistro is closed all day."

More wine and more laughter followed until the phone rang at eleven.

Chapter Seven

After a hearty dinner, Ben sat in the den quietly talking to his father.

His father stood and stretched. "Well, I'll say goodnight. Got a load of work first thing in the morning."

Yawning, Ben pulled himself upright. "I'm right behind you." Then his phone pinged with a text: Fatality at 34a Wilson Circle - Bistro cook

Normally he wouldn't be called for a death unless it was related to his investigation "Bistro cook" made it damned related. Suspicious circumstances must be involved. "On my way," he responded. "I gotta go, Dad. Don't know when I'll be back. Don't wait on me for anything."

His dad nodded. "Take care."

"Always."

Wilson Circle was a middle-class part of town. The area consisted of well-built single homes and several brick duplexes. Yards were neat and well-kept. Ben parked his rented SUV outside the crime scene perimeter. He noted neighbors were clustered in small groups just outside the cordoned area.

He showed his badge to the deputy and ducked under the tape.

Outside the residence, he donned shoe covers and gloves before entering the crime scene. "What've we got?"

he asked Vince who had just emerged.

"Looks like a burglary gone wrong. But I'm doubtful, given all that's happened. It's too pat."

"More like an execution staged to look like a burglary."

"That's my thinking."

Ben shook his head. He'd known Eva Johnson all his life. She'd been the elder Wheatons' cook before they'd retired. She'd been at the Bistro ever since it opened and was the main reason for its success. Not counting the loss of a much-loved friend and employee, her death would hit the business hard. No doubt that was someone's intention. "Her family been notified?

"Yes, one of her daughters, Sophie, lives on the other side of the duplex." Vince jerked his head in the direction of a woman surrounded by crying children and neighbors.

"I need to call the Wheatons. Beth and Lola need to know what's happened."

Vince nodded is approval. "Go ahead. They'll be devastated."

Wilson Circle was blocked with sheriff department vehicles. "This is a nightmare," Beth said, maneuvering the Maxima through the vehicles to find a parking spot.

Beside her in the front seat, her sister was sobbing too hard to respond. Kelly sat in the backseat

Beth swiped away her own tears. She'd had the least to drink of the three, but the nightmarish phone call had sobered them pretty quickly.

Lola jumped out as soon as the car stopped even before Beth could turn off the key. Running, Lola slowed long enough to duck under the yellow tape and bounded toward Eva's home.

Feeling helpless, Beth watched as Will caught her sister in his arms. She was close enough to make out what he said. "You can't go in. You'll contaminate the scene."

Lola struggled in his arms and beat on his chest, screaming, "I have to. She can't be dead. It's a mistake. Do CPR. Do something!"

The chief deputy shook his head. "I'm sorry, Lola. She's gone."

"I'll see what's happening," Kelly said. Unobtrusively, she got out and headed toward the yellow tape.

"Thank, Kelly." As the ranger strode away, Beth watched her sister collapse against Will's chest. Eva had been a mainstay most of their lives, first at home, then at the Bistro. More than a cook, Eva had taken care of both Beth and Lola while their parents had kept the Merc afloat through some rough years. Eva loved cooking, and she loved children. Her greatest joy had been becoming a grandmother.

Glancing over at the neighbors, Beth spied Eva's daughter, Sophie. Making her way through the crowd, she wanted to run and give Sophie a hug, but she hesitated. Was Eva's death related to the break-in at the Merc? Was it their fault Eva had been killed? For one thing, Ben hadn't said how Eva had died, but it couldn't be from natural causes.

The cruel irony of fate? Wrong place. Wrong time.

Instead, she hung back, not wanting to intrude. Eva's daughter looked up and glared, her body trembling with fury. "This is all your fault, Beth Wheaton. My mom told me how she was going to start carrying a gun just so she could be safe at that damn store of yours. You were responsible for her safety. She took care of you and your sister all those years. Pity you couldn't do the same for her. And now she's dead. Murdered in her bed!" Sophie spat on the ground.

Beth's jaw dropped. Once upon a time, she and Sophie

had been friends. Played together. Gone to school together. Now, the woman hated her. "I'm so sorry for your loss," she managed to get out, before breaking down. She ran back to the car, leaning against it while sobs wracked her body.

Kelly emerged from under the tape. "I'm so sorry."

"What happened? Can you tell me anything?"

The ranger opened her mouth to speak, then hesitated with a shake of her head. "It's an ongoing investigation. It's suspicious. That's all I can say." She glanced around. "Where's your sister?"

"Right now, I'm not sure. The last time I saw her, she was with the chief deputy, Will." Beth sighed. "They have something in common now."

"Pardon?"

Had she actually said that aloud? "Will's girlfriend was murdered last year. Now we've lost Eva. Lola was even closer to her than I was. I'm afraid someone is trying to send us a message. Ben was right when he said they—whoever *they* are—were just getting started."

"I'm so sorry for the loss of your friend. But I'm afraid Ben's right. And it *will* get worse before it gets better."

"I hate to think what could be worse than this."

"There's always worse. No, you don't want to think about it. It's disgusting what some people will do all in the name of power and greed."

Over Kelly's shoulder, Beth saw Ben come out from the duplex. Apparently, he spotted her at the same time, because he nodded and headed in her direction. His expression was grave as he approached. She waited until he ducked under the tape before going to him. "Ben, is this my fault?"

He shook his head. "No, someone *chose* to take her life. You didn't do that."

She stared into a navy blue night sky. Bright stars

twinkled, oblivious to the horror of the scene below. "But with everything that's happened, I feel responsible. Her daughter certainly blames me."

"She's upset and grieving. People say all sorts of things they don't really mean."

"Or wouldn't normally say aloud. Because she meant *every* word."

"Why don't I take you and Lola home? There's nothing you can do here." His voice was tender and as comforting as a warm embrace.

But this wasn't the time or place.

"Kelly, too," she said, remembering. "She's staying with us tonight."

"She is?" His eyes widened, then his brow furrowed.

Beth rushed to explain. "Well, I put her to work right away. She didn't have time to find a B&B, but that's all sorted. We found her a spot at the Yellow Rose."

He nodded, his gaze rested gently on her, making her feel warm and cozy as if his arms were around her.

"How did it happened? What happened? Can you tell me that?"

He gave a long sigh. "Her daughter, who lives on the other side of the duplex heard a noise. She went over to check on her. Back door had been forced. She found her mother in bed."

"Was she...?" She couldn't bear to ask if Eva had been assaulted.

"She wasn't raped. That's all I can tell you." He dropped his tone. "She didn't suffer." Thank heaven for that." She heaved a small sigh then craned her neck to see over Ben's shoulder. "Where's Lola? I don't see her anywhere."

He surveyed around the crowd of onlookers. "She's over there," he said, "sitting in Will's truck. She's pretty upset."

"We both are." She finger-combed her untidy curls.

"And I need to call mom and dad. They'll want to come back for the funeral."

"I'm sure Eva's family will appreciate that," he said gently.

She rubbed away the goosebumps on her arms. "I don't know. Soph's so angry."

"Give her time."

"But she's not wrong. I *am* responsible." He slid an arm around her waist, pulling her close. Even though she'd just hoped he would do just that, now he had. And having his arm around her was so much better than she could ever have imagined. If only it hadn't taken Eva's death...

"No. You're not. You wouldn't wish something like this on your worst enemy, much less a friend."

"You're right, of course." No. She wouldn't have wished being murdered on anyone, not even Ben's bitchy ex-wife. No. Not even spiteful Zoe deserved such a fate. "But I can't help feeling like I didn't do enough.

"Let's pull your crew together and get you home." He turned to walk over to his brother's truck.

"No." She tugged on his wrist. "Don't. Lola's right where she needs to be."

Ben stopped. He stared for a second. Then he nodded. "I get it."

"Don't tell anyone I said this, but she's been pining over Will... for quite a while." She clapped her hand to her mouth. "I can't believe I just told you my sister's deepest, darkest secret."

A smile played about his sensual mouth. "Don't worry. Your secrets—and your sister's—are safe with me."

His playful tone. His hard masculine body. His heady masculine scent. They all played hell with her senses. No matter how she tried to present herself as a hard-shell businesswoman when in the proximity of one certain Texas

Ranger, she was a soft and gooey caramel on the inside.

He must've realized she was near the melting point because he ushered her to the Maxima and opened the door. "Wait here. There's something I need to check with the sheriff. I'll round up your posse whenever they're ready."

"Thank you," she managed to murmur as he strode away. His view from the rear was almost as inspiring as from the front. Broad shoulders, trim waist, firm butt, and those long legs. What a man.

Oh, God. And how shallow was she that she could engage in such thinking when dear Eva lay dead in her own home, the one place where she was supposed to be safe from harm?

Lola's reappearance interrupted Beth's stream of thought. She glanced over her shoulder. "Where's Kelly? Is she coming with us?"

"Ben's rounding her up," Beth said. "If she sticks around any longer, she's going to blow her cover." She gazed into her sister's teary blue eyes. "Are you all right?"

"Sure fine." She shrugged as if brushing away Beth's concern.

"You were pretty cozy with Will, for a while there."

"I was a mess. He took pity on me." Lola opened the door, sat, and leaned back as if determined to play it cool and collected.

"Took pity on you?" She raised a skeptical brow. "Is that what it was?"

"That's all it was. I couldn't risk being in his arms any longer. I felt like I was taking advantage of him. The horrible way he lost Darla..." She let out a huff. "At least Eva didn't suffer. Precious little consolation for a lost life. 'She didn't suffer.'"

Beth reached over to hug her sister, but Lola shook her head. "I'm all right. Really. I am."

"Pfft." Beth couldn't help but scoff. Her sister was too stoic. Too determined to keep a stiff upper lip. And minutes ago, she'd fallen apart. Being in Will's arms—pity or not—had helped.

Break-ins, extortion, and now a murder. And they'd barely started construction on the casino.

Ben shook his head. He was in danger of losing his head over a woman. And here that same woman was caught up in a situation she had no control over. Way in over her pretty head. Unlike his ex, Beth possessed an aura of sharp intelligence with an underlying goodness, all wrapped up in a tidy bundle of curves and curls. More than anything, he wanted to shield her from the ugliness to come. If he had his way, he'd send her on a year-long vacation. But would that be long enough?

What he wouldn't give for that casino project to fall by the wayside.

Get real. The casino was a done deal. A year from now, Kenton Valley wouldn't be recognizable as the same small town he'd known all his life. An influx of who-knew-how-many eager tourists, eager to gamble away their life savings, would change the Valley forever.

More break-ins. More extortion. More murder. This was just the beginning.

Somehow, he had to root out the instigator of the Valley's present troubles. If he could just cut off the head of the snake before it multiplied...

He strode over to where Vince was talking with the coroner. "Find anything else?"

"Damn little evidence. Other than the clumsy break-in, it was a professional job. Double-tap to the head. No one heard the shots." Vince shrugged.

"Used a suppressor." Ben clenched his jaw. "Now who in this town has contacts with a professional hitman?"

"Alonzo Griggs for one."

Ben shook his head. "Griggs is small time. I see a larger guiding hand in all this. Whoever's behind everything that's happened could go through Griggs or that lawyer, Deacon. But for a hit, using a middleman is risky. That means he's heavily connected enough to go direct to Yuri Makarov."

"So,, you believe someone in town is stirring up trouble, making inroads for the Houston mob?"

"Don't forget the cartel connections. The way I see it they're both involved."

"What you're really saying is someone in town—in Kenton Valley—is using both the mob and the drug cartel to what? What would be the point of destroying this town?"

"Power and greed." He'd seen it too many times in too many towns. "There's been a construction company connected with everyone we've arrested, both the Diaz brothers and Gonzalez."

"Briggs Construction? "Vince shook his head. "I can't imagine the mayor would have anything to do with any of this."

"Excuse me, sir." Ranger Donovan stood at Ben's side, almost at attention. "I'm going to see that Beth and Lola get home safely."

"You do that," Ben said with a curt nod. "Remember, you're here for a job. Not a slumber party."

"Sorry, sir. I won't forget." She flushed darkly, then tucked her head and strode off toward Beth's vehicle.

"She's a young one," Vince said with a sigh.

"Don't I know it? They get younger all the time." Dammit. He'd been newbie once upon a time, too. All it would take for Donovan was a single warning. He had faith in her abilities. And she wouldn't disappoint him.

A frown crossed the sheriff's face. "Before we were interrupted, you mentioned a connection with the mayor or more specifically his construction company."

"He owns the largest construction company in the county." Ben nodded. "And has a major contract with the Bureau of Indian Affairs."

"I've known Carlton Briggs all my life. He's been a good, though not great, mayor, but he's always seemed to have the town's best interest at heart. Why would he want to destroy his home town by forming alliances with the cartel and the mob? Doesn't compute. Not for me."

"Same answer as before. Power and greed."

Vince shook his head. "Sorry, the idea of the mayor ordering a hit on a middle-aged cook is too long a reach."

"The mayor, or whoever, is playing the long game. This is just the beginning."

"Or someone high up in the company. Someone who's using the mayor's construction business as a cover for his own gain."

"There's one other person in the mix that I'm still uneasy about, Matt Freeman."

"Interesting." Vince shrugged. "Like you pointed out, there *are* some troubling gaps in his history."

"He came of nowhere at just the right time to insert himself into the Valley at the very moment when all the trouble started."

"Yeah, that bothers me too."

"I'm going to have another go at Freeman. I hate coincidences." Ben gave a curt nod. "See you at the office."

"Right."

Activity at the crime scene was dying down. Ben stepped out of the way to allow the coroner's men to remove the victim's body. The victim—such an impersonal term.

She had a name. A life. Now all she had left was the mystery of who killed her and why.

He watched them load Eva Johnson's body into the coroner's van. *I'll find him, Eva. Or I'll die trying.*

Unfortunately dying was always a possibility in his line of work.

Early Sunday morning, the eastern sky was beginning to lighten when Beth parked the Maxima behind the Mercantile. "I'll wait until later to call mom and dad. If I call this early, it'll only alarm them."

"No point in going to bed," Lola said. "Why don't I make us a big pot of coffee?"

"Hurry," Beth said, rubbing her arms. "I'm feeling chilled."

Kelly chuckled. "I don't care how hot it is. Make it strong. Then I need to pull myself together and move over to the Yellow Rose."

"Strong and hot coming up," Lola said and fled to the kitchen.

Kelly gave herself a dope slap and then plopped on the sofa. "Dammit. I forgot to tell Ranger Rasmussen about the spy cam." She pulled the cell phone from her jeans pocket. "I'd better let him know right away. He already thinks I'm goofing off."

Turning to Kelly, Beth set her purse on the kitchen island. "Why would he think that?"

"Because I was going to spend the night with you all. He warned me I wasn't here for a slumber party." She huffed. "As if."

"That's not fair." Beth set her hands on her hips. "I told him it was my fault you didn't have a place to stay. I mean I put you to work right away. Men!"

"It'll be all right. I think he was only halfway serious. He's really worried about you—and Lola, of course. He'll be even more worried now."

"Anyway, I'd better call him. For one thing, we need to know how to handle the guy who installed the damn thing, and I have a feeling Ranger Rasmussen will want to handle that dude himself."

"Call him." Beth gave an encouraging nod. "Well, I'd certainly like to wring Matt Freeman's neck myself, but I'm sure Ben won't think that's the best way to go." At least, he'd only installed a camera in the living room and not in the private areas. Still, their privacy had been invaded, and there was quite a bit she'd like to say to the handsome stranger who was becoming less handsome and more strange by the second.

"You can wring his neck," Lola yelled from the kitchen, "and I'll knock his block off."

Kelly paced while she talked to Ben. Beth hovered over the ranger's shoulder, anxious to hear his response. The ranger nodded and repeated, "Yes, sir" several times before disconnecting.

"Well?" Beth asked.

"He's on his way. He wants to see the camera for himself."

"What else did he say?"

"Doesn't bear repeating." Kelly's cheeks darkened with a full-on blush. "I mean, it really doesn't."

"He gave you a hard time?" Leaning forward, Beth probed sympathetically.

"I deserved it." She took a deep breath. "Basically, I lost focus. I should've maintained my cover as a civilian at the crime scene. And I didn't tell him right away about the camera. Those are the worst of my sins."

"Anyway, he's coming over." Beth tried to keep the excitement from her tone. "We were distracted, all of us."

"I can't afford the distraction. I lose focus and someone else gets killed."

"Hey, Eva's death isn't on you. If anything, it's my fault. They, whoever *they* are, are coming after us—Lola and me."

"Ranger Rasmussen and I aren't going to let anything happen to you and your sister."

"Brave words," Beth said. "And in spite of your assurances, I'm not feeling too brave right now." Truthfully, she was half scared to death. If someone was determined enough to kill an innocent woman, all bets were off. Anything could happen. Eva's murder had brought it home, big time. These fuckers weren't fooling around.

At dawn, traffic was non-existent. Ben sped down Main and turned into the alley behind the Merc. He parked and exited his vehicle. He bounded up the steps to Beth's apartment and banged on the door. "Beth!"

No excuse for Donovan's lapses. Still, she was a young ranger, and this would be her one and only mistake. If she screwed up again, she'd be out of the Rangers. He'd see to it.

He heard the click of the door camera in operation. Then Beth opened the door. A mass of blond curls fell to her shoulders. Her dark brown eyes were red from tears and lack of sleep. His heart pounded at the very sight of her. He took a breath. Best calm down and save Donovan's real ass-chewing for a time without civilian witnesses.

"Come on in."

"You used the camera. Good."

"Of course." She stood back, allowing him to enter.

"Coffee's ready. Want some?"

"Always." Resisting the very real urge to scoop Beth into his arms, he stepped into the cozy living room and glanced around. "Now where's this camera?"

"Here." Donovan produced a zippered plastic bag. "I've recorded the name, model, and serial number on my phone. It looks brand new."

"Meaning Freeman left it behind when he was installing the security system." He clenched his jaw. That man had a lot to answer for. "You're sure there aren't any others?"

"Not as far as I can determine, sir."

Ben hid a smile. Donovan was duly chastened and respectful. She wouldn't make any more mistakes. He'd bet on it. "I'll take it and research its origins."

"I'll be happy to do that, sir." She bit her bottom lip, as if uncertain she still had a job. "I'm moving into a B&B this morning. The store won't be open today," she glanced at Beth, "or for several days I imagine."

"No, we'll close until after the funeral." Beth turned to her sister. "Okay with you?"

"Absolutely." Wiping away a tear, Lola shook her head. "I don't know how we can open the Bistro without Eva. She's irreplaceable."

"Let me know what you find on the camera's origins. And stick close to Beth and Lola. You're an old friend from college, visiting and helping out." Better she should be a bodyguard to protect the woman he was growing more and more fond of. "And if it seems appropriate to spend the night here, you'll hear no more from me about slumber parties." And Beth would be safer.

"Yes, sir." She gave him a quizzical smile.

"First, show me where you found it."

Donovan pointed to the AC vent near the ceiling. "I took a photo with it in place before I removed it. Sorry, I didn't mention it sooner."

"Couldn't have checked into it until now anyway," he said, inclining his head. And that much was true. Her phone call had diverted him from going to the sheriff's office. Vince would be wondering where he was.

Beth brought him a cup of coffee. He took a seat and accepted the hot brew gratefully.

"Do you think Matt Freeman actually left this behind when he was installing the security system?" she asked.

"It's a distinct possibility," he said through clenched teeth. He took a sip of hot coffee. Whether imagined or not, he felt the jolt of caffeine.

God, he needed that.

"Finding that camera has given me the creeps. Someone has been watching us. If not Matt, then who?" Beth walked over to one of the windows overlooking the alley. "Personally, I'd like to smack him, but Lola's preference is knocking his block off."

"That's not half of what I'd like to do," Ben said, clenching his fists. The thought of Freeman spying on Beth and Lola sent a hot burst of rage to his gut. Son of a bitch had a lot to answer for.

"What are you going to do? I mean, what *can* you do?" Lola brought in a tray with more cups of coffee and set it on the cocktail table.

"I'll be talking to him. Today."

"Just talk?" Beth screwed her pretty face into a fearsome mask.

Ben gave her a grim smile. "The *talk* will determine the final outcome."

"Spying on someone without their permission—it's illegal," Beth said. "We know that, for sure."

"Yes, it is."

He stood, ready to head over to the sheriff's office.

"Donovan, get yourself checked into that B&B and follow up on the camera. I'll take care of Freeman."

Ben stormed into Vince's office. "Damn Freeman! He left behind a spy camera in Beth and Lola's apartment. Donovan was suspicious of him. She suggested they change their Wi-Fi passwords, and she even went further. She scanned their apartment and found a bug in the living room's AC vent."

"Whoa!" The sheriff's eyes widened as he leaned back in his chair. "You don't say. What are you gonna do about it?"

"I'm going to bring him in. Have a talk with him, but I need to do some checking first."

Vince shoved the Sunday issue of the *Kenton Valley Messenger* across his desk. "I'm guessing you haven't seen this."

Ben read the headline. **BRADLEY ANNOUNCES RUN FOR SHERIFF**. "I thought you were running unopposed."

"I was. Keyword: *was*. Deadline to file was Saturday. I guess he made it under the wire."

Bradley? Not a familiar name. "Who's this Bradley guy?"

"Eugene Bradley, head of Security for Briggs Construction. He hails from Houston." Vince frowned. "What do you think of that?"

Another connection to Briggs Construction and Houston. "I bet Carlton put Bradley up to running for your job. What've you done to piss him off anyway?"

Scowling, Vince leaned forward. "He wanted to purchase the land Abby had the title to. He did his damnedest to talk her into selling it to him, instead of donating it to the BIA."

Ben nodded. "I'm beginning to see the light." Briggs was up to something, no doubt about it. "Now it's time to have that chat with Freeman."

Vince nodded. "Damn straight."

"There's one more thing. Just an idea really," Ben said. "What if someone's after all the other businesses, and the Merc is just the first?"

"Good point." Vince rubbed his forehead. "More and more, it's looking like someone's—whether it's Briggs or not—is consolidating power."

Ben pointed at Vince. "Bingo! Greed and power is the name of the game."

Seated in the corner of Vince's office, Ben waited, drumming his fingers on the chair arm. Freeman was taking his sweet time. Maybe he was making a run for it after Ben's insistence he should come down to the sheriff's office, right away.

Vince's line buzzed. "Yeah. Send him back." He nodded. "He's here."

Freeman ambled into the sheriff's office and gave a polite smile. "Sheriff Tate. Ranger Rasmussen. What can I do for you gentlemen on this *early* Sunday morning?"

"You can start by telling us what you know about this." Ben pulled the zipper bag containing the bug from his pocket and tossed it to Freeman.

Freeman played it cool, turning the plastic bag over. "It's a Zetronix 3219 with Wi-Fi, video and audio capabilities. Obtainable online and from any shop that sells this kind of equipment."

"Any idea how it came to be installed in an apartment

you recently wired for a security alarm?"

"Hold on. The only apartment I've done is for Beth and Lola Wheaton."

"That's right. This bug was discovered last night."

Freeman held up his hands. "Don't look at me, guys. Not one of mine. If that's what you're thinking, you're barking up the wrong tree."

"Mighty coincidental that you show up in a town just when you're needed most. I don't like coincidences," Ben said. "Don't trust 'em. Or you, either."

"I know how it looks. But that bug isn't mine." He started to pace. "I installed hidden cameras only in the Mercantile and in the Bistro. They're a different brand and series altogether. I can show you the paperwork on what I installed." He stopped pacing long enough to open his tablet and scroll. "Here's the bill for what I installed. If you've already checked the device's model and serial numbers, you'll know—"

Ben's phone rang. Donovan. "I have to take this." He listened and frowned as he terminated the call. "Sold in Waco. Buyer as yet undetermined."

"See. It's not mine. I order directly from the manufacturer." Freeman gave an affable smile as he turned from Ben to the sheriff. "Not guilty."

"Still a coincidence," Ben said. He focused his gaze on Freeman who didn't seem intimidated. "Where're you from, Freeman? Why're you in Kenton Valley specifically?"

Freeman gave an I'm-a-good-guy smile. "After college, I spent some time in D.C. My boss thought the Valley, as you like to call it, could use a good security man."

"Your *boss*?" Vince scowled, his disbelief. "What does anyone in Washington, D.C., know about Kenton Valley?"

"More than you might expect. My boss is Hamilton Stone—"

"Assistant Director of the DEA," Ben supplied. "I knew it. You had to either be a Fed or a crook."

Freeman pulled out an ID. "I don't normally carry this when I'm undercover, but from the tenor of your call this morning, I sensed it was time I checked in with local law enforcement."

"About damn time," Vince said with a shake of his head.

No matter who this guy worked for, Ben didn't like him. He didn't trust him. More specifically, He didn't want him around Beth.

Freeman pulled up a second chair and took a seat. "We've been hearing a lot of chatter about the cartel moving into the Hill Country as well as someone with connections to the Makarov crime family in Houston. Stone thought it was time to put a man in place before the casino opened and matters got hot and heavy."

"The Texas Rangers cooperate fully with the DEA to bring down drug dealers. What I fail to see is why you, as an agent of the DEA, haven't shown us the same courtesy. You're days late in notifying us of your presence."

Freeman had the grace to appear ashamed. "I came to town and was just feeling my way around, setting up my cover story. Events snowballed," he said. "The Mercantile was broken into."

"That was the third incident, and now we have a murder to contend with." Furious with Freeman, Ben added. "If you'd had the courtesy to follow protocol and notify the sheriff and the Rangers of your presence, I wouldn't have wasted my time checking you out. Time that could've been used following other leads."

"Part of my cover is to appear a little shady in order to attract attention. I assure you I didn't install that camera. But obviously, someone did."

Meaning it was up to Ben to find out who'd been spying

on Beth and her sister. "I have someone who's researching that."

Freeman rose and gave a curt nod. "Gentlemen. I'll leave you to it." He strode from the office.

"I still don't like him," Vince said. Frowning, he picked up the newspaper and tossed it into the trash.

"I don't either." Ben stood. "I'm checking into the Sleepytyme. I'll be closer to town. Easier to reach." And closer to Beth.

"Good enough." Vince sighed. "Now I've got to spend time mounting some kind of re-election campaign, or come fall, I'm out of a job."

"Good luck with that." Ben set his hat on his head. Dealing with the politics of an election campaign would be a headache. Why now was someone running against a damn good sheriff? Why one of Briggs's employees? Why was Briggs after Vince's job? Was it merely a matter of the land, or was there a bigger issue at play?

Dammit. He already knew the answer to that question. But the hard part would be proving it.

Slipping her phone into her pocket, Beth walked into the kitchen. "Kelly just called. She's settled at the Yellow Rose Inn," Beth said. "I'm going to place a sign on the door, that the store is closed until after the funeral. What do you think?"

Lola took a sip of coffee, then set the cup aside. "But *when* will the funeral be? How long will they keep her body? Can we afford to stay closed that long? People in town depend on us."

"You have a point," Beth admitted reluctantly. "If the situation was normal, it would just be until Wednesday or

Thursday at most."

"This situation is anything but normal. Won't they do an autopsy? And won't her body have to be sent to the state lab in Austin?"

Beth's hand went to her mouth. "I hadn't thought about that. No telling how long the autopsy will take. Besides, I'm pretty sure we won't be welcome at the funeral. Sophie was *so* angry."

"She said things in the heat of the moment," Lola said. "Besides, it was my bright idea to go armed, not yours."

"Whatever, I just feel we need to be at the funeral. To show our respect. After all, she raised us right alongside her own kids, Sophie included."

Lola took another swallow of coffee, then sighed. "What would you think if I went to stay with Mom and Dad until the funeral? There's no Bistro without Eva."

"You want to take some time off?" Beth opened the fridge and pulled out a pack of bacon and a carton of eggs. "I sort of understand that."

"You have Kelly here to help in the Merc if you do open. Please, Beth. I just need to clear my head. I'm the one who's really responsible for Sophie's rant."

Beth closed the fridge and walked over to the stove. "How are you responsible? Eva wasn't killed because you were going armed. She was killed because someone wants to take over this town, one store at a time. And they don't care how they do it." Opening a cabinet, she pulled out an iron skillet.

"I'm sure she is. I just need a few days away to get my head straight. That's all. I'm not dumping everything on you. I'll be back. This is still my home."

Beth arranged strips of bacon in the skillet then turned on the burner. "Sure. I do see your point." *Even if I don't have the same luxury.* "Go on. Call mom and dad. Why don't you pack while I fix breakfast? There's no point traveling on an empty stomach."

Ben strolled into the Sleepytyme Motel. "I need a room."

Jeff Ocala, the undercover ranger, looked up in surprise. "Yes, sir. How long will you be staying with us?"

"Let's say a week, possibly two. Can you give me a weekly rate?"

A stricken expression crossed the operative's face. "I'll have to ask my boss. Otherwise, it'll be Seventy-nine dollars a night."

He frowned. True, he could expense part of it, but he might as well get the best deal possible. "Call your boss."

Hank McKennitt emerged from the office, scratching his ginger head. "What's this about a special rate?"

"I'll need a room for at least a week, more likely two. I'll pay in advance. You won't be stuck."

"I could go for a ten dollar per night discount, that would be four-eighty-three dollars per week."

"How about a twenty dollar a day discount? Other than clean towels, all I'll need is the linen changed once a week if I stay beyond a week."

"That'd be only four-thirteen." He shook his head. "Can't do that. But make it four-fifty and you've got a deal.

"All right. Four-fifty a week it is."

"Give 'im a key," McKennitt instructed Ocala.

"I prefer an end room."

"Fine. Twenty-four's at the far end, and it's just been cleaned."

"Much obliged, Hank." He took the key from Ocala. Ocala played the part of a clueless, newbie desk clerk well.

Good choice.

Ben opened to door to his temporary digs. The odor of pine cleaner hit his nostrils. He opened the bathroom door. Clean. All in all, he'd seen worse. Spreads were a tad faded. But clean enough. He pulled the linens back and checked the mattress for bed bugs and any sign of bloodshed.

All right. So far. So good.

He tossed his go-bag in the corner. Now. Time to check in with Beth. Time to figure out who planted that damn bug in their apartment. Who besides Freeman had access?

While Lola packed a small bag, Beth scrambled the eggs. The aroma of fried bacon still lingered in the air, and her stomach growled. "How long a drive is it to Mom and Dad's place?" She'd often spoken of her parents as having retired to RV land, but the truth was they had a nice two-bedroom condo in a gated community and only used the RV when they traveled.

"About three and a quarter to three and a half hours. That's driving the speed limit."

"Which you never do." Beth opened the oven door and checked on the biscuits. Nice. The tops were just beginning to brown.

She set the platter of crisp bacon and scrambled eggs on the table and was ready to check on the biscuits again when the doorbell rang. Running to do the door, she spied Ben in the door cam. Her heart revved just a bit—okay, a lot. Now what?

She opened the door, then darted back to the kitchen.

"Excuse me. Oven," she called over her shoulder.

Ben wandered into the kitchen. His face lit up with a wide smile when Beth set a pan of hot biscuits on a trivet. "Mm. I see breakfast is ready."

"Yes, join us. There's plenty." She set another plate on the round oak table. "Lola's going down to mom and dad's place until it's time to come back for Eva's funeral. Is that okay with law enforcement?"

"Shouldn't be a problem." His gaze grew warm. "You'll be here *alone*?"

"Yes." Should she make something out of his inflection of 'alone'? Was it her imagination? Probably her imagination. "But I'll have Kelly to help with the store if I decide to open before the funeral. That's her cover, right?"

"Right," he said with a nod.

"There's no question of opening the Bistro until we find another cook. And given the circumstances, finding one may take a while. But we won't even talk about looking for another cook until Eva's been put to rest. We both feel a lot of guilt where she's concerned."

"You shouldn't, but it's natural to feel responsible, even when you aren't."

"Lola," she called, "breakfast."

Lola strolled into the kitchen wearing black jeans and a black T-shirt, and boots. "You think the gatekeeper will let me inside, dressed like this?"

"Goth cowgirl? You'll be fine." Beth sat in her usual spot while Lola took hers across from Beth.

Ben removed his hat and sat to Beth's right. "I didn't drop in just so y'all could feed me," he said with a half-grin. "I have a reason for being here."

"Of course you did. My cooking is world-famous," Beth said with a grin. Breakfast she could do, but that was the extent of her culinary skills.

She passed the pan of biscuits to Ben. He split and buttered the hot biscuit then spooned on a dollop of blackberry jam. "Donovan has been checking on the spy camera. It was sold to a store in Waco. We don't know who purchased it, but she should find that out on Monday when the store opens."

"What about Matt Freeman?" Lola asked, spreading jam on her biscuit. "What did *he* have to say?"

"He's cleared," Ben said. "He showed us the receipts for what he installed here and at the Merc. He orders direct from the manufacturer. So, my question to you is who's had access to your apartment recently? Cable installers? Phone men. Anyone *else*?"

"Well?" Beth glanced at Lola. "We remodeled the apartment before we moved in. That was two years ago. We had electricians, construction workers, all manner of folks in here then."

"And since then?"

Beth shook her head. "I can't think of anyone. I'll need to go back over our personal receipts. I might be able to figure it out. Otherwise, it appears the camera might've been here since the remodel."

Ben shook his head. "No way. Date of sale was three months ago. It wasn't in place any longer than that."

"Three months. Three months." Beth shook her head. "There's something tickling in the back of my mind, but I can't quite figure it out. It'll come to me," she said with a nod. "Sooner or later."

"Sooner would be preferable." He bit into a crunchy strip of bacon. "This is heaven," he said, giving a moan of pleasure. "Sorry," he chuckled. "Everything is delicious."

Pleased by the compliment, Beth beamed. Even more pleased by his moan. If only...

Stop it. Even if he was chowing down, he was here

because of the hidden camera.

It's just business.

Ben pushed back from the table. "I'm afraid I've made a pig of myself. Your cooking really hit the spot, Beth."

Lola laughed as she rose from the table. "Just so you know, breakfast is her *only* meal."

Zoe's idea of a hearty breakfast had been half a grapefruit and half a slice of toast. "I have to say a breakfast like this would be enough for any man." Sitting across the breakfast table from Beth would be enough for any man, whether she could cook or not. The lack of sleep hadn't seemed to dim her natural beauty or her sweet nature.

"I'm going to get on the road," Lola said, heading to her bedroom.

Her comment snapped him out of his daze. Without realizing it, he'd gotten lost in the depths of Beth's warm brown eyes. "Right." He held back a smile.

"Do they know what time to expect you?" Beth asked.

Emerging from the bedroom with her bag, Lola nodded. "I just sent mom a text. Now, you two behave yourselves. I won't be here to chaperone, so don't have too much fun without me."

He smiled when Beth's chin dropped and she blushed prettily.

"*Lola.*" She fanned her cheeks. "You're embarrassing Ben."

"Not at all," he said. Lola's sisterly teasing was welcome and comforting.

"Go on." Beth made a shooing gestured. "Good-bye. Ben is here on business. And you know it." She walked over to the roll-top desk. "I have to check through our receipts so we can figure out who planted that damn camera."

Beth's sister let out a peal of laughter. "Whatever. I'm outta here." She picked up her bag and left them alone.

Alone. As in alone at last?

Beth let out a huff. "Ben, I'm so sorry. Lola's just incorrigible. She has this crazy idea that—"

He closed the distance between them. "—that we should be together. It's not a crazy idea. Your sister's right."

Her chin trembled. "She is?"

"So many times, I've come close to—"

His phone beeped with a text. Dammit. Zoe wanted to see him. So what? One good thing about being divorced, he could ignore his ex's annoying texts.

"How dare he not respond to my text?" Zoe fumed while she drove around town. Being twice divorced didn't suit her at all. What was wrong with the men in her life, anyway? She was beautiful. A knockout. What man wouldn't want her? Especially one who'd had her and knew what delight she could give.

Of course, she should've known Jose would be a hound dog. After all, he'd been married when she first started seeing him. But once they'd married, he should've changed. She was the perfect wife. She kept a beautiful home, not a spot of dust anywhere—well, the maid did the dusting and cleaning, but Zoe supervised. Everything must be just the way Señor Vayden liked it.

And still, he'd run around.

Ben had never been unfaithful. She was sure of that. Now, she wanted him back. Daddy had told him as much. But he still wouldn't respond to her calls or texts.

How freaking difficult was it to text anyway?

She'd just have to take matters into her own hands.

Hmph. The Merc was still closed. He'd better not be with that little blonde Wheaton tramp. Ben had always preferred blondes. That much hadn't changed.

She turned into the alley that ran behind the main street stores. The Maxima parked behind the Merc must belong to one of the sisters. Such a pedestrian taste in cars. A Maxima couldn't hold a candle to her precious, silver Porsche 911 GT3.

And a strange SUV. Ah. She spied the rental agency sticker in the rear window. That must be Ben's. Daddy had told her about Ben's wrecking his truck. But why was he spending so much time hanging around trashy Beth Wheaton? She ran a grocery store, for Pete's sake.

"Okay, one more chance, buster."

Chapter Eight

Ben's phone beeped again. I'm right outside. I need to see you. Now!

Outside? Ben reined in his irritation. Zoe just wouldn't give up. Dammit.

"If you want to..." Beth said, gazing up at him sincerely.

"That's just it. I don't. It's my ex. I definitely don't."

"But it could be important." She gave a little shrug. "I guess."

"Never is." He fumbled for the words. The mood was broken. Damn Zoe.

Okay, try again. Don't lose this moment. "You've been on my mind for a while now, and—" God. Could he sound any more inane? What he really wanted was to pull Beth into his arms and kiss her until they were both senseless.

"I understand."

"What? You understand what?" Confused, he stumbled ahead. "Do you understand I'm scared half to death that something will happen to you before I can find who's behind these attacks? And if you understand that I'm falling in love with you, then yes, you do understand."

"You are?" Her chocolate brown eyes shone brightly as she gazed up at him.

"I am."

He rested his hands on her waist, pulling her closer until her breasts touched his chest. His breath caught in his throat. He caressed her cheek. "I've never known anyone like you. You're so beautiful."

"But I'm a blonde." She gave a chuckle. "You swore off

blondes."

"A guy can always change his mind." He inclined his head and captured her mouth with his. Soft. Responsive. Sensual. His mind reeled. Kissing her was pure heaven. Maybe not that pure. His groin tightened. His breathing grew rapid.

Beth pulled at his belt and was unzipping his pants when a car horn blared. And blared.

Reluctantly he broke contact and stepped back.

"Dammit. My car alarm. She's really determined to piss me off."

Anger rushed through him as he struggled to zip his pants and buckle his belt. "To be continued," he said, dropping a quick kiss on her forehead.

So close. But a kiss was a kiss. And what a kiss it'd been until Ben's car alarm blasted. Beth sighed and walked over to the window to see what was going on.

Just as she expected, none other than Zoe Briggs Rasmussen Vayden. And dressed fit for *hunting* in a low-cut lace top that revealed her obviously surgically enhanced breasts to their full advantage and a short skirt that showed off her long legs. What a witch. Rumor had it she was in town following the breakup of her second marriage. So, she was after Ben.

Again.

You'll have to try harder, sweetie. I'm a Wheaton and we don't give up so easily.

Ben flew down the back stairs, taking them two at a

time.

Sure enough, there was Zoe, wearing next to nothing and standing proudly, tire iron in hand, where she'd bashed his window.

"Dammit, Zoe." Thoughts of strangulation came to mind. Gritting his teeth, he dismissed murder as a solution. She stood with feet apart, her hands on her hips. "I'll have you know Dammit is not my first name."

"Do you see what the hell you've done. You broke my damn window. I'll have to pay for that." He shook his head. "No. *You* will."

She jutted her chin. "I'd like to see you make me try."

"Okay, cut the crap. What do you want?" He unlocked the driver's side door and started brushing glass from the seat.

"You ought to know what I want. I'm really sorry about how things ended. I made a mistake. I want you back." Her words ended with a definite whine. Yes, he remembered that whine, as annoying as a fingernail on a blackboard.

"Zoe, that ship has sailed. In fact, that ship has crossed the Atlantic."

"You loved me once." She crossed her arms under her breasts. "You couldn't get enough of me."

"I was young and stupid. But I've been cured of that affliction. I'm immune."

"Affliction?" Her bottom lip stuck out in a pout. "You're comparing me to some kind of disease. Really?"

"Yes." The anger and the humiliation had evaporated long ago. In fact, once he'd accepted who and what she really was, his recovery had been rapid.

His ex began to pretend-cry. Not a single tear. "But I love you. I'll be a better wife this time."

He shook his head wearily. "I've seen this movie before. It's over, Zoe. Go on and let me be. We are stick-a-fork-in-it done."

Zoe's face flushed a bright red. She whirled and brushed against Beth's Maxima, ensuring the metal studs on her bag scratched the vehicle's finish.

Another flash of anger. More thoughts of mayhem. "You did that on purpose."

She turned all dewy-eyed innocence. "What?"

"You scratched Beth's car."

"Oops." She jumped into her over-priced sports car, gunned it, and raced down the alley.

What had he ever seen in her? It was obvious from her behavior any maturity that normally came from life experience had passed her by. Two marriages had crashed and burned, and the best she could come up with was a rerun of the first.

Beth watched the scene below in disbelief. Ben's ex had actually broken the window on his rental. She shook her head. Zoe Briggs was not only an airhead but also a little scary.

Oh, well. Forget about Zoe. Forget about Ben's kiss? Not so easily done.

Still, the receipts. She walked over to the desk and had a seat. Hm. Here it was: a work order from the gas company. Two—no, almost three months ago there'd been a gas leak reported in the downtown area, and a gas company employee had requested access to check the apartment after he checked the stove in the Bistro. Nothing out of the ordinary. But while she had let him into the apartment, she hadn't remained. They'd been in the middle of rearranging the store. Instead of hating the new layout, customers actually had commented on how much more efficient it was.

She sorted through the rest of the recent receipts. Nothing. It had to be the gas company thing.

So, if he was checking for a leak downtown, he would've checked with the other businesses along Main Street.

Fine. She'd just go across the street to the drug store. Maybe Abby would remember. She glanced at her watch. It wasn't noon yet. Abby might still be at home.

She picked up the phone and called the Tate Ranch. When Abby answered, Beth asked, "Can you remember anything about a gas leak downtown, almost three months ago. What I mean is, did someone from the gas company come by to check the drug store?"

"No. We heat with electricity and don't have any gas appliances. Why?"

"Oh, I'm just checking on something. No big deal. Sorry to have bothered you."

"No problem. I'm bored to death. Vince won't let me leave the ranch until things in town are a little more settled."

"What about the drug store?"

"I've had to reduce the hours we're open, and my evening person is still working overtime. As things are, it's a real hassle."

Beth agreed and quickly terminated the call. Maybe she should check—

The door cam beeped. She'd forgotten Ben was still outside. She ran to the door and let him into the apartment. "I think I've found it."

"What?" He raised a brow, his curiosity obviously piqued.

"Almost three months ago, someone came to check on a gas leak. I just need to check with the other business owners downtown to see if he checked with them too. But I still don't understand why."

"Hold on now. You've done enough. I'll check with the

gas company tomorrow."

"But I want to know if any of the other owners—"

He stopped her flow of words with a quick kiss. "That's my job. I'll check with the other business owners, as well, but at this point, you're the only one who's been involved."

She rubbed the chill bumps on her arms. "It's still weird to think someone was watching and listening to us for the last three months. I mean, it's beyond sleazy."

While she and Lola didn't make a habit of cavorting around in the nude, it wasn't unusual to be half-dressed on occasion.

Ben's mouth crooked up in a half-smile. His eyes glittered.

"I know exactly what you're thinking, Ben Rasmussen, and we don't."

"I guess my imagination got the better of me."

"Don't let it happen again," she said, pouting. Teasing and flirting with Ben seemed so natural. If only everything in the Valley wasn't falling apart.

Ben's phone beeped with another text. He scowled, the frown marring his handsome face.

"Zoe again?"

"No. The sheriff. Something's come up. Needs to see me right away."

"Of course. You must go." As she said the words, she meant them. He had a job to do. And he was the breed of lawman for whom the word "determined" was defined.

"Sorry." He reached forward and caressed her cheek. "We keep getting interrupted."

She nodded. "Yes, we do. But duty comes first, and personal concerns have to take second place. I understand that."

"You really do." He added ruefully, "My ex never did."

"Go." She gave him a big smile with a gentle nudge.

"Before I regret letting you off so easily."

Leaning forward, he landed a quick kiss on her forehead. "Lock the door behind me."

"I will."

With a sigh, she watched him go and secured the door. Then she called Kelly. "I think something's up. Ben just got a text from the sheriff. He left in a hurry."

"Want me to come over? If I'm to keep my cover viable, I can't just show up at the sheriff's office for an update."

"Right. Do come over. Lola has gone down to mom and dad's place." Frankly, now that Lola had left, having Kelly here would certainly make her situation less risky. Besides, Kelly was quickly becoming a friend.

Ben strode into Vince's office. "What's up?"

Vince shook his head. "I can't believe this, but my contact in Judge Garrison's office just let me know a warrant is being prepared for my arrest on corruption charges."

Ben did a double take, then sank into a chair. "What?"

"That's right. If someone is determined to shut down our investigation into increased criminal activity, this should just about do it."

"It's politics." He shook his head. "As much as I will hate seeing you in the pokey, my part of the investigation can't be shut down that easily." Playing politics with the Texas Rangers wasn't the same as local politics. No matter how much money was involved.

"Then be warned. You're next. And their next gambit may not be through the courts."

"In other words, watch my back." A chill zapped up Ben's spine. He'd already had one run-in with someone.

"Exactly."

"Then *you* need to call your lawyer, and but first get Will in here. We'll update him on everything we've learned." Then he remembered Beth's supposed gas leak. "What do you know about a gas leak nearly three months ago—in the downtown area?"

"Nothing. Why?"

"Beth had an employee from the gas company in her apartment about the time the camera was installed. They were busy in the store, so she didn't stay with him while he checked it out."

"That's it then. Since I'm about to be detained, you'll have to check with the gas company tomorrow."

"Will!"

Ben and Vince spent the next ten minutes briefing Will regarding their investigation into Briggs and his ties with Los Malos Dios and the Makarov mob.

Will shook his head. "I can't believe someone thinks *you're* corrupt. What are you supposed to have done?"

"Apparently I'm responsible for all the crime in the county. Drug running. Bribes, and a host of other infractions." He sighed.

Just what his friend and fellow lawman needed with a pregnant wife at home. Vince was, without a doubt, one of the most honest lawmen Ben had ever known. Taking Vince out would slow the investigation down, but it wouldn't derail it.

"Will, whatever you do, don't make an issue of defending me when they come to arrest me, for your own sake," Vince warned. "Otherwise, you could be suspected of collusion. I *have* to leave someone I trust in charge."

No sooner had Vince said the words when the intercom buzzed.

"Sheriff Tate, the assistant state's attorney general to see you."

"Send 'im in." Vince gave a resigned shrug. "Here we go."

The Assistant State's Attorney, Neil Johnstone, entered, along with two Texas Rangers Ben recognized from the Public Corruption Unit, and Mayor Briggs on their heels.

Ben nodded to his fellow Rangers. "Gentlemen."

"How can I help you, gentlemen?" Vince asked quietly.

Ben held his tongue. Damn, the man was a hell of a lot calmer than he'd be in the same situation. Planting a fist amid Johnstone's florid face came to mind. Briggs—his suntanned countenance was entirely too smug. Corruption? The mayor wore tailored silk suits. Vince Tate wore a uniform and badge. Anyone with one eye, much less two, could see which man was more likely to be corrupt.

Without so much as a 'Howdy-do,' Johnstone pulled paperwork from his coat. "Sheriff Tate, I have a warrant for your arrest and a search warrant for your computer along with your work and personal phones."

"What are the charges?" Vince's tone was even and measured.

"For a start, corruption," Johnstone said, then read Vince his rights. Johnstone eyeballed Will. "Chief Deputy, until further notice you're the acting sheriff."

Vince stood, removed his badge and gun, then set them on the desk. He pulled his phone from his pocket, hesitating. "I need to call my wife."

"You'll be allowed a phone call once you've been booked."

Vince flushed. His jaw tightened. Setting the cellphone on the desk, he gave Ben a sideways glance.

Ben gave the barest of nods, but then he couldn't hold back any longer. "This is damn inconvenient. We're in the middle of a joint investigation."

One of the other Rangers spoke. "Major Innes will be

contacting you shortly." Innes was head of Company F.

"Good to know." Not necessarily good. Interference from his superior wasn't high on Ben's list of favorite things. "I definitely need to update him on certain facts of our investigation." More like tell him he'd lost his damn mind. And charging Vince Tate with corruption was absurd. Oh yeah, he'd have plenty to say about that.

"Where will I be held?" Vince asked, obviously hoping his incarceration would be local.

"Austin. You'll be arraigned tomorrow," Johnstone said. "Cuff him."

"Surely it's not necessary to lead him out of his own office in cuffs," Will said, scowling.

"It'll serve as an example to all. This is what happens when you're crooked," Johnstone said.

Will's hands clenched. Ben patted a calming hand on his brother's shoulder as a reminder.

The Rangers confiscated Vince's laptop and cellphone. He stood and was cuffed like a common criminal. Ben tamped down the rage that threatened to engulf him. "Ed Jenkins," Vince said.

Ben nodded. Ed Jenkins was the best criminal attorney in the Hill Country with a reputation for performing miracles. For the most part, law enforcement despised him, but he was the go-to man for anyone unjustly accused.

"No interference," Johnstone said.

"Calling the sheriff's attorney and his wife. How is that interfering, unless you're well aware this is a bogus charge manufactured by someone with an agenda?" Ben glared at the mayor.

Yeah, you.

Then the interlopers led Vince from the building.

Once they'd gone, Will exploded. "This is outrageous! It was bad enough last year when he was suspected of murder and I had to take charge. That was sort of understandable. The bodies were found on his ranch. But corruption? No way! I just can't wrap my head around it."

Ben walked over and closed the door. "Hold on. Has to be a setup. First, someone is running against him in the election, and now someone has decided he needs to go. Why can't they wait and see if he's re-elected? I'll tell you why because, for one reason or another, their timeline sped up. And Briggs is in this up to his eyeballs."

Will took his seat at Vince's desk. "At first, I thought y'all must be nuts for suspecting the mayor. But did you see the smirk on his face when Vince was arrested? We're taking Briggs down if it's the last thing we do."

Ben straddled a chair leaning on the back. "Yes, we will. But we gotta be smart about it. Someone in this department is bound to have manufactured the evidence they're using against him. Let's go over the roster. Who's most likely to have ties to Briggs, the cartel, or the Makarov mob?"

"We need my laptop." Will left long enough to retrieve his computer, then pulled up the department's roster and scrolled through the names of his fellow deputies. "Garcia is embedded in the Hispanic community. But I've never seen him take a wrong step. There could be ties to the cartel through a relative, though. Someone could've threatened his family. You never know."

"Personally, I've always liked Luis. We played football together in high school. But we'll keep him on the list for the time being." Ben read further down the roster. "What about Powell? I don't know him at all."

Will chuckled. "I played soccer with him in school. Does that mean he gets a pass?"

"Of course not." The real problem with finding a traitor in one's midst was that these were all men Vince had hired and trusted to do their duty. But Briggs had to be working with someone in the Sheriff's Department. A mole.

Will stood abruptly. "I've got to see Abby. She needs to hear about Vince, face-to-face. I don't want her to hear about it on the news."

"I agree. I'll call Ed Jenkins. He'll have to go to Austin for the arraignment and argue for his release. We'll meet back here to finish going over the roster."

"I'll be quick." Will set his hat on his head and took off in a dead run.

After notifying Jenkins of Vince's arrest, Ben pulled Jacob Powell's personnel file.

A little light reading. Let's see what you've been up to, fella.

Grew up in the Valley. High school. Played soccer. Two years of college in Austin. Police force there four years before coming back to serve in the Sheriff's Department. Wonder why he left?

All it would take to find out was a single call.

Carlton Briggs smiled as he threw his hat on the hall table. "Guess what I did today, baby girl?"

"What, Daddy?" Zoe sashayed into the hallway and gave him a big hug.

"I got the sheriff arrested and carted off to jail."

Zoe smiled. "You arrested the sheriff? What on earth for?"

"Well, darlin'. I didn't arrest him myself. I merely nudged the assistant state's attorney in his direction." He paused for effect. "For corruption."

"Phooey! So what?" She stopped chattering long enough to check her makeup in the hall mirror. "I would've liked it better if you'd arrested Ben. Surely if Vince Tate is crooked, then his good buddy Ben is too."

"The Rangers are already looking into him. They'll look a lot deeper than I can. If he's bent, he'll go to jail too." He walked from the hall into his study. His study was a true cattleman's retreat, complete with the skull of a longhorn bull over the seldom-used fireplace and a cowhide rug.

His daughter pouted. "Ben certainly deserves to rot in jail. He's treated me so badly. "

"I know, darlin' girl. I know." He grinned and wagged a finger in her face. "But if I remember correctly, *you're* the one that left him for a married man." He had no delusions about his darlin' girl. Her morals were as loose as her mother's had been. Still, she could be useful in ways his late wife never was.

"I'm giving a dinner for some very important guests. I want you to arrange everything. Set it up. Be my hostess. Tuesday night. I know it's short notice. Can you do it?"

"Oh, yes! No problem." Zoe gave a squeal. "That sounds like fun. How many guests?"

"It'll be small. I'm inviting the two men who are my silent business partners."

"And their wives?"

"No wives. Now, no one must know. This is very hush-hush, but I want the best of everything. Order from Dallas to keep people around here from knowing. This is wheeling and dealing at the highest level, my girl. "After dinner, we'll retire to my study and talk business. You'll make yourself scarce."

Zoe nodded. "I'll make it special. Who's coming?"

"I'll tell you tomorrow morning. Less chance of a slip-up. That's all for now."

She spun around giddily. "We'll serve the finest beef the ranch has to offer...and lobster. I'll have it flown in from Maine."

He waved his hands, dismissing her. He'd heard enough yakking. "Don't bother me with the details. You handle everything." While he wanted her to be really nice to one of his guests, he could depend on her libido for that. He wouldn't have to tell her which one, either. Yes, he knew his daughter. And yes, she would be very useful.

Damn. Ben heard a commotion in the outer office. He glanced up in time to see Will storm into Vince's office. "Those bastards! I was too late." He slammed his fist on the desk. "Those bastards served a search warrant on the ranch. They took his computers, everything regarding the ranch's business accounts. Abby's in a hell of a state." He plopped into one of the guest chairs. "They almost arrested their housekeeper when she tried to keep them out with a twelve-gauge, no less."

Ben shook his head. Damn the mayor and whoever he was mixed up with. "Is Abby all right?"

"She's mad all right. Outraged is more like it."

"That's not good for the baby. But I may have come up with something." He slid the file over for his brother to see.

"It better be good because I've had enough shitty news today."

Ben closed the door. "Deputy Powell spent four years with the Austin PD. I got to wondering why he left to come back here."

Will straightened, his expression alert. "Well?"

"Seems he informed on some of his fellow officers. The charges were investigated and didn't stick. Seems his charges were completely unfounded. Considering the amount of time and resources involved in the investigation, he was asked to leave."

"Was Vince aware of his history?"

"Seems he was, but he agreed to give Powell another chance. During his time here, Powell's been written up twice for use of unacceptable force. There's a warning in his file if it happens one more time, he can find another position, preferably outside law enforcement."

"So, he has cause for a grudge. But surely the assistant state's attorney wouldn't get involved without evidence. How has Powell manufactured evidence?"

"I don't know. I'd like to get a forensic accountant from Waco to dig into Vince's records, but since they've seized his computers both here and at home, that won't be possible. I suspect they've frozen his bank accounts, as well. That's what I would do if I were handling the investigation."

Will nodded. "Right. I warned Vince's brother Chase that might happen. He says he'll put the ranch up as collateral for Vince's bail."

"Smart move, little brother." Ben reached for the phone. "Now, I already talked to Ed Jenkins. He's on his way to Austin, as we speak, but I need to let him know what I discovered on Powell."

One way or another, they had to get Vince back home. It might take even longer to get his job back, but at least he could be with his wife. No matter how corrupt the assistant state attorney might think Vince was, he wasn't a flight risk, not with a baby on the way.

Sunday Evening

Beth paced from one side of the living room to the other. "I can't explain it, but something's wrong." All evening, she'd been unable to settle. Normally, she enjoyed watching *Victoria* on Masterpiece Theater, but somehow, the Victorian Era and the beautiful clothes seemed so far away and so unconnected to the events surrounding them. Or maybe not. Being surrounded by politics and scheming seemed to be pretty familiar themes, then and now.

"You might be right," Kelly said from her spot on the sofa. "Ranger Rasmussen just texted me that he needs to update me on something. I told him I was over here. Is that all right?"

"Of course." Beth couldn't refrain from smiling. Honestly, she felt like beaming, but she resisted. "I'll put on some coffee. It's been a long day. Eva's death. Lola's leaving—you know that really wasn't like her, taking off like that."

"She *was* pretty upset," Kelly said. "But maybe she wanted to give you and a certain ranger some time and space."

"Maybe. But you have to understand my sister. She's pretty pushy when she thinks she knows what's best. I may be the older sister, but she's the strong one." Beth flopped on the sofa. "Anyway, I'll put on the coffee and give you some privacy with Ben. He won't want to reveal things about the investigation in front of me, given I'm a civilian."

"That's the way it should be, but I don't think he sees you as just a civilian." Kelly gave her a knowing smile.

Beth pulled her feet up and got comfortable. "I'm never really sure how he sees me. We were just getting closer this afternoon when he received a call and had to leave in a hurry."

"It's never easy being involved with a law enforcement officer."

"We're not exactly involved. Not really." And that was fudging the truth a bit. He'd told her he was falling in love with her, but life kept getting in the way of their getting *involved.*

Kelly laughed. "You might not be an official item, but there's definitely something going on between you."

"Yikes. I said I'd put some coffee on." She sprang from the sofa and headed to the kitchen. The conversation was getting into personal territory, and Ben was Kelly's superior. He might not appreciate Beth's spilling her guts to his subordinate.

Ben inhaled the aroma of fresh coffee. "You made coffee. Thank you."

"I figured you could use it," Beth said with a shy smile. He could see the fatigue in her eyes but just seeing her beautiful face lightened his heart. Her soft honey-colored hair waved about her shoulders, giving him the urge to run his fingers through it.

Focus.

He took the hot cup of coffee, his fingers touching hers so briefly, but brief or not, there was a spark that jolted up his arm. He steadied his grip on the cup. "If I could mainline this stuff, I would."

"I'll leave you two alone so you can talk about the investigation." Beth turned away to leave.

"No." He grasped her wrist to keep her from going. "You can hear this. In fact, you need to know. Earlier this afternoon, the assistant state's attorney arrested Vince for corruption. It'll be on the news tomorrow, so there's no reason to keep it a secret."

"Oh no! Abby." Beth covered her mouth with her hands. "She must be devastated."

"That'd be putting it mildly." Energized by Beth's nearness, he reminded himself to focus. "But we know Vince isn't corrupt. Someone's trying to take him down. To keep him from investigating what's really going on in town."

"What *is* going on, Ben? I don't understand why, all of a sudden, things seem to be going to hell in a handbasket around here."

"I have my own thoughts on that, and those I *can't* share with you. I want to warn you both. I may be investigated as well, so don't be surprised if you begin to hear negative things about me.

"I would never believe anything bad about you, Ben." She gazed up earnestly. "No one who knows you would."

Beth's faith in him was more than reassuring; it touched him on a deep level, warming him and yet the reality of how fragile trust could be was always in the back of his mind. He'd trusted Zoe once, not for long, but long enough he still remembered the hurt. "Evidence can be manufactured. Computers hacked. If someone is really determined, anyone can be made to look dirty."

"Then how can we trust anything we're told?" Beth gazed up at him, her eyes shining with emotion. "All I know is, down deep inside, I know you and Vince are both good and honest men. I'm trusting *you* with my life...and my heart."

Kelly sprang from the couch. "Okay, folks, this is where I leave. G'night." She headed to what was probably was one of the bedrooms.

"You don't have to leave," he said, feeling his face start to heat up.

"Oh, yes. I really do." Kelly stopped at the doorway and gave him a knowing grin. "I am so out of here."

"Sorry," Beth said. "I didn't mean to spoil things."

"You didn't spoil anything." He bent to kiss her sweet mouth and got lost in the sensual lure of her lips on his. He pulled her closer until he could almost feel the rapid beat of her heart against his chest. Fragile or not, her trust was everything a man needed. Everything this man needed.

Shaking her head, she broke away. "That wasn't what I meant. I meant you came here to update Kelly in her capacity as a Ranger. I let my personal fears and concerns intrude on Ranger business."

He let out a chuckle. "No. I wanted to see *you*. A phone call would've sufficed to update Ranger Donovan."

"I'm glad you came by." Her arms stole around his neck. "Because I really want to do more of this." She tiptoed and ran her fingers through his hair. Her touch, like lightning, sent a burst of lust to his groin. "Whoa, are you sure?"

"Very." She looped her thumb into one of his belt loops and started to lead him to the bedroom.

Dang. Donovan picked that moment to emerge from the other bedroom. "Hey! Do y'all smell smoke?"

Chapter Nine

Ben sniffed the air. Yes. That was smoke all right. "Donovan, call 911!" He turned to Beth. "Fire extinguisher?"

"Under the sink." Beth glanced around the apartment. "The fire's not up here. Must be the store. Oh no!" She rushed for the front door.

"Gotta get out now. Fire burns upward. Come on!" He opened the cabinet beneath the sink and grabbed the extinguisher. Probably wouldn't be sufficient. He checked the tag. At least it wasn't expired. "Just in case."

Donovan dialed 911 while all three ran from the apartment and down the steps.

Down here, the acrid smell of smoke was stronger.

Beth started to race for the rear entrance to the store. He snatched her wrist just in time. "No! Open the door and you'll add oxygen to the fire. There's the danger of flashover." Beth and Donovan's vehicles were too close to the building. "Move your cars," he ordered. "Anyone else living over the other stores? This whole block could go up."

Beth shook her head. "No, we're the only ones."

The Merc, like with most of the historic buildings on Main Street, was primarily a wooden structure. Well-maintained, but wood, nonetheless.

"Fire department is on the way," Donovan said, then pulled her keys from her pocket. The new fire station was a good ten blocks away, but he could already hear the faint whine of a siren.

He shook his head. They'd be too late to save Beth's store. Dammit. She and her sister had worked so hard to keep the store up-to-date and yet retain the country general store feeling. Was this fire part of the new reign of terror someone had decided to heap on his hometown? Or was it more personal?

Time would tell. Thankfully those new security cameras had just been installed. He'd know who set the fire, sooner rather than later.

Once the vehicles had been moved to safety, Beth circled the block and ran down Main Street until she reached what was left of her store. Flames of orange, yellow and red licked at the signboard above the storefront. "Oh no!" Dazzled by the flames and roasting from the heat, she fell to her knees. Tears streamed down her cheeks. "It's all gone. Everything my family has worked for the last hundred and fifty years. Who did this? How could anyone be so cruel...and reckless?"

Right behind her, Ben pulled her to her feet and put his arm around her waist. "Just be glad you got out in time." He pressed a kiss atop her head.

The lead firetruck pulled in; the firemen dismounted and scrambled about their assigned duties, hooking the hose to the fire hydrant and producing ladders and fire axes.

Near collapse and shivering in spite of the inferno, she watched the horrific scene. If Ben hadn't held onto her so tightly, she would've surely lost it. "It's a total loss. Everything's gone."

Soon enough, but never really soon enough, the firemen hosed down the flames.

Finally, after what seemed like hours later, the fire was contained. The fire chief reported that the businesses on either side had minimal smoke and water damage, but the

Merc and the Bistro were gutted. The upstairs apartment had also been gutted with the roof open to the air.

"I want to see." Determined to see for herself, she tugged on Ben's hand.

"No." He stood stock-still. She couldn't budge him. "The chief said the building's not stable. And there are still hotspots."

"I *need* to see." Her clothes. Lola's clothes. Furniture. Mere things, but things which had made up a majority of their lives. The Merc and the Bistro too. All gone. She stared up at Ben. How could he not comprehend the loss? "I'm-I'm homeless."

"For now. But we'll find you a place to stay."

A place to stay? She wanted her home back, the cozy home she'd taken so much care in decorating. "The fireman said the back stairway to the apartment is fine, but with a lot of smoke and water damage. I need to get my stuff." She didn't care about smoke and water damage. She just needed something of her own to feel whole.

Ben shook his head. "You can't go inside the apartment. The chief says most of the floor is gone, and the building, what's left of it, is unstable."

"Someone set this fire on purpose. I *know* they did." What good was all the security she'd had installed if it couldn't keep an arsonist from having a field day with her life? "Is there any chance the security system recorded who started the fire?"

"There's every chance it did. Your recordings upload to the cloud?"

"I'm sure I remember Matt saying something about that. That way we didn't have to keep track of tapes or discs or anything like that."

"Then we're in business," he said giving her an encouraging smile. "We'll find who set the fire."

"But what if it was just some flunky? Who actually gave the order?" Her eyes brimming with unshed tears, she gazed up at him. How could he be so calm?

"Flunkies turn on their bosses every day. Let me catch the flunky, and I'll soon know who's behind the fire and probably everything else that's happened."

Kelly came up and touched Beth's shoulder. "I spoke to Karen at the Yellow Rose. You have a bed for as long as you need it."

Ben gave Beth a reassuring smile. "See. You're not homeless anymore." He nodded. "Thanks, Donovan."

"Thanks, indeed, Kelly. I just want to go to bed." If she could sleep at all. Someone wanted to ruin her life, if not actually take her life. Who could be so freaking ruthless?

Somehow. Someway. Someone was going to pay for this. If it was the last thing she ever did, she'd make someone pay.

For a while, he raged. Who'd had the balls to set that fire without his say-so? He, sure as hell, hadn't given the order. He leaned back in his cowhide leather chair, and then he laughed. Someone had done him a favor. They'd burned the Wheatons' store, almost to the ground. The fire certainly couldn't be traced back to him. But it did give him some ideas about how to proceed.

Now for the next phase.

Beth drove over to the Yellow Rose Inn with Ben following closely. The quaint three-story Victorian was painted yellow with white gingerbread trim. It was the perfect house for a bed and breakfast. Situated on a leafy green street, Karen had opened it only last year, a month before her husband died in a car accident. She'd often told Beth, having the B&B to run was the only thing that kept her sane during the terrible months after his death.

After parking in the side yard, Beth let her head fall back against the seat. Before she could rouse enough to open the car door, Ben opened it for her. Gratefully, she smiled up at his handsome face. "You didn't have to come all this way."

"But I did. I need to know you're safe for the night." He pulled her from the Maxima and walked with her to the side portico where the owner of the Yellow Rose waited.

"Come in. Come in," Karen said, ushering them into an all-white kitchen equipped with professional-grade appliances. A vibrant woman in her mid-thirties, she radiated warmth and comfort from her auburn hair cut in a no-nonsense bob to her neat floral blouse and tan slacks. "For tonight, I've put a cot in Kelly's room." Karen turned to Kelly, "If that's okay?

Kelly nodded. "Sure."

"Tomorrow, you'll have your own room after a couple of guests check out."

Relief surged through her and gratitude as well. "Don't worry. I'll pay you the going rate. I don't want you to lose business because of making room for me."

Karen waved away Beth's concerns. "We'll sort all that out tomorrow. Tonight's on me. It's only a cot."

"I'm so tired I could probably fall sleep on the floor." Indeed, Ben's strong arm around her waist was about the only reason she was still on her feet.

"Thankfully, that won't be necessary," Karen said. "I have a clean nightshirt you can wear. I've already placed extra towels in Kelly's bathroom so you can shower to your heart's content."

Beth glanced down at her T-shirt and jeans and sniffed. "I smell like smoke. I'll definitely take you up on that shower and nightshirt. I can't tell you how much I appreciate you for going out of your way like this."

"That's what small towns are all about. Neighbors helping neighbors." She chuckled. "Oh, my. I sound like one of those greeting card ads."

Beth smiled up at Ben. "Now you see that I'm well taken care of, I know you have more important matters to deal with than where I'm going to spend the night." Truly, she didn't know how she could've dealt with everything that had happened without him. This was a man she could depend on. More and more she wanted him in her life, in her arms, and in her bed.

He smiled and pulled her close to his muscled chest. "Get some sleep. I wouldn't be able to focus if I didn't know you were safe. Stay safe." He pressed a kiss on her forehead. Not an overwhelming, earth-shattering kiss as kisses went, but she felt the tenderness behind it. And there was the fact of his innate reticence keeping him from being more demonstrative in front of his fellow ranger and the B&B owner.

She watched him leave, his reluctance written in his body language and in the glance full of longing he gave her as he shut the door.

He wanted more. As did she. Oh, so much more.

And now, for a task she dreaded. Calling Lola.

Zoe turned into the long drive to the ranch where she'd grown up.

What a rush!

She could barely believe she'd had the nerve to burn down that little blond skank's store. That should take her down a notch or two.

Who knew setting a fire could be so simple? She parked in front of the three-story, multiple- columned brick mansion her daddy liked to call home.

Now, there was absolutely no reason for Bethany Renee Wheaton to stay in the Valley. No store. No livelihood. No apartment over the store. No home. Perfect.

Of course, there was that family house over on Spring Street, but someone else was living there. So, it wouldn't be very nice to burn that down too. Or would it?

Of course not. Besides, it was an old Victorian, another reason not to burn it. She'd just have to leave well enough alone. With Beth out of the way, Ben would be sure to fall back into Zoe's loving arms.

She would have to punish him a bit before she took him back, though. She'd make him beg. Yes, that was it. He'd have to get down on one knee and grovel.

But first, she had a dinner party to plan. She couldn't help but wonder who his guests were? He trusted her to be his hostess for a special and secret meeting. Now that was really something.

Ben opened the door to the motel room then locked it behind him. Stripping to take a hot shower, he literally ached with need. Need that could only be slaked by one woman.

Better make that a cold shower.

He stepped into the bathroom, turned on the shower, and stepped in.

The shock of the icy cold needles of water woke him up

all right.

Focus. Seeing two Rangers from the Public Corruption had unsettled him. Would someone from Public Integrity be looking over his shoulder next? A separate unit, Public Integrity investigated crimes committed by state officers and state employees, while Public Corruption investigated public officials and law enforcement officers, and others who held a position of public trust.

While Ben knew he was as clean as any Ranger alive, if someone was out to take over the town, they had a head start. They'd already taken down Vince. While Ben's younger brother was smart and on the ball, the political part of the job wasn't his forte. Vince had been in the job long enough he'd developed a deft touch when it came to handling the mayor and the city council.

And they often needed handling.

Ben had an uneasy feeling he might be next. While he believed his fellow Rangers were honest if there was even the tiniest chance that one of them was a bit bent... God, he hoped not.

The Texas Rangers were a premier law enforcement group. Their reputation was paramount, alongside the RCMP and Scotland Yard.

One bent ranger with an agenda could do a hell of a lot of damage to that reputation.

He turned off the water and stepped onto a mat and toweled off. Pulling on a pair of shorts, he took a deep breath and trudged from the bathroom.

Time to call the Major.

Past time. Ten-thirty. The Major would still be up. The man never seemed to sleep. No matter what time Ben had ever called him, he'd always sounded wide awake.

"Major. Ben Rasmussen."

"What?" Innes never wasted words.

He proceeded to update his superior with the latest news about the fire.

"Need more help?"

"Could use an army, but I'll settle for another ranger. I have two newbie rangers cooling their heels undercover, but they're needed where they are."

"Monday morning. Ranger Stirling."

"He's a good man. Much appreciated." He hesitated. He was about to tread on dangerous ground. "About Sheriff Tate. Was arresting him really necessary?"

"You're questioning my judgment?"

"Hell, yeah, I am—sir."

The major grunted. "I take it you know this sheriff."

"All my life. He's as honest as the day is long. Someone behind the scenes has an agenda, sir. We are in the middle of an investigation into who's behind the upsurge of criminal activity in Kenton Valley. Indicators are the cartel and the Makarov's are working together with someone local and powerful. Someone in the Sheriff's Department is dirty, but it's *not* the sheriff. This person has manufactured whatever evidence was used to obtain Tate's arrest warrant."

Silence... "Let this play out."

'Play out?' Was the major serious? "It could ruin his reputation. He's up for re-election."

"Not if he's as honest as you say he is. Got a good lawyer?"

"Ed Jenkins. He should already be in Austin."

"The *miracle* worker?" Innes swore, quite colorfully too. "He'll need him."

"They may come after me as well." Might as well be upfront about it.

"Hmph! Let it play out. We'll deal with it."

"Yes, sir." Fuck it. Not an exactly reassuring response.

What had he expected? "Uh, tell Stirling, depending on what time he shows up, I'll either be at the Sleepytyme Motel or at the Sheriff's Department."

"I'll call him now." Without wasting more words, the major terminated the call.

Letting out a sigh of relief, Ben set his cellphone down on the nightstand. Now if he could just get a decent night's rest.

Monday morning

Ben rose at six and dressed hurriedly. Light gray slacks. Pale blue shirt. And as always, his white cattleman's cowboy hat. Fortunately, he'd taken time before going to bed to hang up his grey sport coat so it could shed any wrinkles overnight. After a quick cup of the worst instant coffee he'd ever had the displeasure to drink, he walked over to the office to touch base with his undercover operative, Jeff Ocala. Sure enough, he was on duty. Apparently, he'd been on the night shift since his eyes were red and his eyelids drooping with fatigue.

Ben arched a brow in the direction of the manager's office apartment.

"He's not up yet," Jeff said, keeping his voice low. The young ranger was thirty-three, but he looked younger, more like his mid-twenties. Fresh out of training, he'd spent ten years in law enforcement in the Houston area before joining the Rangers. With his fresh face, black hair and lively brown eyes, he was an asset to the Rangers.

"I heard about a fire in town. Anyone hurt?"

"No. injuries. Lots of damage though."

Jeff glanced over his shoulder. "Well, there's nothing going on here. I haven't seen anyone who might even look like an extortionist. This place is *dead*. Hank spends a lot of time on the phone, though. He should be getting up soon. We'll hear him coughing and hacking. Are you sure this the best use of my time?"

"For now." *That might change.* "You always work the night shift?"

"No. He likes to split my work hours up. Once he's on duty, I'll grab a few hours of sleep and come back around noon. I never know what kind of mood he's in, or when he wants me to work from one day to the next."

"Stick it out. Maybe another week. If no one approaches him by then, we may need to move you. Things are heating up in town."

"Murder. Arson. I'd say."

The sound of hacking and coughing broke the early morning calm. Jeff nodded. "That's it. Hank's up."

Ben nodded. "Later."

He left the motel office and stepped out into a brilliant Texas morning. The temperature already in the low eighties, according to the temperature gauge on the wall, presaged a hell of a hot day to come.

Carlton Briggs sat in his study with his daughter across the desk, her pen poised to take notes. He restrained the laughter that built in his throat. His daughter was so anxious to please him. So anxious to get back in his good graces.

"All right, Daddy. Tell me who your guests are. I'm ready to do you proud."

He leaned forward and lowered his voice. "First of all, I cannot stress how important it is that you tell no one about my guests or even about this dinner."

"Of course. I'm so honored that you want me to be your hostess for this important dinner." She gave him a beaming smile.

"One of my guests is Yuri Makarov. He's an international importer from Houston."

Her gaze widened. "Really? What kind of goods does he import?"

"Never you mind what he imports. My other guest is Reynaldo Reyes. He's a wealthy landowner just south of the border. I think you'll really like him. I'm told he's very handsome."

Zoe smile. "I'm sure I will. Is that all you can tell me?"

"That's all you need to know, my darlin' girl."

"Fine. Be secretive. Now, I've ordered catering from Dallas, the finest wines and food. I'll do you proud."

"I'm sure you will." He stood and walked around the desk. Smiling he leaned forward and patted her cheek. "That's my girl."

Ben strode into the Sheriff's Department and nodded at the blond dispatcher. He made his way to the sheriff's office where his brother Will was already sucking down a hot cup of coffee. He jerked his head toward the coffee pot in the corner. "Have some. It's fresh."

"Quiet night?" he asked. Must've been, since he'd slept the night through without interruption.

"For once. Waiting to hear about the ME's report on Eva Johnson. The ballistics report is in, though. We have a winner. Same gun was used in a contract killing in Austin and one in Lubbock."

"That fits with what we suspected. Professional job." He hitched a hip on a corner of the desk. "I have another ranger,

Dave Stirling, coming in this morning to give me a hand. We'll need more space."

"Take my desk in the bullpen, at least until Vince is back on the job. The desk he ordered for you is scheduled to arrive around eight-thirty. Stirling can use that one." He shot Ben a wry smile. "I came in early to make room." He picked up a stack of papers and started flipping through them. "Now, I've gone over the statements of Miz Johnson's family, and there's nothing to indicate she had any enemies. Honestly, my gut says her killer's gone back to whatever sewer he normally hangs out in."

"Reckon you're right." With a scowl, he eased off the corner of the desk. "The only way we'll find her killer is to root out whoever's behind the break-ins and now this fire. I need to check the Merc's CCTV footage. We're bound to have caught the perp who set the fire on video. Since the video equipment is pretty much useless at the store, I'll call Freeman. He should be able to access the footage. I want to see the bastard face-to-face who set that fire. He could've killed Beth and Donavon both."

"Yeah, but you'll be looking at another henchman. It won't be whoever's behind it all."

"Right." Ben leaned forward on the desk. "But the more pieces of this jigsaw we put together, the better. Sooner or later, we'll have the full picture."

"Amen to that." Will set his cup of coffee aside to begin going over what few forensic reports he'd received. "What're you up to now?"

"After I put in a call to Freeman, I'll touch base with Donovan. Spoke to Ocala this morning. All's quiet on that front."

Will looked up and gave him a rakish smile. "Meaning you're really going to check in on Beth."

"That too," he admitted. While he'd slept the night

before, he'd also dreamt of Beth. Dreams best put out of his mind if he was going to adequately function as a lawman.

Will's phone buzzed. He answered, nodded, then said. "We're expecting him. Send him on back."

"Ranger Stirling?"

"You got it."

Dave Stirling strode into the office with a wide smile and his hand held out. "Nice little town you got here. What's going on? The major said you'd bring me up to speed." The ranger was in his late thirties, tall, well-built with a heavy muscular frame. His once dark hair was a decided salt and pepper. He possessed pale blue eyes that took in more than one might guess. The only mark against his handsome mug was his large nose that canted slightly to the left ever since an altercation with a fugitive bank robber.

Will got out of his seat, leaned across the desk, and shook hands. "Welcome. You might change your mind about that."

"Man, am I glad to see you." Ben took Stirling's hand and pumped it. "Let's talk and walk. I'll bring you up-to-date on the happenings." He turned to Will. "Do me a favor, put in a call to Freeman. Tell him what I'm looking for."

His brother nodded. "Will do."

They left the department and stood for a moment on the sidewalk. "So, what's going on?" Stirling asked.

"Just break-ins, extortion, a murder, and last night arson."

"Damn. You need an army." He chuckled. "Good thing I'm here."

"My thoughts exactly." This wasn't the first time he'd worked with Stirling. Dave was a standup guy. Good to have a man like him covering his six.

***

Beth yawned and stretched. The cot had a thick mattress, but it wasn't her luxurious pillow-top, which probably now reeked of smoke and would have to be discarded if weren't already burnt to a crisp.

Maybe she could rent one of the new condos until the Merc could be rebuilt and the apartment restored to its former glory. As lovely as it was, a long-term stay at the Yellow Rose wasn't a viable solution to her and Lola's housing situation.

The ringing of her phone interrupted her yawn. She sat up and looked around. Okay. Where was the damned thing? She found it on the floor beside her cot. "Hello."

"Still safe and sound?" The low rumble of Ben's voice sent a thrill through her as nothing else could.

"Yes. Safe and sound." She tried to keep the sound of breathy anticipation from her voice but failed. She was about to ask when she'd see him, but his next statement put the kibosh on that.

"I'll be busy today. I have another ranger in town so we can get a handle on everything. As long as I know you're safe, I can function without distraction."

"Of course," she scoffed. No point in being a distraction. Is that all she was? A *distraction*. Anger flashed through her before she could tell herself she was being ridiculous.

"I need to speak to Donovan."

"Then you'd better call on *her* phone because I'm about to step into the shower. She's already gone down to breakfast." Might not be the actual truth, but Donovan wasn't in the room so Ben could figure it out for himself. "Bye." She tapped the end call icon. "Fine."

As if she didn't have enough to do herself. Really? He wasn't the only one affected by what had to be an attempt on her life. If the fire marshal would let her back into the store, she needed to see what, if anything, could be salvaged.

Then there was the insurance company to notify. Lola was coming back today anyway. When Beth had called her after the fire, she'd been more than upset. The Bistro was her baby and now with Eva's murder *and* the fire, Beth wasn't sure her sister had the heart to proceed with a rebuild after two hard blows.

All Beth knew was that *she* wasn't giving up. No break-in, no fire would keep her from reopening the Merc. They'd have to kill her first.

A shudder ran through her body. A real possibility. Whoever was behind all this crap wouldn't hesitate to kill again.

But before anything else, she wanted a shower.

But one thing she would not do was distract a certain lawman from his job.

What had he done? What had he said? One-minute Beth was purring into the phone, the next she was hissing like a scalded cat.

Ben cleared his throat. How much of his conversation had Stirling overheard? No matter. Checking in with Donovan was next anyway. He punched in the ranger's number. "Donovan. All quiet?" The major's terse pattern of speech was rubbing off on him.

On hearing her affirmative response, he nodded. "Good. Stick with your charge and keep her out of trouble. Call me if you have any problems." He ended the call and stuck his phone back in his jacket pocket.

He flashed Stirling a wry smile. "Ready for the tour?"

"Lead on," Stirling said with a brow that angled upward. "Donovan's charge—a good friend of yours?"

He responded with a grunt.

They walked from the new office city park toward Main Street, a matter of a few blocks. The rise in temperature was already making itself known. Ben unloosened his tie and unbuttoned his top button. "Could say that." Although given her present pissy mood, who the hell could tell for sure?

Best keep matters on a professional level, he continued, "It's not a big town as towns go. According to my calculations, it's ripe for growth what with the casino under construction. As of the last two weeks, there've been three break-ins, attempted extortion after one of the break-ins, a woman murdered who cooked at the Bistro, and now, a fire at The Mercantile and Bistro on Main. That's where we're headed now. The owners of the Mercantile and Bistro installed high-end security after the first break-in. I'm waiting to hear about the CCTV footage from the man who installed it. I was suspicious of him, had him brought in, but it turns out he's undercover DEA."

"That sucks. Why were you suspicious?" They stopped at a corner waiting on traffic.

"New in town. Johnny-on-the-spot. In fact, Beth—she's one of the owners of The Mercantile—was having dinner with him at the time her store was broken into. Just didn't sit right with me."

Stirling gave a knowing, "Uh-huh. So, is this Beth-person the one Donovan's in *charge* of?"

"She is."

"Uh-huh." Traffic cleared. They crossed the street. Another block and they were at the burned-out Mercantile.

Stirling blew out a breath. "Who-ee! Really did a number on it."

"They did." Ben stopped. The building was still barricaded. He pulled out his phone and called the fire marshal. "Safe to enter the Merc?" he asked. "Okay, roger that." He turned to Stirling. "First floor only."

The acrid smell of the fire damage hit Ben's nostrils. "This store's been here since the late 1800s, owned and operated by the Wheaton family ever since. I really hate this. It's a fixture on Main Street."

"Someone's sending a message, all right."

"Yeah, loud and clear." He scowled. "I mean to send a message too. Whoever *someone* is, he's not taking over this town."

Matt cued up the CCTV footage from the alley cameras behind the Mercantile. He'd had to use his backdoor password in order to access the footage. Apparently, someone, possibly the ranger, had advised one of the owners to change the password he'd assigned. But since it was his software and his installation, he could still access it. He fast-forwarded to the time shortly before the fire erupted. He leaned forward, rubbed his eyes.

Would you just look at that?

Here was an example of leverage, pure and simple.

Grinning, he reached for the phone to call Chief Deputy Rasmussen. "Deputy, Matt Freeman here. I've cued up that footage, and there's a problem with it. The heat from the fire must've damaged the router. I may be able to clean up the images from the cloud, but it's going to take some time. I have some software that may do the trick, but it isn't a quick solution. I know you want to know who set the fire ASAP."

"It's vital," the Chief Deputy responded. "Do your best."

"Will do." Matt ended the call. "Yeah, I'll do my best all right." Opening the desk drawer, he pulled out a burner phone and called information for a certain number. Then he plugged in the voice changer.

Fortunately, the lady herself answered, "Double Bar B

Ranch. Zoe Briggs speaking."

"You've been a very bad girl. Playing with matches. Very naughty."

"Who *is* this?" she shrieked in his ear.

"Just think of me as someone who has a proposition for you. I have some very damaging footage of you setting a fire, and if you'd like to keep me from turning it over to the Sheriff's Department, we'll need to come to terms."

"You're crazy. Who is this? I don't know what you're talking about."

Ignoring the panic in her voice, he went on to describe every single step she'd taken to set the Merc afire. "Now do you believe me?"

"What do you want?"

Much better.

"Don't you mean how *much* do I want?" He chuckled, knowing how evil it must sound on her end of the call. "Five-hundred thousand to start. But it won't be the last payment. I'll need occasional top-offs."

"Where would *I* get that kind of money? My husband just deserted me. I'm penniless."

"Surely not. I'm sure your very rich father will be more than happy to keep you out of jail. You work on him. I'll call later with instructions on delivery." With a self-satisfied grin, he ended the call. "That should put some wind up her skirt." He replaced the burner in the drawer, then locked it.

And just in case that smart Texas Ranger decided to access the footage himself, he copied it to his personal cloud storage and then altered the original image to an unreadable state.

When he'd completed his task, he pushed back from the desk with a feeling of great satisfaction. That ought to do it.

Chapter Ten

Beth parked in front of the Merc. Seeing it in its present state sent a stab of pain to her chest. Considering Wheaton's Mercantile had weathered untold misfortune over the last century and a half, she was tempted to sit down and weep. Instead, she sucked in a deep breath. No point in acting like a ninny. She squared her shoulders. Like her ancestors, she was made of stronger stuff. Lola was already on her way back from Mom and Dad's. Together they'd tackle the mess.

"We can't go in yet," Kelly reminded her. "The fire marshal will have to okay it."

Wiping away the soot from a pane in the door, she tiptoed and peered inside. "I see movement. Someone's already in there. Fire marshal or not, I'm going in."

Beth jerked open the door and was greeted by the sharp smell of smoke. She gasped. The damage was even worse than she'd imagined. If as much as a can of corn was salvageable, she'd be surprised. The fire had burned a hole in the ceiling extending through the roof. She could just make out one of the kitchen table's charred legs.

Echoing from the back of the store, she heard a noise. "Who's here?" she shouted. "I'm calling the sheriff if you don't come out, right now." She planted her feet and clenched her fists. She was ready to fight. Just let someone try something.

Through the dark interior of the store, made darker by the charred shelves and walls, she spotted movement. "I'm dialing right now." She pulled out her cell phone, ready to make good on her threat.

"Hold your horses, Beth. I have permission to be here. You don't." Ben's familiar form walked toward her. He glared at Kelly. "Donovan, you're supposed to be riding herd on her."

"Yes, sir." Kelly shot him a half-smile. "Easier said than done."

Setting her hands on her hips, Beth jutted her chin. "I just needed to see the damage. Now I wish I hadn't."

She spied another figure just over Ben's shoulder. "Hmph. I see you have some help. Maybe now you can focus without *distraction*."

"Now, Beth..." he began, in that rich baritone of his, reaching for her.

"All right, we're done here. I need to find a place to live. Let's go, Kelly." She spun and left the way she came. "Ride *herd* on me," she muttered. "Really?"

"He just wants you safe."

"So, he's not 'distracted.' He thinks I'm a *distraction!*" She wasn't sure, but she thought she heard Kelly emit a groan. "I'm in the mood to rent a condo. Insurance will surely pay for some of it. That way I won't be taking up a bed at Karen's."

That's right. She had things to do. Who needed a man anyway? Especially, one who thought she was interfering with his work.

After the whirlwind aka Beth stormed out, Ben shook his head. "Sorry about that. I don't know what's gotten into her."

"She's a fiery one. I'll say that for her." Stirling clapped Ben's shoulder. "It's not easy when things get personal."

Before their conversation could travel into more

uncomfortable areas, Ben's phone signaled a text. He read it. "Dammit. The CCTV footage is a no-go for now. But the guy who installed the cameras is working on cleaning up the images."

"What about the cloud? If it's a new system, it should've uploaded to the cloud."

"Freeman gave me some BS about the heat damaging the router. Does that sound right?"

"Maybe we'd better have a talk with this Freeman guy. What d'ya say."

Ben nodded. "Never liked him. Not for a minute. DEA or not, he needs to step up and give us a face and a name. I want to know who set this damn fire." He mopped his forehead with a handkerchief. "Let's get back to the office and get you set up for work."

He had entirely too much on his plate to worry about what trouble Beth was getting into. She was becoming dangerously more blonde than ever. Donovan was here for a reason. He couldn't be in five places at once. Surely, she ought to understand that much.

Monday noon

The Texas sun was high in a cerulean-washed sky interspersed with delicate wisps of white clouds. The summer heat was definitely giving the car's AC a workout. Beth reached to turn the radio station down low enough so they could talk.

"I'm so glad to get all this done. A good day's work." She gave an emphatic nod. With Kelly riding shotgun, Beth had rented an unfurnished three-bedroom condo at Cottonwood Acres, located on the outskirts of town. Then after a trip to the local furniture rental store, she'd signed a six-month contract for enough furniture to furnish the place. Heaven only knew how long it would take to sort through the insurance issues and then rebuild the Merc and Bistro.

"I still think you should move in with us," Beth suggested. "The third bedroom will just sit empty if you don't."

Kelly wrinkled her nose and slanted a sideways glance. "I'll have to see what Ranger Rasmussen thinks about it."

"I'm sure he'd approve." Beth gave an eye roll. "That way it'll be *so* much easier for you to ride herd on me. Just promise me you'll think about it."

"Like I said, it's up to the boss man."

"We have some time. The condo is ready now, but it'll be Wednesday before Briscoes can deliver and set up the furniture. It'll certainly be comfortable, although you might miss Karen's lovely breakfasts."

"That's the truth." Kelly licked her lips. "What's next on your agenda?"

Beth stopped at a red light. "Okay. Insurance. A place to live. Furniture. All done." She took a moment to consider. "Clothes. I definitely need clothes. Lola too, although—"

"Go." Kelly nudged her. "Light's green."

"Yikes." She quickly moved her foot from the brake to the gas pedal, putting the car in motion. "I really have no business trying to talk and drive at the same time. As I started to say, Lola will have some clothes with her. If she needs more, which I'm sure she will, she can shop after she gets back. Ought to be soon." She glanced over at Kelly. "Would you text her and see where she is? If she's close, tell her we'll either be at the shopping mall or at the Yellow Rose after that."

Kelly frowned. "If she's on the way, she probably won't stop to answer a text."

"Then I should just call her."

"Why don't you wait until *you* can pull over?"

"Good point." Beth pulled into Kenton Valley's only strip mall, although it might not be the only one for long. Rumor had it that before too long, someone would be groundbreaking on a new mall. "Call Lola," she said using the onboard phone.

"I'm almost there," her sister answered. "Are you still okay?"

"Sure. I just pulled into the Valley Mart to pick up some undies and stuff."

"You're staying at the Yellow Rose?"

"For the next couple of days. I'll tell you more when I see you. I'm going to hang up and get my shopping done." Beth ended the call, then turned to Kelly. "All right let's make this a quick trip. I'm hungry."

Beth had just crawled from the Maxima when the sound of sirens pierced the air. An involuntary shiver ran through her, raising goosebumps on her arms. "What now?"

"Someone walk across your grave?"

"That's what it felt like." She rubbed her arms. "Let's make this quick."

"You want to see what's happened?"

"You betcha!"

Ben eyed the desks, positioned back to back. "That should do it." Thanks," he said to the movers who'd shown up an hour later than promised. Turing to Stirling, he jerked his head toward the supply closet. "Will said we can use their supplies, as long as we don't go overboard."

"Good enough." Stirling nodded. "Very generous." He twisted his mouth to the side. "So, do you trust that security/DEA guy or not?"

Ben curled his lip. "No. I'd like to see that footage for myself."

"What about a password?" Stirling cast a knowing grin. "Or has your *friend* already given it to you?"

Clearing his throat, Ben said, "Ranger Donovan gave me the link and password for the Merc. Those alley cameras are tied to the store's system."

He took a seat and keyed in the URL, then the password. "Resolution looks great," he said when he first brought up the footage. He fast-forwarded to the time right before the fire. "Damn. Freeman's right, you can't tell anything about who set the fire." He leaned back and let out an exasperated grunt. "But by coincidence, why would the cameras go wonky before the fire started?"

Stirling shrugged. "Could've used some kind of scrambler and activated it before starting the fire. Makes sense."

Ben swore.

At that moment, the dispatcher rushed by them into the sheriff's office. Stirling's brows shot up to his hairline.

Will emerged, white-faced and tense. "Another fire. Sleepytyme Motel."

Already Ben could hear the fire engines screaming through town. His heart felt as if it were lodged in his throat. "Let's roll. One of my newbie rangers is undercover there."

When they arrived at the motel, Ben braked sharply. After turning off the ignition, he opened the door and got out. Fearing the worst, he ran to the nearest fireman.

"No further," the fireman warned with an upraised hand.

He produced his badge. "Any injuries?"

"We've got a severely burned clerk. The hotel owner's apartment is fully involved. We're not sure what we'll find there."

"That desk clerk is one of mine," Ben said. "I need to see him." He brushed by the fireman .and ran to where Ocala was being loaded into an ambulance. Ocala's face was covered with an oxygen mask. Black traces of soot surrounded the edges of the mask. "What the hell happened?"

"Don't know for sure," Ocala gasped. "Explosion. I don't think Hank made it out."

"That's enough for now," the EMT warned.

Ben turned the air blue. "Take good care of him. He's one of mine."

He turned to Stirling. "Have to let Major Innis know. I don't want him hearing this on the news."

He keyed in the major's number. "Major, Ocala's injured. Smoke inhalation and severe burns, according to the EMT. Explosion at the motel where I assigned him. He's on his way to the hospital. One probable fatality—the motel owner. Waiting to find out. I'd appreciate it if you'll authorize the bomb unit."

After receiving the Major's okay, Ben ended the call and walked over to his brother's side; Will had arrived on Ben's tail. "I've requested the Ranger bomb unit. They'll be able to determine what kind of explosive device was used, and if we're lucky, the signature of the bomb maker."

"Sure." Will swept off his cowboy hat and arrowed his fingers through his hair before replacing the Stetson. "I'd like to know who the hell we're dealing with? Why has the Valley become such a hotbed of criminal activity? Never seen anything like it. I don't mind admitting I'm in over my head what with Vince being arraigned today."

"We've got your back, Will," Stirling said, clapping

Will's shoulder. "Don't we, big brother?"

Ben's thoughts were running along the same track as Will's. Matters were escalating at a precipitous rate. If he could just talk Beth into taking a vacation until things settled down. More than anything, he didn't want her hurt. She'd already too close.

Over his shoulder, he observed firemen removing a body from the destroyed office. He shuddered. He'd come close to losing one of his new rangers. Too close.

He turned to Stirling. "Dave, check around the back of the office. See if you can tell where the bomb went off. Check for surveillance cameras. Looks as if only the office and the first two units are affected. The rest of the units appeared to be affected only by smoke and water damage."

The fire chief, Nelson White, trudged over in his PPE. He was a tall barrel-chested man with long skinny legs, his Personal Protection Equipment making him appear top-heavy.

"Any civilians injured?" Ben asked.

"Other than the desk clerk, who I understand is one of yours, there's a single fatality. The civilians vacated their rooms, right after the explosion. The Red Cross will find them alternate lodgings."

"That's well and good, but I need statements from everyone who was staying at the motel." He turned to his brother. "Can you take care of that?"

Will nodded and rushed off to corral the motel inhabitants.

"Any chance I can get in there now, just to have a look around. The Ranger bomb unit will be here soon."

"Considering a bomb is most likely involved, there could be additional explosive devices. You're not going in there. Not now. Not until your bomb unit clears it."

"All right, Chief." Not about to mess with White. At a

fire his word was law, and his no-nonsense gray gaze wouldn't brook attitude from anyone, not even a Texas Ranger.

Ben pulled out his phone to update Donovan, but as he turned away from the scene, he spotted Beth's Maxima parked on the opposite side of the road. Beth and the ranger, who was supposed to be minding her, stood with their arms folded, leaning back against the vehicle.

Shaking his head, he trudged across the road. "What the hell are y'all doing out here?" He gave Donovan his best evil eye.

Donovan squared her shoulders. "Sir, we heard the sirens and followed the ambulance. We're not in the way. But I wanted to see if I could be of any assistance." Her chin trembled. "I-Is Jeff okay?"

So, that's how it is. Ben remembered that Donovan and Ocala were in the same class. Were they romantically involved? Wasn't that something he should've known before assigning them to the same case?

"He's alive," Ben said gently. "Smoke inhalation and some substantial burns. He's on his way to the hospital."

Keeping his eye on Donovan, she seemed to take the news calmly. Biting her bottom lip was the only sign she gave of upset.

More to the point. "Why is Beth here?"

Beth jutted her chin a notch. "Reckon it's kind of hard to ride herd if said herd is somewhere else. After the fire, as you might imagine, I needed a few clothes. We were at the strip mall when we heard the sirens. I hope I'm not distracting you too much." She gave him a sugary sweet smile that made him wish he could turn her over his knee and apply a good smack to her pert bottom. While that might be considered fun for some, he didn't think she'd enjoy it, at all.

He held back any words she could take the wrong way. Pissing her off was not his intention. "It might be prudent if you were to consider whether you ought to be ambulance chasing and head back to the strip mall for those clothes."

Beth gave Donovan a side-eye glance. "Maybe you're right."

"Perhaps," Donovan said tentatively, "we could check on Jeff at the hospital afterward?"

"Definitely, we should do that," Beth said with a bit of attitude. "Okay with you, boss-man?"

Honestly, even when she was doing everything she could to try his patience, she was like fireworks in the night. "Beth..."

She smiled up at him, her wide brown eyes full of warmth. "Yes? You have something to say to me?"

He let out a sigh of exasperation. "Be careful. Whoever this is, isn't messing around. Please, just be careful." Jeez. Repetitious. Inane. Boring. How could he ever share the emotions he felt when it was never the right time or the right place.

"Careful." She tapped her chest. "Yes. That's me, all right." She opened the car door and slid inside. Donovan followed suit.

"Lock it." He shut the door and shook his head as she pulled into the road and raced away in the wrong direction. Then he grinned as she'd apparently made a U-turn and was speeding back toward town.

Somehow. Someway. Sometime, he needed to sit her down and have a real conversation. His feelings weren't going away. If anything, the danger heightened his emotions and threatened to choke him every time he saw her.

The main thing was to keep her safe. She was a target. And whoever was behind the break-ins, extortion, and the fires wouldn't stop at murder. One woman had already been murdered, and now the motel owner was dead. No way could he risk Beth being the third victim of this vendetta.

After they drove back to the Sheriff's Department, Ben had just sat down when his phone rang. "Rasmussen." He listened, then ended the call and nodded at Stirling. "So, the bomb squad has confirmed it. It was an explosive device at the motel. Pretty simple as such things go. But effective."

"What are your thoughts on who's behind it?"

"Behind the bomb or everything?"

"Both."

"Someone in town is making a move, in advance of the casino. The break-ins, the fire, the bomb, intimidation to the point of murder." He leaned forward on the desk. "We have a couple of small-time players, and they may be involved, but they're not running the show. And it's only getting started. Whoever he is, he's not messing around. We need to check public records. I want to see if any single person is buying up property or businesses."

"Have any of the affected owners been approached to sell? What about your friend, Miss Wheaton? Has anyone tried to buy her out recently?"

Ben tried to remember if she'd mentioned anything like that. If someone had made Beth and her sister an offer, without a doubt, they would've turned it down without a second thought. Sell their family's business?

No way in hell.

"If she was approached, she didn't mention it. Why don't I drop you off at the courthouse? Find the City Clerk and have her go over the recent land purchases and business license changes. I need to get over to the hospital and check on Ocala."

***

After her shopping expedition was accomplished in record time, Beth stowed the shopping bags in the trunk. "I was hungry. Now I'm starving. Since the Bistro is no longer an option, why don't we go to the country club for lunch?"

Kelly looked down at her jeans and t-shirt. "I'm not exactly dressed for the country club."

"Duh!" Beth gave herself a dope-slap. "Neither am I. What do you say we hit the market and pick up some salad and sandwich stuff... and chips? I'm really dying for some chips and salsa." She got into the car. "Karen won't mind if we bring in a few groceries."

Kelly worried her bottom lip. "I don't suppose we could make a quick stop at the hospital first?"

"OMG! I'm sorry. I'm so dense. We should've done that first. I'm *really* sorry. I'm way too focused on my gut. We'll go right now and check on your...friend?"

"H-He's more than a friend. We—uh, got really close during training."

Beth grinned. "Far be it from me to stand in the way of romance. One stop at Los Marcos General coming up."

"Is it a good hospital? He's severely burned..."

"It is. I mean, it's not like a big city hospital, but the nurses and doctors live locally in the Valley or out in the county. They really care. It's not impersonal, at all. You'll see what I mean."

Beth trailed behind as Kelly rushed through the E.R. doors and up to the reception desk. "Jeff Ocala—he was just brought in with burns and smoke inhalation."

The receptionist gave Kelly a sympathetic smile. "He's

in treatment room four, but the doctor is with him. If you'll just have a seat—"

Beth sighed. The ranger wasn't about to have a seat until she laid eyes on her man. She ran to the fourth room and peered through the window. "Just hang on." Beth slid her arm around Kelly's waist. "It's really crowded, and they're treating his burns. You don't want to get in their way."

"No. I just needed to see him." Her eyes shone with tears. She bit her lips. "The burns—they look bad."

"It's hard to tell from here, and we're not medical. Why don't you wait until the doctor comes out?"

"Will they even talk to me?" Tears began to stream down her cheeks. "We're not married, not even engaged.

She tugged on Kelly's elbow. "Look." Ben emerged from room four. "I bet they talked to him."

"You're here!" Wiping away her tears, Kelly ran to Ben. "I didn't see you when I looked into the room. How is he?"

"I was in the corner, doing my best to stay out of the way."

"How is he?" she begged. "What can you tell me?"

"It's not as bad as it looks," he said gently. "Burns over 30 percent of his body. Smoke inhalation. All treatable. He's not going to be a happy camper for quite a while. It'll take time, but he'll survive this."

Letting out a sigh of relief, Kelly sagged and slid down against the wall. "Thank heaven." Then pulling herself together, she got to her feet. "Sorry. Just a weak moment, there." She squared her shoulders. "May I see him? *Will* they let me see him, for just a minute?"

How could anyone with a heart refuse the desperate young woman? Beth wondered. Now, if it were Ben who was lying on that gurney...

"I'll see." Ben walked back into the room where Ocala

was being treated, spoke to one of the nurses, nodded toward Kelly, and then came back out. "Just for a minute. He's groggy, but he's awake enough to know you're here."

Beth watched as Kelly eased into the treatment room and took her place by Jeff's side. His eyelids flickered, and he managed to give his partner a brave smile.

She gazed up at Ben. "This is what it means to be in— uh, involved with a lawman. Isn't it?" She'd meant to say, 'in love with a ranger,' but she'd stopped herself just in time. She still couldn't help but imagine herself in Kelly's place. What if something happened to Ben? He *was* a Texas Ranger, after all. Anyone close to him would have to deal with the uncertainty. The worry. The knowledge that anything could happen. Anytime.

"It's part of it." The words seemed to catch in his throat. His low baritone deepened. "I put that young man in harm's way. Logically, we're in harm's way every day, but I can't help but feel responsible."

"I'd say whoever started that fire is responsible," Beth said, her spirits rallying.

He cleared his throat. "I know this is off the subject, but have you had any recent offers to buy the Merc?"

She angled her head, looking up at him. "What?" She thought for a moment. "Yeah, as a matter of fact. The mayor himself made me an offer. But I didn't think he was serious. Why?"

"We'll talk about it later," he said.

Kelly walked into the hallway outside the treatment room. "He's in good spirits. He says he may have to have some skin grafts, but at least, he's going to be okay. I'm sorry, Ranger Rasmussen, for my lapse of professionalism. It won't happen again."

Ben slid an arm around each of them. "Damn professionalism. Your partner was hurt. It bothered you.

Hell, it bothers me."

Beth smiled up into his bright blue gaze. There was such comfort in his embrace, even if she was sharing. Then her stomach had the temerity to growl.

He roared with laughter. "Damn, woman. When did you last have something to eat?"

"Breakfast. I do feel just the tiniest bit hungry. Kelly?"

Giving a sniff, Kelly nodded. "Now that I've seen Jeff, I think I can manage to eat something."

"Buy-Rite here we come." She took Kelly's hand and headed to the E.R. exit.

"Be careful," Ben called after them.

Beth pulled out of the E.R. parking lot and headed north to the Buy-Rite Grocery, a small mom and pop operation that served the north end of town. Dan and Sylvia Liston were in their sixties and were well-known for their friendly service and generosity. So far, they hadn't been affected by the crimes that were becoming all too frequent in the Valley. And if Ben and his fellow rangers could get a handle on who was behind it all, they never would be.

Beth pulled into the Buy-Rite's parking lot, parked the car, and turned to Kelly. "Did you see that GOING OUT OF BUSINESS sign?"

"Who could miss it? Are there a lot of grocery stores in the Valley?" Kelly asked, climbing from the Maxima.

"More than you might expect." Beth opened the door and got out. "The Merc doesn't have a monopoly on groceries. There've always been enough customers to go around. I'm surprised at Dan and Sylvia's selling up, though. I'm sure that's what they've done. Maybe they're retiring. They're the right age for it."

When they entered the store, the cashier was leaning back on the register and reading a paperback. "What's going on?" Beth asked. "I can't believe the store's closing."

The cashier shrugged and gave a sniff. "Me neither."

"Are Dan and Sylvia around?"

"Try the office," was her off-hand reply.

"Thanks." Beth nodded, then turned to Kelly. "Why don't you pick up whatever you're in the mood for while I have a quick chat with the Listons. Whole wheat bread for me."

"Sure thing." Kelly nodded and took off with a shopping cart.

Dan and Sylvia would be much more likely to talk to Beth than a stranger. She walked to the back of the store and knocked on the office door.

Dan motioned for her to enter. He stood and gave her a hug. "Beth, what a nice surprise. Sylvia's not here. She'll be sorry she missed you." Dan's polite friendliness was what anyone could expect from the short, slightly chubby man. "Have a seat. How can I help?"

"We came for some sandwich and salad fixings, but I have to say how astonished I was when I saw your sign. Why are you closing the store?"

He leaned back and let out a sigh. "We had such a great offer. It would've been crazy not to accept it. I'm sixty-four and Syl's sixty-two. It's time we packed it in."

She leaned forward and lowered her voice. "It's not because of the break-ins and fires, is it?"

"Not at all." He shook his head. "In fact, the offer was made before all that started. But to tell the truth, after seeing what's been going on, I'm glad we accepted it."

"Who bought the store? Are they going to keep it going or what?"

"I don't rightly know."

"You don't know *who* bought the store?"

He let out an amused chuckle. "Oh, sure. Of course, I know who bought it. A company called—let's see now—TexMak, Inc."

"Never heard of them. Are they local?"

"Well, I'm pretty sure they are, since the mayor is on the board. In fact, we dealt with him and his lawyer. Sam Dunaway handled our end of the purchase. He said the deal was a fair one, not great, but we took it."

"Sam's a good man," she said, approving of his choice. "He's my lawyer too." *The mayor, again.* Very interesting. What was the man up to? Maybe the offer he'd made a couple of months ago was a serious one. After Ben's question earlier.... What was going on?

"And what do they plan to do with the store?"

Dan's brows drew together. "Don't quote me on this, but I think his honor, the mayor, is set on accumulating power. Though I don't have a clue how our little store would fit into a power grab." He straightened a stack of papers on his desk. "And I don't care. Syl and I are buying an RV, and we're hitting the road. We've been stuck in this store for twenty long years and haven't seen a dad-blamed thing of this great country of ours."

"That's wonderful. You'll be missed, for sure." She rose and extended her hand. "Thanks for talking to me, Dan. And I hope you and Sylvia have a wonderful retirement."

A power grab. Was that the mayor's plan? Maybe she should invite him to make another offer. What would happen if she did? Would it be lower or higher? Stupid question, considering the store was nothing more than a blackened ruin. Best talk to Ben. See if he was thinking along the same lines.

The mayor?

Talk about corruption. Was he behind the break-ins,

the fires, and the deaths of two people? To what end?

She walked back toward the front of the store. Kelly was at the checkout, about to pay for their late lunch. "No. This is on me," Beth said and inserted her debit card into the card reader. Then she lowered her voice. "Before we eat, I need to talk to Ben. Something's definitely up."

Gathering up the bags, Kelly said, "Tell me."

After leaving the hospital, Ben met up with Dave Stirling at the City Clerk's office and then drove back to the Sheriff's Department. "Anything of interest?"

Stirling gave Ben a wide smile. "You could say that."

"Let's take it into the office. No point in sharing this with all and sundry."

"You got that right."

Ben tapped on the glass. Will raised his head from a stack of paperwork and motioned for them to enter.

Ben pulled up a chair and straddled it. "We've—or I should say Dave—has found some very interesting transactions.

Stirling closed the door behind him and took a seat. "I checked with the City Clerk on property sales and business licenses during the last few months. And I came across something pretty interesting. A company by the name of Tex-Mak, Inc. has been systematically buying up land all over the county. They've already made several purchases of businesses in town, as well. The Buy-Rite Grocery, for one, and Cherry's Hardware, for another."

Ben interrupted, "I checked with Beth, and she said the mayor offered to buy her out a couple of months ago. Like I figured, she laughed it off. I also checked with the owners of the Tidy-Kleen, and they also admitted someone made them an offer which they refused. Given Hank McKennitt is dead, we can't ask him. Who is this Tex-Mak, Inc.?"

"Man goes by the name of Carlton Briggs. Say, isn't Briggs your mayor's name? Any relation?"

"None other than the man himself," Will said. "I can see where this is headed. Who else? Who's the Mak?"

The Mak of Tex-Mak—who else could it be? "What about Yuri Makarov?" Ben suggested. "I can see him trying to get a foothold in the Valley, now that the casino is under construction."

"The company filing papers don't list anyone but Briggs."

"He's got to be a silent partner. Briggs owns a big construction company, but I doubt he's pulled this together on his own."

Will's office phone buzzed. "Yeah?"

"Someone to see you, Sheriff."

Will gave an eye roll. "*Acting* sheriff," he said with a growl.

"They really asked to see the Ranger," the dispatcher said, "but he's with you."

"Send 'em in."

Looking over his shoulder, Ben spied Beth, along with Donovan. He shook his head. What now?

He stood, offering her his chair.

"No thanks." She shook her head, her warm brown eyes with bright with excitement. "We're not staying, but we have something important to tell you."

"And I thought y'all were headed out for food." Ben gazed down at her, all the while wishing they could have five minutes alone. So much he wanted—no, needed to say.

"We did. We stopped at the Buy-Rite. Did you know it's going out of business? Dan and Sylvia have sold out to—"

"—the mayor. We know."

"Well, it's a company, but Dan Liston says the mayor's behind it because he did the deal with the mayor and his lawyer. Dan's lawyer said it was a fair deal, though. I don't remember what the mayor's offer was. I didn't even let him finish." She gave a sigh. "Considering everything that's happened since then, I might've made a mistake in not selling." She sank into the chair, after all.

"No, you can't give in to thugs. Mayor or not, he's nothing more than a thug," Ben said. "It's extortion by fear with menaces."

She chewed on her bottom lip for a second. "Eva Johnson might disagree. At least, she'd still be alive if I'd even listened to his offer."

Will's office phone buzzed again. "I'm ready to throw this damn thing through the window." He picked up the handset. "Yeah?" Then his face broke into a wide smile. "That's great. Thanks for letting me know."

"Well?" Ben raised a brow. "Little brother, we could use some good news."

"That was Vince's lawyer. Vince was just arraigned and released on his own recognizance."

"Hot damn!" Ben slapped his thigh. "At least the judge had the good sense to do that."

"He can come back to work?" Beth asked. "What does 'on his own recognizance' mean exactly?"

"That means that after reviewing Vince's case and his standing in the community, the judge deemed Vince wouldn't be a flight risk. All he would have had to do was sign a written promise to appear in court. No bond, even. He's still suspended, but he's not cooling his heels in an Austin jail."

"Great. At least he can be home with Abby until the baby comes." Standing, she smiled up at Ben, sending his heart rate soaring into the stratosphere. "And since you already know about the mayor, we're heading to the Yellow Rose. I'm still starving." She motioned to Kelly. "C'mon. Before we faint."

Ben let out a bark of laughter. When he thought of Beth, he thought of a strong feisty woman, not one inclined to faint, no matter how hungry she was.

His brother out and out cackled. "She's never fainted in her life. You'd see me faint before she would."

"She's a Texas woman, born and bred. Need I say more?" Ben asked with a knowing smile.

Stirling nodded his agreement. "And what would we do without 'em?"

Considering his first foray into not-so-wedded bliss had failed so miserably, Ben shook his head. "Can't live without 'em. Can't kill 'em."

"Sad but true," Stirling agreed. "The way I see it is every lawman's entitled to at least one failed marriage. It makes him cautious and more aware of what to look for in number two... or three." He elbowed Ben's ribs. "I should know. Right?"

"Right," Ben agreed with a smile. Stirling was on his third marriage, this time to another ranger, and it appeared as if this one would take. Did Beth have what it took to be a lawman's wife? Could she withstand the late dinners, the interrupted dinners, the completely missed dinners without seeking comfort elsewhere as Zoe had? He'd bet his silver badge; Beth would remain true blue.

Chapter Eleven

Monday afternoon

Beth carried two bags of groceries into the kitchen at the Yellow Rose, while Kelly brought up the rear with another two. "I hope you don't mind. We brought some salad fixings and sandwich stuff."

Karen turned from the stove and wiped her hands on a floral apron. "Girls, you didn't have to. I'm doing a nice roast loin for your dinner."

"No. That's not right. We don't expect anything other than your wonderful breakfasts."

"Of course, I do. Why don't you have your lunch—petty late lunch at that—out on the patio. Don't eat too much because I make a mean pork loin."

"We got side-tracked," Beth said. "So much has happened."

"I'm aware your store and home and the bistro are basically gone—for the time being anyway. You will rebuild, won't you?" She took one of the bags from Beth and started unpacking it. "By the way, your sister is up in your room getting settled. You'll be in the Bluebonnet room. It's right next to the Pink Peony room where you spent last night." She let out a giggle. "Oh, I do rattle on. Why don't I make your salad and fix a tray of the meats and cheeses while you touch base with your sister? Goodness! You bought enough for an army."

"Okay. That's what I'll do." She turned, anxious to see how her sister was taking the latest upheaval.

Kelly said, "Why don't I stay and help Karen. That'll

give you some time with Lola."

Not only a damn good ranger, but she was sensitive, too. "Thanks," Beth said, then ran upstairs and opened the door to the Bluebonnet room which had been painted a pale blue. A duvet and matching draperies were covered with a delicate bluebonnet pattern. The queen-sized bed meant she and Lola could share. But where was her sister? She glanced around. "Lola?"

The bathroom door opened, and her sister emerged. "I was putting stuff away." Her shoulders were down, and her expression was blank. "I drove by the store."

"I know. It's awful. I've already talked to the insurance agent. We're covered. We can rebuild..." she hesitated. "But I think we should take our time." She quickly filled her sister in on the events that had occurred since she'd left.

Lola sank on the side of the bed. "Honestly, I don't know if I care anymore."

Because they'd worked together side-by-side, Eva's death had hit Lola harder. How could she pull her sister out of this funk? Lola had always been so strong. "We can't give up. I just think we should take our time and let Ben and the sheriff arrest whoever's behind all this. From the way he talks and the questions he's asked, I'm pretty sure the mayor is up to something. Whoever he's working with—well, they haven't shared that particular bit of information with me. Not yet anyway."

"I should've stayed with mom and dad." Lola shook her head wearily. "But I didn't think it was right to stay there and leave you saddled with all the responsibility."

"It's all right. You can go back if you'd rather. I've rented a condo, but don't let that keep you from doing what's best for *you*." She slid an arm around her sister. "I can handle things on this end. Go back. Be with mom and dad. Let them take care of you."

"Come with me." Lola's eyes shone with tears. "Leave this one-horse town. It's not the same town where we grew up. It'll never be the same."

As tempted as she was to do as Lola suggested, she couldn't. "I can't. I won't let the mayor, or whatever yahoos he's working with, run me out of town." She straightened her spine.

"But you're in danger. You're so freaking stubborn, what if they kill you next? I couldn't live without my sister." Lola's body heaved with great sobs, leaving Beth desperate to comfort her sibling.

"I'll be fine," she said gently. "Kelly is on the job, and Ben—he's keeping a very close eye on me."

"He cares about you. At least, you have that going for you." She gave a sniff and pulled Beth into a ferocious bear hug. "Promise me you won't do anything stupid."

"Now *that* would be impossible," Beth said, giving an eye roll. "Go wash your face. Then come downstairs and have something to eat. I'm freaking starving."

Lola released her hold and rose from the bed. Finger combing her hair away from her face, she wrinkled her nose. "You're always hungry."

"That's probably true." Beth leaned back against the padded headboard and let out a sigh. She'd thought Lola's going to stay with mom and dad was a solution. Away from the Valley, she'd perk up, surely. But it wasn't going to be that easy. If anything, Lola was in the depression stage of grieving for her friend—their friend really. But either Beth was in the denial stage or maybe she was just numb. Too much had happened, too fast.

Ben left Will's temporary office and called Major Innes

to update him on their findings and suspicions, as well as let him know Sheriff Tate had been arraigned and released. He purposefully kept his voice low since what he had to say was sensitive. "I know this is the last thing you want to hear. Arresting a corrupt mayor is no picnic."

"Picnic? It's a shit storm is what it is. You don't have enough solid evidence to do anything other than piss the man off. We need to know who he's in business with. You're right about one thing. Yuri Makarov is a sure bet, but you need proof. Bastard is slicker than an eel packed in oil."

"We need a surveillance team on him."

"You already have one. You and Stirling and that new agent Donovan. See if you can keep this one uninjured. If there's anything I hate more than telling a mother her son or daughter has been injured or killed in the line of duty, I can't imagine what it would be."

"All heart, sir," he mumbled.

"What was that?"

"Nothing, sir."

"Then bring me some hard evidence so we can charge this corrupt mayor of yours."

"Yes, sir." Ben ended the call and heaved a sigh. "Good news and bad news."

"I'll take the good," Stirling said with a wry grin, "if it's all right with you."

Ben leaned forward, still keeping his tone low. "Surveillance team has been authorized. And the bad news is you, Donovan, and I are it."

"You mean you and I are it. You're not going to take Donovan off her current assignment, are ya?"

"Hell no."

"Twelve and twelve, then?"

"No other choice." Ben shrugged and felt like throwing up his hands. It was almost as if he were being penalized for trying to do his job. Being given the go-ahead but not the resources he needed to be successful.

"What about the mayor's residence? How close can we get?"

"This isn't New York City. A surveillance van is going to stick out like a sore thumb. He lives on a ranch, about five miles west of town. Set in a valley. There's a grove of cottonwoods fairly close to the house if Briggs hasn't cut them down. We might have to ride in and set up old school surveillance. Keep track of who comes and goes."

"And if the mayor leaves in a vehicle. We sure as hell can't follow him on horseback."

"We may need Donovan, after all." Ben scratched his head. "Let's drive out there now and see what the situation is. I haven't been to the ranch for months, not since Zoe and I split up."

"Are you sure you want to pull Donovan off her current detail?"

"I may have to. The major figures we should be able to handle surveilling Briggs. Beth and her sister are staying at a B&B. I doubt anyone is going to mess with them there.

With glasses of iced sweet tea on a table between them, Beth and Lola sat in comfortable lounge chairs in the Yellow Rose Inn's screened-in back porch. The heat of the day had lessened a bit, and a gentle breeze drifted in from the north. Overhead a ceiling fan spun lazily. "What are you going to do? Move into the condo with me or go back to mom and dad's?"

Lola let out a low groan. "Do I have to decide right this minute?"

"Of course not." She reached for her sister's hand and

gave it a squeeze.

Responding with a wan smile, Lola asked. "Do we know when Eva's funeral is?"

Beth gave a shake of her head. "Her body hasn't even been released yet."

"I really need to see Sophie and pay my respects. Running away isn't the solution. I'm staying."

"I'm glad. But you don't have to stay because of me. I'll be all right." In spite of her reassurances to the contrary, Beth was thrilled Lola had agreed to stay. And Lola was right. Running away was never the best solution.

"Anyone need more tea?" Karen came out with a pitcher of sweet tea, and Kelly followed with a plate of chess squares.

Beth held out her glass for a refill with one hand and snatched a chess square with the other. "This is the life. I always thought I was born to have servants. Maybe I was switched at birth?"

A giggle erupted from Lola. "And here I thought I was your servant all these years." She bit into one of the rich squares and gave a little moan of pleasure.

Inside the house, the sound of the phone ringing sent Karen dashing away to answer. She returned with the phone. "Lola, it's for you."

Lola sat up. "For me?" She took the phone and answered, "Hello?"

Beth watched and waited as Lola nodded. "All right. Thank you for letting me know."

"Who was it? What's going on?"

"That was Will." There was the slightest tremor in her voice. "He called to let me know Eva's body has been released to the funeral home. Arrangements are incomplete, as yet."

"That was thoughtful of him," Beth said. "He's such a

sweetheart. He was thinking of you and how close you and Eva were."

"I'll call Sophie tomorrow. Maybe she'll have calmed down by then."

Biting her lower lip, Kelly set the plate on the round table between Beth and Lola. "I have something to tell you. I just received a text from Ranger Rasmussen. He needs my help with some surveillance."

"Then you must go where you're needed," Beth said. "Now that we're away from the action downtown, I don't think anyone is going to give us a second thought." Out of sight. Out of mind, she hoped.

"I'm not really of any use here. I mean, yes, it's comfortable, and I'm enjoying hanging out with the two of you. That being said, my original assignment was to work at the Mercantile and keep an eye out for someone trying to extort money from you. The Merc is gone, and I need to support my fellow rangers."

"We'll be moving to the condo Wednesday, anyway." Beth turned to their host. "Karen, can you put up with us that long?"

"Of course. You're no problem. I don't have any new guests scheduled until Thursday."

"I just hope we're not endangering you by being here."

Karen's hand went to her throat. "Two more nights? What could happen?"

A sinking feeling centered in the pit of Beth's stomach. What indeed? "Kelly, when do you…"

"I'm to meet them at the Sheriff's Department at eight. That's all I know. The text was brief and lacked detail. It's seven-thirty, so I need to get ready."

"You're still welcome to stay with us when we get moved into the condo," Beth offered. Safety in numbers came to mind. "Or move in with us. Your choice."

"Thanks. We'll see how things go." She gave them a quick wave and left.

"Tell me about the condo," Lola said.

"It's the Cottonwood Acres. Three bedrooms, three and a half baths. Never been lived in. Furniture's being delivered Wednesday. Sound okay?"

"Sounds perfect."

Perfect? Hardly perfect. Two more nights and they would be out of everyone's hair with new temporary digs. Certainly not how she'd expected to spend her summer, dodging arsonists, extortionists, and killers.

Ben glanced at his watch: five 'til eight. Donovan should be here any minute. Will had just given them the bad news that forensics hadn't found any additional evidence from the Johnson murder scene. Other than a small sample of touch DNA on the bullet which was of little value until they had a hit in the DNA database or someone to compare it to. No other evidence at all. Not surprising since they'd already determined it was a professional hit.

Upon hearing surveillance had been approved for Briggs and how short-staffed the rangers were, Will offered Deputy Longworth as a fourth member of the surveillance team.

Fearful that obtaining a warrant on the mayor's ranch and landline would possibly tip him off, they decided as a group that old-fashioned surveillance was the only way to go.

"Two on the house and two to surveil the mayor as he goes about his daily routine. Longworth and Donovan can alternate twelve-hour shifts at the house. Dave, you and I will dog him around town," Ben said.

A tap on the door made Ben turn around. "Good. Donovan, you're here. Need you to run surveillance on Mayor Briggs ranch. Deputy Longworth is taking the first shift, but you're to relieve her at six in the morning. You'll need to ride in. You have a horse?"

"Not *with* me."

"Never mind, I can get you one from my cousin Luci's dude ranch. Just keep track of who comes and who goes. Particularly if you see anything out of the ordinary. Or either of these two men. I just sent their photos to your phone."

"Roger that." She glanced down at her phone. "Yuri Makarov, I know. Who's the other dude?"

"Other one is Reynaldo Reyes. From south of the border."

"Cartel dude?"

"Most definitely a cartel dude," Ben said. In fact, he's the head of the Malos Dias and reputed to be interested in expanding his territory into our backyard."

"Okay, six am. Briggs Ranch. Would love some directions and a horse."

"We'll get you rigged up. Before I run you to my cousin's for a horse, though, we'll drive by the Briggs ranch. The Hendrix dude ranch is his nearest neighbor."

Donovan nodded. "I'm ready if you are."

"Keep your phone charged and ready. That's how we'll communicate. I don't want to risk being overheard." Ben glanced out at the deputy bullpen. "You never know who could be on someone else's payroll."

Beth had just drifted off to sleep when a noise awakened her. She levered onto her elbow. "What was that?" Her feet hit the floor. She grabbed her robe from the bedside chair and pulled it on over her shoulders. Looking around for some kind of weapon, she gave an exasperated gasp. Other than a lamp, there wasn't anything. "Lola!"

"I wasn't asleep." Lola sprang from the bed. "Sounded like a window breaking."

Beth ran to the door, opened it, and sped down the hallway to the staircase. From her vantage point, she felt a draft from where the door glass had been shattered.

Karen emerged from her bedroom, carrying a shotgun. "Let me at 'em. I'll fill 'em full of buckshot." She picked her way downstairs. "Shoes! There's glass in the foyer."

Beth ran back and slid her bare feet into a pair of sandals, then dashed from the room and down the stairs with Lola following.

"Where's Kelly?" Beth asked.

"She's not back yet," Karen said. "Y'all stay back. There's a brick with a note on it." Carefully, she picked up the brick, unwrapped it, read the note, then handed it to Beth. "Must be from your fan club." She gave a shake of her short red bob.

Get out of town now, or there'll be another fire.

"We *have* put you in danger," Beth said, the note trembling in her hands. "We'll leave. We'll go now."

"Don't be silly. You're not going anywhere. First, I'm calling the sheriff's office," Karen said. "And then, we'll see who this sick bastard is on my security cameras."

Beth sucked in a deep breath. "You have security cameras?" *Great. Now we're getting somewhere.*

"You bet your bottom dollar I do. There's one at each door. Follow me. Watch the glass." Karen strode into the den where a laptop sat on a desk in the corner. "I use it for B&B business, so we should have something soon." She sat and booted up the computer.

Beth and Lola peered over Karen's shoulder. "Our

bastard is a woman," Beth said. "I can't make out her face for the hoodie, but that's definitely a woman running away."

"A woman?" Karen gazed up at Beth. "Now before I call the authorities, think hard. Who have you P.O.'d?"

"Beats the heck out of me." Beth thought for a minute. "This is kid stuff. It can't be the same person who broke into the store or a stone-cold killer who murdered Eva in her bed." But could it be the same person who set the store on fire? Why stop at throwing a brick? Why not another fire?

Hiding across the street and smiling widely, Zoe rubbed her hands together. Now *that* should send the bitches running out of town. As the newly elected president of the Kenton Valley Historical Preservation Society, she couldn't bear the thought of setting fire to the historic Yellow Rose Inn. Hopefully, the threat of another fire would be enough to get them moving. Then she could work on getting Ben to fall in love with her again.

Still a little high from the excitement, Zoe ran the two blocks to where she'd left her Porsche. She was fumbling for her key fob when her cell phone rang. "What?"

"Little Miss Zoe. You've been a bad girl again. Now, I want a quarter of a million dollars to keep my mouth shut."

"What? Have you been following me?"

"You could say that."

"Who are you?" She glanced around, unable to see anyone in the dark of night. "Where are you?"

"Never mind where I am now. Meet me tomorrow morning with money in hand. Your bank opens at eight-thirty. Meet me at nine."

"I can't possibly come up with that much money. Not that fast."

"You'll think of a way."

"Meet you where?"

"Central Park by the gazebo. I'll be wearing a black hoodie and red running shoes."

"Tomorrow is a really busy day for me. I—"

"I don't care. Just be there with the damn money. Or else."

Just be there with the damn money.

Damn him, whoever he was. As bad as she hated it, she'd have to go to her father. He was the one with wads of cash stashed in the safe and probably all around the house. Heaven only knew where he kept all his ill-gotten gains. "I'll be there," she said through gritted teeth, then ended the call. Daddy would have to take care of the guy. He was trash. A blackmailer. Whoever he was the world would be better off without him.

She had no illusions about how her father would take care of him, either. The blackmailer wouldn't be her first problem daddy had solved.

Matt leaned back and chuckled. Whatever bone to pick the mayor's daughter had with the Wheaton sisters, it had to be over a man. More than likely, a certain Texas Ranger who'd been sniffing around the little blonde owner of the Mercantile. The same blonde Matt had taken to dinner and would've taken to bed if certain events hadn't overtaken them.

If he was of a mind to do it, he had enough evidence to send little Miss Zoe's elegant ass to prison. Arson. Vandalism. Heaven only knew what else she'd been up to.

But no, that didn't suit him at all. She was more like an untapped piggy bank. His personal retirement plan.

***

Will and Ranger Stirling were still in the office when the dispatcher informed them of an act of vandalism at the Yellow Rose Inn. Will sprang from his chair. "That's where Lola and her sister are staying. Damn, I swear someone has it in for them. Better call Ben and let him know."

"We can handle this," Stirling said, pointing to Will and back to himself.

"No. You *really* need to let my brother know there's been another incident involving the Wheaton sisters."

Stirling gave Will a knowing glance. "Okay, I get your drift. I'll call him, but we can handle the call. He needs to get Donovan's horse situation resolved."

"*I* will handle this call. More of the sheriff department's jurisdiction, if you get my drift. Besides, you need to get some shut-eye if you and Ben are going to start surveilling the mayor."

"All right." Stirling raised his hands in surrender. "You don't have to kick me out of here twice. I'm going. By the way, I'm staying at the Kenton Valley Hotel. Call if you need me."

"Will do." Will gave the ranger a curt nod. Now to get over to the B&B and see if Lola was all right, and Beth, of course. Lately, it seemed as if the cloud left by Darla's horrific death was beginning to lift, and his thoughts often turned to Lola Wheaton and her slender dark beauty. But now he had a job to do, and if it concerned her, then all the better.

Carlton sat in his study watching the late news. More war. More crime. So what? He reached for his coffee when he heard a tap on the door.

"What is it?"

Zoe opened the door with her sweetest smile. "Daddy, I have a problem."

He glanced up from his newspaper. "What is it, darlin'? How can I help?"

"It's kind of a big problem." She shut the door. "Now I know you're gonna be mad, but honestly, I just couldn't help myself."

He let out an exasperated sigh. For Pete's sake, she was dressed like a street person in a sweat suit and a hoodie. "Where have you been? What have you done, this time?"

Sheepishly, she sat across from him on the sofa. As succinctly as she was capable, she told him she'd set the fire at the Mercantile. So, that had been his daughter acting out. And the blackmailer after being seen on the store's security camera, and oh yes, she'd thrown a brick through the front of the Yellow Rose Inn."

"Why not another fire?" he asked. "Why hold back?"

She bristled. "Surely you understand as the newly elected president of the Kenton Valley Historical Preservation Society, I couldn't bear the thought of burning down such a lovely old historic house. I hoped that the threat of another fire would encourage Beth Wheaton, the skank, to get out of town. Daddy, I know Ben and I are meant to be together. I know I shouldn't have done it, but I couldn't stand seeing him playing up to her all the time. I want her *gone*. I know this isn't a good time, and your guests are coming tomorrow—"

"That's for damn sure," he growled. Where was her freaking head? Up her ass, as usual.

"But, Daddy, you need to take care of this guy who's blackmailing me. He wants a half-million dollars."

A half-million? The nerve of the fucker. "Where and

when do you meet him?"

"Nine by the gazebo in the park. He'll be wearing a black hoodie and red running shoes." She rose.

"Fine. He'll be taken care of. But I'm telling you, this is the very last time I'm going to clean up one of your messes."

He let her make it to the door. "Hold on, missy. What do you get in return? Did you tell him you want all the footage?"

A puzzled expression crossed his daughter's face. "I didn't think of that."

"You should've. Anyway, if you don't meet him, he'll call again. What he wants is money, not you in jail. Then, you tell him what you demand in return for my half a million dollars."

"I don't have to go and meet him?" She sounded relieved, as she should've.

"No. Set another time. Demand the footage. He'll be met, but it won't be by you." He sighed, then returned to watching the news. "Now, go to bed." Honestly, she was almost as dense as her mother had been.

"Oh, thank you, Daddy." She leaned over and planted a kiss on the top of his head.

"I'll take care of it, don't worry."

He always did.

Flashing blue and white lights lit up the late evening sky. "There." Beth nudged Lola and pointed toward the window. "It's Will. He's alone." She tried to hide her disappointment. Where was Ben, and why couldn't he be bothered to come? Had something else happened to divert his attention? She shuddered at the thought.

Beth watched as Ben's brother came to the door. "Sure

made a mess of your door, Mrs. McAfee. Did you touch anything?"

"Well, I'd like to say I didn't, but my curiosity got the better of me," Karen said. "I picked up the brick and unwrapped the note around it, so my fingerprints are all over the note. It's not like I don't watch all those crime shows. I should've known better. I'm so sorry."

"And mine," Beth admitted and cast her gaze down at her toes peeping through her sandals. "Sorry."

"We have her on video," Karen said. "If that helps. I guess it won't, though. You can't see her face."

"A *woman*?"

"Yes! She definitely runs like a woman." Lola motioned toward the den. "The computer's in here."

Will nodded. "I guess I'd better have a look at this video."

They followed Karen into the den where she sat down in front of the laptop. "The footage is already cued up," she said, striking the enter key.

"You're right. Definitely a woman." Will turned to Karen. "I need to take the footage. We might be able to clean it up a bit."

Karen ejected the disc. "It's all yours, Sheriff."

"*Acting* sheriff," he corrected. "Also, I need the brick and the note you say were attached." He pulled two evidence bags and a pair of gloves from his pocket. "I'm also going to have to fingerprint all of you for purposes of elimination."

"I'm so sorry. I should've known better. You just never think you'll be in a situation where you need to worry about fingerprints." She took a breath. "I have a tendency to rattle on, especially when I've nervous. Don't mind me."

Half asleep, Beth yawned while Will labeled the evidence. "I'll be back," he said. "Print kit is in my vehicle."

Will returned quickly with the fingerprint kit. "It's

messy, but not permanent."

"Where's Ben?" Beth asked, then added, "And Kelly? Are they all right?" As much as she didn't want to appear needy, she really wanted to know where Ben was and if he was okay.

Pressing her right thumb into the ink and then onto the print card, Will looked up. "He took Kelly out to our cousin's dude ranch to get a horse she could ride on surveillance starting tomorrow morning. Maybe that's more than I should've said, but it's not like you're going to tell anyone."

"Nope." Beth made a zipping her lip gesture. "Quiet as the grave, that's me." She waited until he'd finished taking all of her prints. "This is part CSI, part Old West, what with Kelly needing a horse for surveillance."

A hint of a smile crept across Will's solemn expression. "You got that right." He handed Beth a tissue. "Next."

Lola stepped forward with a smile. "I didn't touch anything, but I'm happy for you to take my prints." She gracefully offered him her right hand like as if she were a Medieval lady honoring her chosen knight.

Beth watched and held back a smile. *My, my, my.* Certainly, seemed like the acting-sheriff took infinite care with her sister's fingerprints. Yes, he definitely lingered over taking Lola's prints.

No fair. Her sister was making more headway with her Rasmussen brother than Beth was with hers. She sighed.

"What was that?" Lola turned around with the smuggest little smile.

"Nothing. All right to go to bed now?" Beth asked, not expecting an answer.

"I doubt they'll return tonight," Will said. "But y'all should board up the door."

"I have a piece of plywood that'll do the trick," Karen said. "After I clean up all the glass."

"Let me do that. After all, I've put you through..." Beth held out her hands. "Just show me to the broom closet." But they had to get out of the Yellow Rose before something else happened. Something worse.

But where to go? Sleeping bags or an air mattress on the condo floor if necessary. Endangering another innocent was not acceptable. Maybe Lola had been right after all. Maybe they should both get the hell out of Dodge. But from the dazed expression on her sister's face, that was looking less like an option by the minute.

Chapter Twelve

Tuesday morning

Instead of going back to the Yellow Rose, Ranger Rasmussen had inveigled a bed for Kelly from his cousin, Luci Hendrix, at the San Saba Springs Dude Ranch. The dude ranch had the advantage of being Briggs' nearest neighbor. So much easier to meet up with Deputy Longworth when all Kelly had to do was ride over from Luci's ranch. The sun was barely over the horizon when she guided the lovely gray mare into the thick grove of cottonwoods.

"Coffee?" Kelly asked, holding out a thermos to the tall blonde.

"You're a lifesaver." Longworth took the thermos. "By the way, I'm Darby. This was such a quick setup that I didn't have time to prepare the way I normally would. I've been dying for a cup half the night."

"Anything to report?"

"Brigg's daughter came home last night around ten-thirty, but everything has been quiet since then." Darby unscrewed the thermos, poured a cup, and then took a long gulp. "You really have saved my life." She recapped the thermos. "There were several deliveries, early evening. I'd say maybe there's going to be a party of some sort, soon." She handed the thermos back to Kelly. "You'll need this. Nothing more boring than surveillance." She spurred the bay gelding. "G'dap."

Kelly watched the deputy ride away then turned her attention to Brigg's ranch house. Pulling a pair of binoculars from the saddlebag, she noted all was quiet. It was going to be a long twelve hours. She dismounted and tied the gray mare to a scrub pine. Might as well get comfortable.

Ten minutes after nine. Zoe tapped her manicured nails against the tabletop. Why hadn't he called? He should've called by now. Then her phone rang. "Hello," she said, tentatively.

"You were supposed to meet me, Zoe. You didn't show up. Do you want me to show this footage to the acting sheriff or maybe to your ex-husband who just happens to be a Texas Ranger?"

"You'll get your money, but what do I get?"

"My silence."

"That's not enough, buster. I want every copy of that footage."

"No can do. It's stored in the cloud on a very secure site."

"But I *have* to have it."

"Sorry, sugar. We do this my way, or you can kiss your freedom good-bye. What's the prison sentence for arson anyway? Have you thought about being in prison? No trips to the beauty salon. No shopping jaunts in Houston. Just snacks from the prison store, if you're lucky."

"I *hate* you. All right. You'll have your money. Let's change the meeting site. I don't want anyone to see me."

"No way, sugar. I want to be out in public so you can't mess me up."

"I don't know what you mean. But all right. I'll see you at nine *tomorrow*. I can't do it any sooner. Daddy's giving a dinner party tonight. I'm his hostess. I'm super busy."

"Just because you asked so nicely. I'll give you until ten

today."

"But—"

The call terminated on his end.

"Thank you for ruining my life!" she screamed at the phone, then threw it against the wall. "I don't think so!"

Carlton sipped his morning coffee and pushed away his plate when his daughter rushed into the breakfast room. Her face was flushed and her motions jittery. Things hadn't gone well.

"You were right, Daddy. He called again. He was pretty pissed, but he set another time to meet. I tried to get him to change the meeting place, but he wouldn't."

"Still at the park gazebo then? What about the footage?"

"He says it's on the cloud or something like that. On a secure site."

"We have to get that footage!" He slammed his fist on the side table.

Zoe jumped. "I can't help it. He threatened to take the footage to the sheriff and to Ben. I told him he'd have his money."

"What time?"

"Ten."

"Tomorrow?"

"No. *Today*. That's all the time he would give me."

He raised his voice. "Today?" Of all the stupid...

"Yes," she replied sheepishly.

"You're not giving me much time."

"Not my fault. He—"

"Get out of here!"

She scrambled. He reached for the phone.

"Timeline has changed. Ten this morning. As before."

Damn, she'd cut it close. Good thing he worked with a pro. No worries.

After his unsatisfactory phone call with the mayor's daughter, Matt walked through the park, just one of many Kenton Valley residents getting his morning exercise. He shouldn't have given her any extra time to come up with the money. But he had a soft spot for blondes, especially blondes who were a little on the freaky side. And she was.

Wait a minute. He caught sight of said blonde, entering the park.

"You're early," he said, then stopped dead. Close up. Not Zoe Briggs. Slender male. Big blonde wig. His reflexes kicked in. He spun, ready to run. The first bullet caught his shoulder, and the second hit his back like a sledgehammer. Spots danced before his eyes. He fell midflight.

The black overtook him.

Ready to inhale his third cup of hot coffee, Ben sank back in the desk chair. He pulled his cell phone from his pocket and punched in Beth's number. She'd had a late night, but it was almost ten. Maybe she was awake by now. He just wanted to hear the sound of her voice.

"H'lo." She sounded half asleep.

"Sorry to wake you. Are you all right? I'm sorry I couldn't get around to seeing you last night."

"It's all right," she said with a wide yawn. "Will explained. Is Kelly okay? She didn't come back to the B&B."

"Donovan? She's fine. What are your plans for tonight?"

"Well, today, we're moving into the condo I rented. And tonight, we'll be using sleeping bags and air mattresses until the furniture is delivered tomorrow. I just can't justify staying at the Yellow Rose and endangering Karen and her livelihood."

"That's very thoughtful. I'm sure Mrs. McAfee appreciates it." He hesitated. Maybe Beth wasn't as anxious to have dinner as he was. Still, he'd give it a go. "I thought maybe we could have dinner if the Valley's criminals will give me a few minutes of peace and quiet."

"Think positive," she said her tone brightening. "I'd love to have dinner with you," she said.

He restrained himself from heaving an audible sigh of relief. "If you'll just give me directions, I'll pick you up at seven-thirty, as long as all hell doesn't break loose."

"It's—"

Before she could give him the address, Will came barreling from his office. "Shooting in the park!"

Damnation! "Sorry. All hell *has* broken loose. I've got to run."

Without another word, he ended the call, grabbed his hat, and ran after his brother. The on-duty deputies scrambled behind him, the thundering of their boots echoing through the building.

Beth hung up the phone. "Something else has happened," she told Lola. "'All hell's broken loose' is what he said." She started to pace. What now? Living in a state of continual fear for the man she cared about was a new experience. And it would always be a part of her life if they continued on their present course. She shook her head. Fear might be a part of their life together, but she wouldn't allow it to control her every thought and movement.

Today, moving into the condo was first on her agenda. "Let's go on and pack. Karen said if we're really intent on leaving, she'll loan us a couple of air mattresses. They'll do for tonight. Tomorrow, we'll have furniture and can sleep in real beds."

Lola walked over to the window, pulled back a curtain, and stared toward downtown. "I wonder what happened? I don't see any smoke, so at least it's not another fire."

"Maybe there's something on the Valley News app." Beth glanced at her phone. "Here we go. There's been a shooting in the park." She let out a sigh. "Ever feel like you're in the middle of a grade B Western movie?"

"Only every day."

"Ben had just asked me out to dinner, but I'm guessing that's a nonstarter, given that, once again, hell's broken loose."

"He asked you out to dinner? How exciting. Don't give up. It's the first step."

"A freaking baby step." No, the actual baby step was when he'd said he was falling in love with her. No. That particular statement was a freaking giant step, but she'd kept his declaration private, hugging that moment to herself alone.

The Cottonwood Acres condo Beth had leased was a two-story townhouse end unit. Landscaping had just been completed in this part of the complex, and it was by no means lush. "I know it looks a little bare, but the bushes look to be of decent quality, even if they're small. You'll love the interior." She unlocked the door and proceeded to impersonate the condo salesperson.

"All-white kitchen with a large island. Quartz countertops. A half bath for guests." She walked over to the French doors. "A compact back garden, complete with a paved patio and a privacy fence."

Lola doubled over with a fit of giggles. "Go on."

"Upstairs you will find the two large bedrooms with an en-suite, as well as a master suite." Beth dropped the sales pitch. "You can have your pick of the bedrooms since I picked out the condo and the furnishings."

"Great!" Lola ran upstairs, and Beth followed, hoping the new surroundings would continue to perk up sister's attitude.

"I already know which one you'll want."

"Oh, great Carmack, which one will I want?"

Beth opened the door into the master suite which included a small balcony. "Ta-dah!"

"Of course. I call dibs on the balcony." Arms outstretched; Lola twirled around. "I'm not sure I'll ever want to leave." She opened to door to the balcony and stepped out. "I can see Silver Lake from here! It's lovely."

At least, she'd brought a smile to Lola's face and maybe lightened her spirit a bit. But there was still Eva's funeral to get through. If Sophie would even allow them to attend.

A crowd had already gathered at the park entrance when Ben arrived. Will had already started directing his deputies to their various duties. "Who is it?"

"Matt Freeman," Will glanced up, shaking his head. "Witnesses are all over the place. Some say the shooter was a man. Some say it was a woman. The shooter ran off and left a blond wig behind, so most likely a man."

An EMT had already placed an IV line and had slapped

dressings on Freeman's shoulder and back wounds.

"Come on, let's get him loaded," the EMT said. "He needed a chest tube, like five minutes ago."

"Someone took two shots at Freeman. No one heard anything. Just saw him fall. Must've used a sound suppressor. Then the shooter bolted out of here like a jackrabbit."

Ben turned to one of the deputies. "Get the names of anyone who saw anything. I want them in the office now. I'll handle the interviews." He nodded at Will. "Why don't you go on the hospital and see if you can get anything out of the victim."

"You're not gonna get anything out of him." The EMT said over his shoulder as he pushed the gurney toward the ambulance. "He's unconscious and going south fast." He and a second EMT loaded Freeman into the ambulance, and then it screamed off toward the local hospital.

"I'm calling Stirling," Ben said to Will. "He'll need to surveil Briggs while I do these interviews. And I have to update Major Innes. A DEA agent shot on our patch is going to thrill him, no end." Yes, he could hear the major now.

Ben had handed out legal pads and pens to all the witnesses for them to fill in their demographics and to write their statements. He began plowing through the interviews, one at a time. He stopped only when his phone rang. Donovan. "What's up? I'm kind of busy here?"

"What's happened?"

"Shooting in the park downtown this morning. Victim's in the ICU. Touch and go, I hear. I'm up to my eyeballs with witnesses."

"Well, something's definitely going down at the Briggs

Ranch. The mayor hasn't shown his face. But I've got two limos and four SUVs. Male, mid-fifties exited from one of the limos, along with a bodyguard. The other limo passenger was male, good-looking, late thirties or early forties. As soon as I hang up, I'll send you photos of the two principals—not the greatest quality due to the distance. I count ten very well-armed guards, not including the limo drivers. I say there's a powwow of some kind about to take place. I'd try to get closer, but with the guards patrolling the perimeter, I can't get within a hundred feet of the place."

"All right. Thanks, dammit."

"What do you want me to do?"

"Keep up surveillance. Longworth will relieve you at six. Then, I want you back here, ASAP for debrief."

"Roger that."

He ended the call, then received the photos. At least, he could definitely identify Briggs's partners in crime. As expected, Yuri Makarov and Reynaldo Reyes. Good to know he wasn't fishing with no bait.

"Next." Ben motioned for the last remaining witness to have a seat. He took the yellow pad and scanned the information, then noted the witness was a young man in his early to mid-twenties, blue-eyed, frosted blond hair, and a fake tan. "Mason Andrew Carter."

"Yes. I'm Mason Carter, and I'm here to tell you that the shooter was definitely a man who sashayed into the park and shot the other man. Cool as a cucumber, he was."

"You're sure the shooter was a man? Most of the other witnesses report it was a woman with long blond hair."

"Honey, I'd had my eye on *him* from the time he entered the park. I was even thinking of asking him for a date, but with hindsight and all, I'm really glad I didn't bother. Besides, he ran by me like his ass was on fire and ripped that wig off."

"You knew he was a man from the start?" Thank God, a reliable witness with eyes who knew what he saw.

"Of course, I can *always* tell."

"So, can you describe him without the wig?"

Carter leaned forward; his expression animated. "I noticed his clothes first. I *always* notice what someone is wearing first. Sequined, faded denim bootleg jeans, a yellow T-shirt with sunflower design, and yellow cross-trainers. He was at least six-foot, two. Slender wiry build, and graceful as a gazelle. His eyes were a cold, cold gray, and his head was shaved clean. Oh, and he had a tattoo on his neck. Mustn't forget that."

Dammit, Carter was observant. "Describe the tattoo."

"I just saw it for a second, but I have a good eye for design. Better yet, I could just draw him. Would that help?"

If Ben had been so inclined, he would've kissed the man. Instead, he smiled. "It certainly would save a lot of time." Given it was a pro hit, finding the perp might be a lesson in futility, but it couldn't hurt to have a likeness to circulate.

Carter set to work, drawing the shooter's face. "Now I only saw him up close in profile, and bearing in mind, faces usually aren't perfectly symmetrical, this is who I saw."

He slid the drawing across the desk for Ben's perusal. Not bad. Not bad, at all. "Thank you, Carter. You've been a big help." He rose and shook the young man's hand. And now, he could get down to work. Without delay, he broadcast a BOLO with the description of the shooter.

Donovan ought to be here soon for her debrief. In the meantime, while he was waiting, he might as well check out the security camera footage captured at the Yellow Rose

Inn. Maybe he could enhance the visuals.

Ben glanced at his watch. Six-thirty. Donovan ought to be here any minute. His fingers beat a tattoo on the desktop. A few minutes later, she strode into the Sheriff's Department and headed straight to Ben's desk.

Finally. He glanced up at her arrival and gave a brief nod. "I see you made it."

"I won't get too close," she warned. "I smell of horse. And sweat."

"The older man is Makarov." He slid a photo across the desk. "The younger is Reyes."

"Figured as much, sir." She nodded eagerly.

"Let me introduce Reynaldo Reyes, head of Los Malos Dias."

"So, the town's mayor is cozying up to the Russian mob and a cartel leader. Can't we just go out and arrest the whole bunch? There ought to be a law against hobnobbing with known criminals."

"We need probable cause. We have nothing on Reyes. So far, he's clean in the U.S. Ostensibly he's a Mexican businessman who imports coffee. But guns and drugs are his real stock in trade. Makarov traffics women, mainly from Eastern Europe. Now tell me exactly how many guards you saw."

"Four SUVs with two men each. Two limo drivers who, I assumed were also armed. The two principals along with their personal bodyguards. From all the activity and deliveries I saw today, there's going to be a hell of a dinner tonight." She pulled the sticky shirt away from her body and blew. "How's the shooting victim?"

"Freeman's on a ventilator."

"The security guy?"

"None other, as well as a supposed DEA agent. On further investigation, the DEA disavows all knowledge of Freeman or his assignment here in the Valley."

"I thought only the CIA disavowed their operatives."

"I don't know who the hell he's working for, but it isn't the federal government. Whoever it is, his cover is good. We're running his DNA to see if we can find out who he really is."

"Witnesses of any use?"

Ben shrugged. "Very little. Forensics has tested the wig for the wearer's DNA, but we have to wait on those results." While the shooter reportedly had a shaved head, he still could've left skin cells behind. "Now lend me your young eyes and have a gander at our perp who heaved a brick through the front door at the B&B." He pulled up the footage to the point where the perp ambled up the front steps and let go with the brick. "Here. Tell me what you see." He angled the screen so Donovan could view it.

"Sure." She leaned over his shoulder. "Slow it down. Go frame by frame. We might catch a glimpse of her face that way."

"You agree it's a woman."

"Oh, yeah. No doubt about it."

"Thing is, a lot of folks thought the shooter was a woman. Turns out, it was a man in a wig. There's no CCTV close to the park, but one of the witnesses was positive it was a man from the start."

Kelly nodded. "There's a difference in the way a woman walks than an effeminate man's gait. Less exaggeration in the sway of the hips, and besides, our brick thrower runs like a woman."

"Shooter ran like a *gazelle*." Playing devil's advocate had the advantage of making them both consider all the possibilities.

"Still not the same." Donovan smiled. "To me, the word gazelle denotes someone who's swift as well as graceful. Our brick thrower is neither."

Ben forwarded the footage frame by frame. "It's no use. That damn hoodie is covering is pulled down too far." As handy as having security footage of the incident was, it wasn't a perfect system.

"Be patient." She pulled up a chair. "Let me deal with this. Aren't you supposed to be surveilling someone?" she asked with a grin.

"First I need to check on Longworth." He pulled his cell phone from his pocket and called Deputy Longworth. "Where's the mayor now?"

She reported the mayor remained at home and was entertaining his guests. In addition, there'd been no additional arrivals, other than those Donovan had observed earlier.

"Sir," Donovan tugged on his sleeve. "I have something."

He quickly ended the call to the deputy. "Show me."

"See the reflection in the porch light. There's a face. Now let me clip it and blow it up. Pray the resolution doesn't go to crap."

He waited while she performed a little computer magic. He leaned forward, his eyes widening. "Well, I'll be damned. Zoe, you twit." He slammed his fist on the desktop.

"Your ex?"

"Afraid so." He let out a huff. "Still, as puny as an excuse it is, vandalism is a crime. Given the historic nature of the house, the charge could be easily elevated to a felony since the replacement of those mahogany doors with leaded glass could run into big money."

"You wanted sufficient cause to interrupt the party.

Let's do it."

He hesitated. "The sheriff needs to apply for this warrant. I'm too closely involved, and it'll likely be denied on those grounds. Vandalism, even a felony, is under Will's jurisdiction."

"Someone mention my name?" Will strode into the bullpen and hitched a hip onto the corner of Ben's desk.

Ben quickly updated his brother and showed him the screen capture of Zoe's heaving a brick through the Yellow Rose Inn's front door. "The repairs on a historic house should elevate the charges to a felony."

"Let me get this straight: you want to me to arrest my ex-sister-in-law?"

"Is that a problem?"

"Hell, no." He let out a chuckle. "I'd love to. Never could stand her."

"Then bring her in for questioning, or better yet, request a warrant. I need a reason to enter the Double Bar B Ranch tonight."

Will's eyebrows shot up. "You don't say. Guess I'd better move my stumps." He shot Ben a sharp glance. "Are you sure Zoe won't interpret this the wrong way? Like maybe you're still interested?"

"If a warrant for her arrest makes her believe I'm interested, she's sicker than I thought." And maybe she was. What if his ex was responsible for setting the fire at the Merc? "Just a thought, have you requested warrants to search Freeman's phone, office, and computers?"

"They're in the works but haven't been granted yet. Why? What're you thinking?"

"Since the DEA has firmly stated, Freeman isn't one of their agents, we can't take his word that the CCTV footage from the fire at the Merc was corrupted. I had a suspicion there was something different about the fire, but I discounted it because it fit with someone trying to set up a protection racket using intimidation. But what if it was one crazy woman determined to eliminate a rival."

"You mean Zoe."

"I do."

"Then I'd better get on the blower to Judge Garrison." Will shook his head. "We're asking for trouble, but I reckon I don't have to tell you that."

"I want an arrest warrant to enter that house, dammit!"

"If that's the case, then you need to wait until the forensics reports are back on the brick and note."

"Screw that. We'll apologize later." Ben stood and slammed his hat on his head. Short of wringing Zoe's scrawny neck, arresting her ass was now his main goal in life. And arrest her he would.

Tonight.

Tuesday evening

Carlton nodded with approval. Zoe had dressed in her usual over-the-top excessive style for the dinner. She'd chosen a revealing full-length, one-shouldered red evening gown with a slit up to *there*. Her jewelry was the best her soon-to-be ex-husband Jose could buy: a large ruby necklace set with diamonds, headlight large diamond earrings, and a honking big ruby ring, also set with diamonds. Sky-high silver stilettoes finished out her wardrobe. She'd even woven a strand of diamonds among the platinum waves.

No man should be able to resist her.

Reynaldo Reyes' eyes widened when he took a gander of his hostess. And from the glitter in his guest's eyes, as he mentally undressed her, she'd have him in her bed by midnight. Maybe a trip to Mexico was what his daughter needed. Maybe Reyes would be so pleased with the slut, he'd keep her out of Carlton's hair, at least for a while.

Zoe gave his guests a dazzling million-dollar smile. "*Señor* Reyes and Mr. Makarov, *Bienvenido* and welcome to the Double Bar B Ranch." She all but curtseyed to the men. "I'm so delighted to meet you, gentlemen. If you'll follow me, dinner is served. We've hired the best caterers out of Dallas. Nothing is too good for my father's business associates."

All through dinner, Carlton noted Reyes was a witty conversationalist. Yuri, not so much. He was rather dour, portly man in his fifties, more intent on enjoying his dinner and drink. Reyes was closer to his daughter's age. Her kittenish behavior said it all. She obviously found Reyes irresistible.

Finally, the five-course dinner was over. Carlton rose and nodded. "Brandy and cigars in my study, gentlemen." He smiled his approval. "Lovely dinner, Zoe. Thank you."

For once, she didn't gush or coo. She simply nodded. "It was my pleasure."

Carlton Briggs swirled the Courvoisier in his snifter while he surveyed his dinner guests. Reyes sniffed the cognac as if he'd probably been told he was supposed to, and Makarov puffed on a fat Cuban cigar. They were nothing more than common criminals he did business with. Common but necessary, even at the higher echelons of criminality.

"Gentlemen are we agreed then. Yuri will handle the gambling and prostitution. Reynaldo will handle drugs and weapons. Once the casino is open, we'll wash half the money through it. Those redskins will never know where their money is going. Until the casino is operational, I will continue buying up business properties in town and use those to wash the proceeds from our combined efforts." He finished with a smile and sniffed his cognac.

His guests rose, and the deal was set. Reyes said, "I've had a long day. If you don't mind, I'd like to go to my room."

Carlton nodded. "Of course." He walked to the double doors and opened them. "Zoe, *Señor* Reyes is ready to retire. Please show him to his room."

His daughter emerged from the shadows. Had she been listening at the door? No matter. She'd never betray him— not if she knew what was good for her. "Of course. Please follow me."

After Reyes trotted off after Zoe like a dog after a bone, Briggs turned to Makarov and nodded. "That's settled."

With a knowing leer, Makarov returned to his seat then nodded in return. "Indeed."

Carlton eased into his cushy cowhide chair and poured himself another cognac when he became aware of the piercing sound of a siren and shouting. He sprang to his feet. "What the hell?"

Chapter Thirteen

Beth plopped down on a folded quilt in the condo living room. With a sigh, she dealt out the deck of cards for rummy. No TV, no Internet, and no furniture until tomorrow. "I don't like being the little woman who sits and waits for her man to come home."

Lola picked up a card from the deck, then discarded another. "You're nobody's 'little woman.' Ben and Will both have important jobs, but *you* are a savvy businesswoman."

"You think I don't know that. I'm just frustrated." Her rummy hand sucked, so she discarded a single card and then picked up the one Lola had discarded. "We were actually going to have dinner tonight. But now, Matt Freeman is in the hospital fighting for his life. And I don't have a clue where Ben is or what he's doing. If he's even safe." She swallowed hard to keep the tears at bay.

"I'm sure Ben is fine. You would've heard otherwise. What I'm really curious about is why Matt Freeman was targeted." Lola discarded two cards.

Beth wrinkled her nose. Her hand hadn't improved. "Me too. Maybe it has something to do with the camera footage from the fire. Ben said Matt told him it was screwed up. And he was supposed to be clearing it up using some kind of special software."

"I never did quite trust him, you know?" Lola's eye twitched. That was her tell for a good hand.

Dang it.

"I was suspicious too, at first. But he did a bang-up job on the store's security system."

"And now the store is gutted, and we're stuck living in

a condo with about as much personality as an empty refrigerator."

"Speaking of which, let's order a pizza." Beth laid down her hand of cards and reached for her phone. "Besides, the fridge isn't empty. It has the basics."

"Pfft! If you call bottled water, a head of romaine, and a bottle of diet ranch dressing the basics."

"Quit whining. I'm ordering a pizza."

Ben stood behind Will when Briggs came to the door. Longworth and Donovan backed them up, but they were clearly outnumbered by all the hired muscle. Hired muscle who for the moment were keeping their cool. All the same, they were present and well-armed. "I'm here to arrest Zoe," Will said. They hadn't been able to obtain a search warrant. Not enough evidence. "Where is she?"

"She's retired for the night," Briggs said, all puffed up. "Ben, I know you're behind this. What's she done?"

"Felony trespass and vandalism. Where's her room?"

"Second floor. You should know. You sneaked up there often enough when you were dating."

"Fine." Ben brushed by Briggs. He took the stairs two at a time, then ran down the hall to Zoe's room. He pounded on her door. "Zoe! Come out. You're under arrest."

No response. He opened the door. "Zoe!" Her bed was empty.

Farther down the hall, another door opened. Struggling with her dress, his ex emerged, wearing a scowl. "What's the meaning of this? What're you trying to pull, Ben Rasmussen?"

"Zoe Briggs Vayden, you're under arrest for—"

Her eyes widened. "I don't care what that man told you.

I didn't set that fire. I didn't."

"What man? What fire? You're under arrest for felony trespass and vandalism for damages incurred at the Yellow Rose Inn."

Her lipstick-smeared red mouth formed an O.

Why the immediate denial about setting a fire? Son-of-a-bitch! Zoe had torched the Merc. But what man was she referring to? Questions to be delved into later, as soon as they could access Freeman's computer.

"This is an outrage!" Briggs bellowed, coming up the hallway, huffing with the exertion. "You can't stand it because my daughter had the good sense to dump your ass. You're doing this out of spite. She threw a brick through a window? So what?"

So, Briggs knew what she'd been up to. "The Yellow Rose Inn is on the Historic Register, and the charges are elevated to a felony. And she's also under suspicion for burning down Wheaton's Mercantile."

Briggs directed his gaze at Will. "I'm sure we can come to some kind of compromise. Will, you're the acting sheriff. Can't we overlook this moment of immaturity?"

"Sorry, Mayor. I agree with the Ranger here. We have a warrant. Zoe's under arrest."

Still tugging on her evening dress, she said, "I can't go like this. I need to change."

Will turned to Deputy Longworth. "See that she changes into something more appropriate, and then cuff her."

"I see you have a new bedroom." Ben strode over to open the door where she'd emerged, betting it wasn't hers at all.

Sprawled on the bed and covered only by a gray silk sheet was none other than cartel leader Reynaldo Reyes. "Hostess seeing to all your needs? How thoughtful." With a smile, he shut the door. So, his ex was up to her old tricks. Divorcing her had been the smartest thing he'd ever done.

After his tearful daughter had been hauled off, Carlton headed back to his study to call his lawyer. "See that my daughter doesn't spend the night in jail. I don't care what strings you have to pull." He slammed down the phone. "Honestly, that daughter of mine..." He collapsed in his chair and reached for the brandy.

Still nursing his drink, Makarov looked up and smiled. "Anything I can do?"

"As a matter of fact, there is. I have it on good authority that..." In no uncertain terms, he told Makarov what he wanted—no needed—to happen.

"Of course," Makarov said with a smile, "my men are at your disposal."

Growing hungrier by the second, Beth glanced at her phone. "I don't know what's taking the pizza guy so long. It's been an hour since I put in the order."

"Gin." Lola laid down her cards then yawned widely. "Maybe they ordered it from San Antonio."

"Pfft! No fair. You always win." Beth stretched, working out the kinks from sitting on the floor.

"No wonder. Your mind isn't on the game."

"I can't help it if I'm worried about Ben."

"Has he even called?"

"No. But I don't expect him too." Beth hugged her knees. "After all, you're the one who reminded me Ben and Will have important jobs. I understand that, and you'd better too if you think you have a chance with Will. Their focus is always on the job, and that's where it belongs. And while we're not the little women waiting at home for our men to appear, I admit it would be nice to see them once in a while."

"It's not having any work to do." Lola picked up the cards, ready to deal, but then set them aside. "Normally, we're so busy. We had the Merc and the Bistro. We didn't have time to worry about sitting at home on a date night or if we even had a date."

"It's *Tuesday*." Beth wrinkled her nose. "Tuesday isn't even a date night." She set down her losing gin rummy hand. "Besides, from what I saw the night Eva was killed, you and Will were getting close."

Lola smiled as if she were remembering. "It's true he comforted me, and I have to say it was pretty damn nice." She stood and stretched. "There's a full moon tonight. I'm going upstairs to see if you can see its reflection on the lake."

"All right. Go ahead, amuse yourself at my expense."

"You gave me the choice of bedrooms. Are you regretting it?"

"Of course not." Anything to make her sister smile. If it took having the best bedroom, so be it.

As soon as Lola had run upstairs, the doorbell rang. "Pizza!" she called, then opened the door.

Big man. Black mask. Big mistake.

While Zoe was being booked and fingerprinted, Ben called Beth's mobile. It went to voice mail. "Uh, hi, it's Ben. I know it's getting late, and we've been a little busy. We made an arrest in the incident over at the Yellow Rose. I thought I'd drop by your new place—"

His phone beeped, signaling a new call...from Beth's sister. What?

He ended the call to Beth to answer Lola's. "What's going on? Why—?"

"Beth's missing!"

He could hear the rising panic in her voice. As calmly as he could, he said, "Tell me."

"We ordered a pizza. I was upstairs when the doorbell rang. When I came down, she was gone! Someone's taken her!"

His heart rate hit the freaking stratosphere, hammering until his head might explode. "Calm down. Lock your door." *Calm down?* That was the best he could do? He grabbed his hat and set it on his head. "We're on our way. What's that address again?"

Lola rattled off the address, adding, "Unit 324. We're on the end."

"Got it." He ended the call. "Will!" He waved to get his attention. "Beth's been grabbed." This had to be Briggs's doing in retaliation for Zoe's arrest.

Body trembling with the need to act, Ben waited for Will to order Longworth to finish processing Zoe. Together they ran for the door. "In mine," Will said, indicating his Durango. He jumped inside and hit the lights and siren.

His heart in his throat, Ben jumped in and rode shotgun. Maybe Briggs's had help from one of his criminal cohorts.

Keep calm. Focus.

Beth was missing. Not dead. Not yet anyway.

The cloyingly sweet smell had faded. Dark. Can't move. No. Hands and feet bound with something. She shook her head to clear the fuzziness. And her body jolted. Where the hell was she?

The pizza man. Right. But it wasn't the pizza man. It was a big oaf who'd clapped a stinking rag over her mouth and nose. So, this was what it was like being bound up in a trunk. Not that she'd ever been remotely desirous of finding out. Still, modern vehicles were supposed to have some kind of trunk release but damned if she could reach it with her hands zip-tied behind her.

At least the trunk was roomy. Small consolation for experiencing a woman's worst nightmare.

Then panic. Her heart raced. She struggled to catch her breath. The dizziness returned.

Think.

How long had she been gone? Where was her phone? She shifted her weight to see if she could feel it in her pants pocket. No. Not there. Of course not. What self-respecting kidnapper would let the victim keep her cellphone in order to lead the police right to her? None.

What about Lola? Had she been kidnapped too? No, probably not.

A glimmer of hope. Lola would call Ben. Of course, she would.

But how would they know where she was?

But Ben would find her. Somehow.

Hopefully, alive.

On arrival at the condo, Ben and Will found Lola on the small front porch holding an ice pack to the pizza delivery guy's head. Will ran to her side. "You were told to lock yourself inside," he growled.

Lola gave a little huff. "After you hung up, he banged on

the door. He was bleeding! I couldn't leave him out here with lacerations and bruises and contusions and what all."

"What happened? How many? What did you see?" Ben fired questions at the delivery guy without stopping for a breath.

"I was delivering a pizza," he said. "Only one guy, but he was big. I mean linebacker big. He came outta nowhere, man. That's all I saw, not counting stars when I hit the dirt."

"What about his vehicle?"

"You know that's the weird thing. There was a limo parked down the street, 'bout two doors. That way." He craned his neck. "It's gone now."

"Did you see him take the woman?" Ben reined in the boiling impatience coursing through every cell in his body. Nothing would be gained by shaking the crap out of this dumbass kid.

The slack-jawed youth gazed up at Ben. "What woman? I didn't see nothing after he cold-cocked me. Man, I was out of it. Don't know how long."

"God!" Fists clenched, he turned away. It was the only way he could keep from smacking the clueless little—

"Lola," Will interjected quietly. "Did you come straight down after the doorbell rang?"

"I might've yelled down first, something about how beautiful the moon was as it reflected on the lake. Then I shut the slider to the balcony and came down."

"That's not long."

Ben sucked in a deep breath and checked his phone. "You called me at 9:48. It's now 9:59. Beth's been gone no more than twelve minutes." He glanced at the front door. "I don't suppose you had time to install any security cameras?" Why hadn't he taken time to see she was protected after all that had happened? No. He'd been too focused on what Briggs was up to. And now...

He shook his head. Anything could happen. Maybe already had.

"I'm not sure. I mean, I doubt it. I wasn't here when Beth rented the condo, so I don't know what security measure they have for residents." She bit her bottom lip. "Wait. There's a folder with information about amenities and stuff. Maybe that'll tell us."

"Where is it?"

"On the kitchen island."

Ben strode to the kitchen and snatched the folder. He scanned the folder's front for a phone number. Damn. "Briggs again." His construction company had built the condos. And his management company sold and/or leased them. He tossed the folder aside. That's how Briggs had found Beth so fast. He already knew where to find her. Son of a bitch.

Furious, he dialed the mayor's home number. Briggs answered.

"What have you done with her, you bastard? Where's Beth?"

"Don't know what you're talking about, Ranger. You've already arrested my daughter. Don't blame me if you can't keep track of your new woman."

"You did this to get back at me. I arrested your daughter, so you kidnapped Beth.

That's the most absurd thing I've ever heard. May I remind you I'm the duly elected mayor of this town. I have connections with the Rangers, my boy."

"Your goons better not hurt her."

"What goons? You act like I'm some sort of mobster. I can have your job with a single phone call to Major Innes."

"Go right ahead. Make your damn call. I won't forget this. If one hair on her head is harmed, I'll see you in prison for racketeering and consorting with known criminals."

Ben stabbed the end call icon. What a waste of time. Briggs wasn't going to admit a damn thing.

Could he get a search warrant? Would there be any point? Briggs had property all over the county. Beth could be anywhere. He turned to the pizza guy. "Come down to the Sheriff's Department in the morning to make a formal statement. What's your name?

"I'm Junior—Bradley." He cleared his throat. "Eugene Bradly, Jr. My dad's gonna have a fit. He works in security for the mayor."

Briggs again! This kid's dad was running against Vince. "Why's that?"

"Never wanted me to take this job. Said it was dangerous."

"Well, Junior, your dad was right." Close to losing control, Ben called for an ambulance and then called the kid's boss to report the incident. In the meantime, Will called Dispatch to broadcast a BOLO for a limo possibly involved in a kidnapping. "There can't be that many rolling around this time of night. I'll call back when I have more detail."

Ben nodded, then picked up the discarded folder. "Okay, here we go. Security cameras at the entrance, the office, clubhouse, and the pool area," he read. "Owners are encouraged to install their own systems for additional security. Damn!" When he thought of all the now-useless security equipment installed at the Mercantile and Beth's apartment, rage filled his gut. Honest-to-God, he wanted to hit something...or someone.

"I'll call the manager's emergency number and get rolling on obtaining that footage," Will said. "A limo's bound to stick out like a sore thumb."

While Will headed over to the office to meet the manager, the ambulance came and picked up Junior.

His gut tied in knots, Ben paced back and forth in the condo. Dammit. Briggs was up to his expensive toupee in everything that had happened in the last week.

"Something to drink?" Lola asked. "I'm afraid all we have is bottled water or Diet Coke."

He shook his head. "No thanks."

"What are you going to do now? How will you ever find her?" She looked around and shivered.

"We'll find her. No point in going off half-cocked." He forced himself to exhibit the patience he didn't feel.

No point in going off half-cocked. What a laugh. That's exactly what he felt like doing. He sucked in a deep breath. "When Will finds the limo on the Cottonwood surveillance cameras, then we'll have something definite to go on."

Something. Do something. Do anything. Lola would still be at risk, even though Beth was apparently the focus. No point in leaving another young woman in danger. He put in a call to Deputy Longworth. "Someone has kidnapped Beth. Will's busy, but could you sit on Lola for the rest of the night. One missing woman is enough." He nodded. Okay, another base covered. "Longworth's on her way."

"Oh, I'll be all right," she said, still shaking.

"Sure you will with Deputy Longworth here."

Her shoulders sagged, seemingly more relaxed.

Then he remembered why he'd been too busy to check on security at their new place. "By the way, when you called that Beth was missing, I was in the middle of leaving her a message. We've arrested someone for the vandalism at the B&B."

"Who?"

"Zoe. When we enlarged the footage from Karen's security camera, her reflection was caught in one of the carriage house lights."

Lola nodded. "I get it. She wants you back, and she

thinks Beth's in her way."

"Something like that." His face heated up.

"You're blushing."

"Makes no sense. Zoe had a dozen reasons for leaving me. Now all of a sudden, she wants me back."

"She doesn't want to be alone. She's one of those women who sees her value in relation to the man in her life."

"I got it." Will strode into the condo. "Limo's registered in Houston under a shell company. I've already amended the BOLO to include the tags and vehicle description."

"When Donovan was surveilling Briggs's ranch, she only could see the tags on one of the limos. But given this one is registered in Harris County; it's bound to be the second limo—Makarov's." The idea of Beth in Makarov's hands, or worse, in the hand of his goons sent a chill up Ben's spine. Among his business interests, Makarov was a sex trafficker, primarily women from Eastern Europe. But a blonde like Beth... A shudder shook his body.

Unable to waste another minute, Ben slapped his thigh. "All right, let's go." He stopped and eyeballed Lola. "Lock the door, for real this time. Donovan will be here in another ten."

"I'll lock it. I will." She cast a protracted look of longing toward Will. "Stay safe, guys."

Will smiled and ducked his head. "Lock the door. And don't open it for anyone but Donovan."

Lola responded with a shy nod. "Yes, sir."

Ben headed for Will's truck, but Will stopped on the porch, then nodded. "She locked it. I heard the deadbolt slide in place."

"Good." Ben climbed into the Durango. "You know, what this town needs are more security cameras like they have in the London."

"Kenton Valley isn't exactly London." Will slammed his

door shut. "Although they would come in handy right now."

"I warned Vince this would happen when the casino opened, but it's already happening."

The comm unit came alive. "Sheriff, we had a sighting of the limo as it passed the bank."

"Copy that. Which bank? What time? What direction?"

"Nine-fifty-one PM. Los Marcos County Bank on Main. Heading north. Nothing after that." The only reason the Sheriff's Department could access the bank's security system after hours was that it was tied into the department.

"That fits the timeline. We just missed seeing the sucker on our way." Ben hit the dashboard with his fist.

"Easy, bro. This vehicle has to last me a while."

"It's my fault Beth is—"

"How the hell's that your fault?"

"I was so damned focused on Briggs and what he was up to that I let Beth and Lola move into that condo without a second thought to their security. Felt like they'd be out of sight, out of mind."

"How were you to know they'd moved into one of Briggs's projects?"

"She's out there, man! Who knows what kind of hell she's been put through?" Dammit. He'd kill the first man that laid a hand on her. He would. And suffer the consequences gladly.

Beth worked at the bindings on her wrists until they were raw. Useless effort and painful besides. Where were they taking her? More to the point, who had drugged her senseless? And why? It wasn't like she was some heiress. Her parents had a nice savings account, but it didn't amount to ransom-type savings.

Why hadn't she done something about security? Why had she just thrown open the door without, at least, first looking through the peephole? Because she was expecting the damn pizza. Pitiful poor excuse and look at her now. How would Ben ever find her? No phone to ping. No breadcrumbs to drop.

So, if he had no way of finding her...

Focus.

Somehow, she'd have to get herself out of this mess. And no doubt about it, she was in big trouble.

Pay attention. They hadn't blindfolded her. Not a good sign.

Don't look at the kidnapper directly.

Would that matter if he aimed to kill her? No. If his plan was to kill her, he could've shot her on the doorstep.

Again, why? Why go to all this trouble?

The car shuddered to a stop. Her gut roiled.

Oh, boy.

Accompanied by his legal counsel, Henry Deacon, Carlton Briggs strode into the Sheriff's Department as if he owned it. Well, he did. Not the entire staff, but one deputy on his payroll was enough to know what was going on at all times. The Ranger's girlfriend had been kidnapped; therefore, he and the acting sheriff were busy trying to chase down her kidnappers.

Good luck with that.

Deputy Powell looked up. His eyes widened. "Mayor, what can I do for you?"

"You know exactly what you can do for me. Release my daughter, right now."

Powell frowned. "I've had my orders. Mrs. Vayden isn't

going anywhere tonight."

He leaned across the desk. "She's coming home with me tonight, or our little arrangement is over—you know the arrangement you find so lucrative."

"And I respect that arrangement, sir," Powell said, lowering his voice. "I'm in a difficult spot."

"You're going to be in a worse one if you don't release my daughter. How would you like it revealed that you're responsible for having Sheriff Tate arrested on trumped-up evidence? You'll never find another sheriff who'll give you a second chance the way he did."

Deacon cleared his throat. "Maybe threats aren't the way to go, Mayor."

"Shut the fuck up. I'm paying you, remember?" Deacon was a hack, a useful one, nevertheless. "Those charges against my daughter are bogus, brought by an acting-sheriff who doesn't know his ass from a hole in the ground. My daughter is not going to spend a night in jail. She's not, or I'll see to it that you will go to prison for corruption instead of the sheriff. Get my drift?"

Powell's hands shook as he opened his desk drawer and pulled out a set of keys.

Carlton smiled. A little intimidation went a long way.

Beth held her breath. The trunk opened. Her heart raced and pounded so loud in her ears she was sure her captors could hear.

Pretend you're still unconscious. Yeah, that's the ticket.

"She still out of it?"

"Yeah. Looks like."

The next thing she knew, she felt a hand on her arm. He pinched hard. "Ouch!"

"She's awake."

"I am now. That hurt." She kept her gaze averted. As much as she wanted to be able to describe her captors, eyeballing them probably wasn't the way to go. Instead, she surveyed her surroundings, making out an airplane hangar. Why had they brought her to an airfield? Why had they kidnapped her anyway?

The goon who pinched her leaned over and scooped her up, then set her feet on the ground. She wobbled a bit, her ankles bound.

"Pretty girl has spirit." He gave an evil-sounding chuckle. "Nice. What we supposed to do with her?"

"Boss didn't say. Just bring her here. Wait for orders."

"We could have fun. She looks like fun-time girl to me." He nodded enthusiastically.

"No." Goon-two jerked his head toward the warehouse. "Inside. Wait for boss."

Of the two scenarios, waiting for the boss seemed the lesser of two evils. As for 'inside,' inside where exactly? The only airfield she knew of locally was the one north of town.

Between them they picked her up and hauled her along, the toes of her shoes skimming the pavement.

They paused long enough for one of the brutes to raise the hangar door. The interior was dark and empty, except for one small plane. "Could I just sit down, please. My feet are getting numb. These things are on too tight."

"Shut your mouth, pretty lady."

"I will when—"

The taller one who cautioned 'wait for boss' drew back his fist.

She clamped her lips tightly and cringed, waiting for a blow that never came.

"Pretty lady is smart lady. Good." They manhandled her over to an office in the back of the hangar. "Sit."

She sat.

The impatient one said. "How long the boss say?"

"Didn't say."

"I say have some fun while we wait."

"*No* fun. Wait for boss. He might want her for himself."

Not a happy prospect.

She began to speak, quietly so as not to anger either of them. "Is it possible there's been a mistake? You see, I'm not rich. My parents aren't either."

"No mistake. Address and description match. That's all we know, pretty blond lady. Many ways to pay ransom." He sniggered, "Are you natural blonde? Always have requests for natural blondes."

She cringed. Women who were sex trafficked were drugged and forced to... She shivered. No point in rushing to the worst scenario here, even though it was the most likely one. Ben would find her before the worst could happen.

He just had to.

Not for the first time, Carlton Briggs wished his daughter had an *OFF* button. He sat in his favorite armchair and poured a fresh snifter of cognac. After listening to Zoe rant and rave all the way home from the county lockup, he needed a drink. Makarov had given up either gone to bed or more likely, he'd gone to take care of the ranger's girlfriend. Whatever...

Zoe paced back and forth like a demented shrew, waving her arms. "I hate him. How dare he arrest me like a common criminal. I want him *dead*. You hear me. I want him killed. I know you have friends who can take care of it. There are a couple of them staying at our ranch tonight, aren't there?"

She stopped in front of him and shook her head. "No. That won't do. I want to kill him myself. I want to take a gun, put it in his mouth, and blow him to kingdom come. You hear me, Daddy. I want him *dead*."

"You'll want to rethink that idea. Murder comes at a high price in this state. With no access to your favorite hairstylist or the high-end Houston boutiques you frequent, you'll soon be indistinguishable from the other losers in the state pen. And don't forget, darlin', in Texas, we still execute murderers with regularity."

"Ridiculous. You'll buy me the best lawyers money can buy. I'll get off easily."

"Don't be too sure." Indeed, having her in lockup would give him some peace. Perhaps, he'd moved too hastily in getting her out of jail. However, seeing the expression on the ranger's face tomorrow morning would almost be worth having to listen to her now.

Ben had Will drive him back to the Sheriff's Department. They were met by an uneasy Deputy Powell who in the middle of a lot of hemming and hawing gave them the bad news.

"Son of a bitch!" Ben got in Deputy Powell's face. "You let the mayor take his daughter home? What were you thinking, man?"

"He's the mayor. His lawyer said to let her out. So, I did."

Will shook his head. "You're suspended, Powell. Give me your badge and weapon."

"But—"

"I don't care what kind of cockamamie excuse his

lawyer came up with. I don't want to hear it. Vince gave you a second chance. And now you've blown it."

Again, Powell tried to protest, "But—he's the mayor."

"He's not above the law, you dipshit."

Red-faced Powell handed over his weapon and badge, his hands shaking with rage. "Sorry, *acting*-Sheriff."

After Powell stomped from the department, Ben shook his head. "I'm not surprised. Briggs thinks he's above the law. In the meantime, forget it. Finding Beth is more important than where Zoe Vayden spends the night." He pulled out his phone. "I'm calling Stirling. Reckon he's had enough beauty sleep. All hands on deck."

Will nodded. "I'm calling in everyone, too."

As soon as the calls had been made, Ben cleared off his desk. "We need to make a list of all Briggs's properties. He's bound to be holding Beth in one of them." He walked over to the wall where a large town map hung. "We'll divide the town into sectors and do a systematic grid search. And then, we'll start checking them out. Eliminate them one by one, starting with those on the north end of town."

While Will cataloged Briggs's substantial holdings, Ben called Major Innes. "Got a problem, Major."

"You wouldn't be calling, otherwise."

"Earlier this evening, we arrested Zoe Vayden for felony vandalism on a B&B where a Ms. Wheaton was staying after her store was torched, as well as suspicious for arson. After the arrest, Ms. Wheaton was reported as being abducted. While the acting-sheriff and I were out searching for Ms. Wheaton, Mayor Briggs brought in his lawyer and bullied one of the deputies into releasing his daughter. Deputy Powell *says* he was bullied, but he could be on the mayor's payroll. I don't believe in coincidence. The kidnapping took place shortly after the arrest in retaliation."

"Mayor Briggs's daughter? You mean your ex-wife?"

"Yes, sir."

"What do you want from me?"

"I want a team of rangers."

"A team?"

"When we arrived at the ranch to pick up Ms. Vayden, Yuri Makarov and Reynaldo Reyes were there as guests."

"The mayor's involved with the mob and the cartel? That's news."

"All indications of it, sir. We've got the entire Sheriff's Department researching for Miss Wheaton. Given the mayor's extensive holdings, I need a team for a systematic search."

"I'd rather send you a team to raid the mayor's ranch and scoop up Makarov and Reyes."

"Sir, Ms. Wheaton is an innocent bystander. Her safety is—"

"You're not involved with this bystander, are you?"

"One the verge of it, sir. More'n likely, that's why my ex targeted her store. Reyes and Makarov have probably already skipped town, anyway."

"All right, I'll send you a team of four rangers for the search."

"Thank you, Major."

As much as he wanted to join the search for Beth, he had one more task before he could. He had to re-arrest Zoe.

Chapter Fourteen

Ben sped to the ranch. All the way up the long drive to the house, he kept a watchful eye for the previous bodyguards. All of the limos were gone, except for the Briggs's. Right. Makarov was probably on his way back to Houston, and Reyes had most likely skipped back over the border. Other than Briggs's ranch hands, there was no one to stop him.

No one was gonna stop him from dragging his ex's butt back to jail.

As soon as Ben slammed the door to his vehicle, Briggs opened the front door. "What the hell do you want now?"

"I'm here to take Zoe. Her release was illegal. The warrant for her arrest remains in effect. The deputy who released her has been suspended pending further investigation."

Briggs flushed red. His chest swelled.

"Step aside, Carlton."

Briggs sputtered. "I'm calling my lawyer."

"Have at it. And while you're at it, better call your doctor. I'd say your blood pressure is up."

Ben brushed past his ex-father-in-law. "Putting you on notice. Your wheeling and dealing has a nasty way of coming to light. The Texas Rangers will be digging into those as well. I don't see you remaining mayor much longer once you're prosecuted for graft and malfeasance."

He strode to the stairway. "Zoe!"

Wearing a black see-through negligee, his ex came slowly downstairs. "I just barely got to sleep, and here you are shouting and caterwauling. I was released."

"Illegally, by someone on your father's payroll who had no authority to do so." He reached for his cuffs. "This is the way it has to be. You belong in jail for setting that fire, as well as felony vandalism."

"You just want to be near me again." She shook her hair. "This isn't the way to do it if we expect to have any kind of relationship in the future."

"Relationship?" He shook his head. Clearly, his ex was delusional. "Just shut up. Remember anything you say can be used against you in a court of law."

"They're too tight," she whined as he clicked the cuffs around her wrists.

"Come on." He dragged her outside. He opened the door to the SUV. "Get in. Watch your head."

"You'll be hearing from my lawyer!" Briggs shouted as Ben started the motor.

One problem down. One to go.

Was it too much to hope that Zoe would keep her mouth shut and ride back to the Sheriff's Department in silence?

"You can't do this to me."

Deliver me. How he'd managed to stay married to her for the two most miserable years of his life, he couldn't comprehend, even now.

"I'm not a criminal. I don't belong in jail. It's all a misunderstanding. It was an accident."

"What part of 'anything you say can be used against you in a court of law' didn't you understand?"

He heard her start to sniff. No way was this heartless creature shedding real tears.

"You're so mean. I don't understand why you're so

mean to me."

"You set the Merc on fire without regard to who might've been injured."

"I knew you'd get out okay. I just wanted to scare Beth."

"Scare Beth? You destroyed her livelihood. You destroyed her home."

"Not my fault that old building went up like a tinderbox."

"You do realize you've admitted to arson? Do you have any idea what the prison sentence for arson is?"

"No. But no one got hurt."

"A first-degree arson conviction run from five to ninety-nine years with a fine of ten-thousand dollars. You could plead down to second with a penalty of two to twenty years in prison."

"Oh."

He heard her move restlessly in the backseat. "What if I knew something? Something you'd want to know and might have to do with what my father's planning?"

What could she possibly know? Surely, her father wasn't stupid enough to include her in his dirty dealings. "I can't make deals. Only the DA can make a deal. But if you know what your father's up to, you'd better tell me, or risk being charged as his accomplice when he's arrested."

"Hmph. I think I'll save what I know for the DA then. But believe you me, you'll want to know everything."

"I didn't know your father included you in his plans." Dig deeper. "Not very smart of him."

"Oh no," she said with a giggle.

So much for her crocodile tears.

"I've never been involved in his shenanigans, but there's an air vent from his study. If I stand in the utility room, I can hear every word that's said in there."

A tendril of hope began to grow in his chest. "Did you

happened to hear who abducted Beth Wheaton or where she's been taken?"

"Maybe," she scoffed. "But I won't lift a finger to help that snooty bitch."

"If you don't help us find Beth and she's injured or worse, you could be held for accessory to murder." Life in prison would be the best you could hope for."

"They'd have to convict me first, and my Daddy—"

"Your damn daddy isn't going to be in a position to help you. Get it through your thick head, Zoe."

More sniffing.

Ben shook his head. "You won't like life in prison. You'll like death row even less."

"You're just mean, Ben Rasmussen," she wailed.

"You have no idea."

The urge to tear his ex limb from limb surged through him. His hands shook on the steering wheel. *Get a grip.*

He pulled into an open space in the town hall lot and parked. Taking a couple of deep breaths to cool down, he opened the door. He emerged and unlocked the rear door. "Get out."

He perp-walked her into the Sheriff's department and personally locked her in a holding cell. Emerging from the cellblock, he told the Dispatcher, the only person left on site, "Ms. Vayden is under arrest, again. And if anyone releases her without my authorization, that person will be fired and prosecuted for obstruction of justice. Am I clear?"

"Yes, sir." The dispatcher nodded. "Crystal."

"Call the DA. Get her out of bed. Ms. Vayden says she has valuable information and wants to make a deal."

Now, to check on the search progress. He called his brother. "What's going on? Any sign of Beth?"

"North sector—we've cleared two warehouses, a beauty shop, three more warehouses to go."

"Text me the address where you're headed next."

"On it."

Almost immediately, Ben's phone pinged with Will's text. "I'm joining the search," he told the dispatcher, then grabbed a walkie-talkie as he ran out the door.

Beth struggled against the zip-ties. Her kidnappers had unfastened the ties around her ankles but instead, plopped her in a chair and rebound her ankles separately to the chair legs. From her spot in the hangar office, she heard the sound of another vehicle. Had Ben found her after all? Or was it the 'boss' her captors seemed to be waiting for. What would happen when he arrived?

A car door slammed. Then the door to the office opened and a dapper man entered, along with a smaller version of the hulks. Definitely not Ben. The boss had arrived, wearing a tailored black silk suit. A beam of moonlight shone through the skylight casting an eerie glow on his stylishly cut silver-gray hair.

"Ms. Wheaton, I presume?"

She stiffened her spine. "You'd be correct unless you happen to see any other kidnap victims in here."

"When I was a young man, I enjoyed a spunky retort, but now that I'm older, I prefer my women to *keep their mouths shut!*"

She shrugged. What else could she do?

His eyes glinted in the moonlight. Dark they were. And deadly like a shark's.

"Your lover has had the misfortune to arrest the daughter of my colleague."

"I don't have a lover." Technically true. But who had Ben arrested? Had he actually arrested Zoe? For what? "I don't know what you're talking about."

"No matter." He leaned in. "Just know that you are mine to do with as I please."

Her heart sank. Her mouth dried. She tried to swallow but couldn't.

"But I haven't decided what that will be."

"Take your time. No rush."

His thin lips drew into a creepy knowing smile. "The most expedient thing would be to drug you. Heroin works well." He paced as he explained. "It makes you compliant, and soon you'll do anything for more. *Anything*." He rubbed his chin considering her future fate, then stopped and lifted a lock of her hair. "A natural blonde. Yes, I'm sure you are. I can get a premium for you in the Middle East."

Her stomach churned with nausea. Sex-trafficked. That was to be her fate if Ben didn't show up soon. Her breathing grew ragged.

"Nothing else to say? Not much to say, is there?" He continued pacing.

"I might've fibbed to your minions. My parents are rich. I mean, *really* rich." Now she was lying for sure, but she had to say something to make him rethink his plan.

He stopped in front of her, his beady eyes alight with greed. "How rich?"

"The store and the land it's on are worth a fortune." More lies.

He shrugged and scoffed, "Store is a burned-out shell."

"But it's heavily insured. My parents still own it. They'd sign it over to you in a heartbeat." More lies. Anything to keep him talking.

He frowned. "Tempting, but business transactions, insurance payouts, they take time. I'm more inclined to sell you to someone with liquid assets."

"You really don't want the Texas Rangers after you.

They always get their man. My lover is a Ranger, and they won't stop until they put you out of business."

"And how will that help you, little dove? You'll be out of the country in a heartbeat if I so choose."

The urge to beg... The words knotted in her throat. No. It wouldn't do any good. This mob boss was too sure of himself and what he could do.

Another sound, and a loud one. The airplane's engine revving.

Oh, God, Ben, where are you?

The mob boss smiled. "Time to go, little dove."

"No!" She drew back. "I'm afraid of flying. Where are you taking me?"

"Don't you like surprises?" Then he chuckled, then turned away. He turned to one of his men. "Put her on the plane. Sergei, you can fly her to the usual rendezvous point. I'll call ahead and make the arrangements."

Sergei nodded.

Her two abductors moved forward in unison. She wasn't the first woman they'd kidnapped. One bent over and release her ankles.

Run.

She jumped up, and immediately, the other one grabbed her shoulders and forced her back onto the chair.

His breath was sour as he leaned and whispered in her ear, "No way, pretty lady."

The other hulk zip-tied her ankles together again. Their boss walked back to his limo and stood watching.

Together, the hulks picked her up and carried her onto the plane and slung her into a seat.

Beth struggled and kicked to no avail. "You can't do this. This is kidnapping. That's a federal crime, you bozos!"

"Enough. Shut her up," the boss ordered.

She cringed and made herself as small as possible, but

hulk number two's backhand smashed across her cheek. Pinpoints of light flickered in her field of vision. She shook her head to clear it.

Queasiness roiled through her stomach and the plane began to slowly move from the hangar.

The walkie-talkie crackled. Ranger Stirling's voice came over the comm. unit. "All north sector buildings cleared except for Industrial Avionics."

"That's where we're headed now."

"Want us to join you or start clearing another sector?"

"Airfield!" Ben barked. "If they're going to try to move her, a plane would be the best way." Even as he said the words, his heart grew heavy. If they transported her by air, no telling where she could end up. It was the last possible place. When last seen, the limo was heading north. If they'd planned on taking her to Houston... Houston was southeast.

The airfield had to be their last best chance to find her.

Industrial Avionics functioned as a private airfield for local businessmen who traveled all across the southwest. It consisted of one hangar and a runway. Ben turned into the airfield just ahead of his brother. In the rearview mirror, he could make out the headlights of three more vehicles coming up fast.

The sound of a small plane engine thrummed through the night. No...

He blasted through the padlocked chain-link fence.

The plane began to slowly taxi down the airstrip.

"It's taking off. I've got to stop it." He floored the gas pedal, positioning his vehicle parallel to the Cessna. He had to get ahead or die trying.

"Don't be crazy, man." His brother's voice rasped through the walkie-talkie. "You'll kill yourself."

Ben gunned the motor and felt it shift into overdrive. Another hundred feet and the Cessna would be aloft. His vehicle inched ahead. If he could just keep pace with the landing gear, he could avoid the propeller. Now!

He whipped sharply into the Cessna's path. The roof of the SUV crashed into the left wing strut, and the hood glanced off the plane side panel. The Cessna careened onto its side as the pilot tried to veer away. The far axle buckled, and the plane tilted over onto its right wing, skidding to a screeching stop.

The airbags deployed, and Ben's SUV shuddered to a stop. He batted the airbags from his face and sat for a moment, shaking his head to clear it.

Beth.

He had to get to her.

He pulled his weapon and slowly exited the SUV.

The Cessna's door dropped open, and he saw feet emerge. Those feet ran away from the plane. How many were on the plane? The pilot, one or two more and Beth?

Another pair of feet, along with two smaller bound feet dropped from the plane. Those had to be Beth's.

"You're surrounded!" he yelled. Using the plane for cover, he eased forward.

Chapter Fifteen

Relief surged through Beth. Ben's voice the most reassuring sound she'd ever heard. She was going to survive this ordeal, after all. At least, her feet were on solid ground again. But it wasn't over, not yet. One of the Russian hulks had his arm around her neck and a weapon pointed at her head. Her heart beat a rapid tattoo and left her breathless. The Russian's beefy arm didn't help.

"Give it up. You're not going anywhere. You're surrounded."

You tell' im, Ben.

She craned her neck to see what was going on around her. In the night, she could make out at least four more law enforcement vehicles, thanks to their flashing blue lights. A number of men had materialized with their weapons drawn.

"Not as long as I have, pretty lady here. Shoot me, you hit her. Not worth the trouble, if you ask me." The mobster dragged her back from the plane. An odor hit her nose. Gas.

"I'm not asking you anything. Release her. Or one of us will put a bullet through your head."

While Ben was engaging with the Russian, another hulk dropped from the plane. Had Ben noticed him easing around the tail of the plane? "Ben! Behind you!"

Ben turned. Then the sound of a shot.

He dropped from sight.

"Ben!"

Another shot.

"No. No. No!"

"Shut up! Boyfriend dead."

Suddenly, the hulk released her. He fell, even before she heard the shot. He lay on the tarmac blood pooling from the back of his head. She scrambled away ducking behind the body of the plane for cover.

"Beth."

She looked up. "Ben." Her arms flew around his neck. "I thought he'd—"

He shook his head. "I'm all right." He stepped back.

She reached for him but stopped short. The metallic odor. Blood oozing from his arm. "But you're bleeding."

"It's known as a flesh wound, through and through. I'll be fine."

She glanced at the hulk on the tarmac. "Who?"

"Stirling took him out while I dealt with his buddy."

"Never have I ever been so glad to see you. You saved me. Heaven only knows what they had planned."

"You're safe now. That's all that matters."

"The mob boss and the rest of his men left in his limo as soon as I was on the plane. I don't know where they went."

"Doesn't matter. We'll get him. There'll be an arrest warrant out for him soon."

She walked around the nose of the plane. "Your rental, it's messed up."

"Yeah, I don't imagine I'll be very popular at the rental agency. My insurance should cover most of the damage."

"You need to see a doctor."

He shook his head. "Stirling will have a first aid kit in his trunk."

Will rushed over and punched his brother's uninjured shoulder. "You dumbass! You could've gotten yourself killed."

Ben fisted his hands and got in his brother's face. "What choice did I have? Tell me that!"

Beth stepped between them. "All right, boys. That's enough. Will, your brother is injured. I'm going to bandage his arm." She turned to Ben. "Now, your brother's upset. You did a crazy thing. You know you did. But I'm so glad you did, or I might be on my way to the Middle East."

"The Middle East?"

"It was mentioned as a likely destination. Seems the gentlemen over there prefer blondes." Her words might've sounded lighthearted, but she'd come very close to being sex trafficked. A hard shudder ran through her. Her knees weakened.

He gathered her to his uninjured side, giving her the support she desperately needed. "I'm not going to let anything else happen to you. I promise."

She luxuriated in the warmth of his embrace for a moment, then added, "And I'm not going to open any more doors without knowing who's there."

"Deal?"

"Deal."

"Back to the cop shop?"

"I'll go anywhere with you, Ben." She smiled. Truer words had never been spoken.

Ben took Beth back to the Sheriff's Department so that she could make her official statement. Afterward, he pulled her into his arms. "We're going to keep you close by until we've arrested everyone concerned. You won't be safe until we've rounded up all of them. I'll call the Marshal's Service to get you into a safe house."

"Sort of like witness protection?"

"Exactly."

"How long?"

"Hard to say. No one can know where you are."

"But you'll know?"

"No. I can't know either."

"But Lola and my parents?"

"*No one* can know. It'll take some time to arrange. Don't worry. You won't be spirited off just yet." He took her to Will's temporary office. "Vince should be off suspension as soon as we can get his charges dismissed." He walked over to the windows and closed the blinds to ensure her security. "You sit tight while I see what kind of information my ex has provided the DA."

Beth's gaze widened. "Did she tell you where I was?"

"Hell no! She said she'd be damned if she'd lift a finger to help you."

With a frown, she folded her arms across her chest. "Charming."

"Zoe doesn't know the meaning of the word." He leaned forward, raised her chin with his finger, and placed a kiss on Beth's soft mouth. "Unlike you. You're charm itself."

She smiled sweetly. "I beg to disagree. *You're* the charmer, Ranger Ben. Thank you for saving my life and risking your own."

"That's my job, darlin'. Protect and serve."

"And that's why—uh, why I love you." Her cheeks reddened. Her hands went to her face. "I can't believe I just said that. I must be—"

He stopped her rush of words with, "I love you too, darlin'. I love you with all my heart. I was so afraid I was going to lose you forever. I could barely breathe when I saw that plane taxiing down the runway." Then he stopped talking and kissed her.

The sweetest damn kiss of his life. Giddily, he held onto her with his good arm and surrendered his heart to his beautiful blonde Beth.

****

Heaving a deep sigh, Beth watched Ben's tall form amble from the office. His broad shoulders, his slim hips—perfection. He'd kissed her. And *wowee* what, a kiss. Her cheeks remained heated from the tender encounter. She picked up a folder from the desk and fanned her cheeks. Plus, she'd told him she loved him. Told him *first*. The words just slipped out so easily and without volition. No telling what he thought of her.

Focus.

Gazing at the folder she held, she started to put it down on the desk. 'Official Sheriff's Department' business was stamped across the front. Reynaldo Reyes, now who was he? Curiosity got the better of her. She peeked inside. Whoa! This Reynaldo Reyes person was an older version of Matt Freeman. Honestly, Matt resembled this Reyes character enough to be his son.

Had Ben noticed the similarity in appearance? Was that why he'd taken an instant dislike to Matt? She'd put his antagonistic attitude down to jealousy. Maybe there was more to it.

The further down the sheet she read, the more interesting it became. Leader of a cartel. No convictions despite several arrests. Also thought to be involved with weapons smuggling as well.

Now, this was something Ben could use...maybe?

Still breathless from kissing Beth, he paused a second, then opened the door to the interview room where Zoe waited with District Attorney Gannon. Eleanor Gannon was in her mid-fifties and tough as nails when it came to prosecuting wrongdoers. He wondered what she made of his ex's tale.

"Well? Was she bluffing or does she have substantial information?"

"I'm sitting right here," his ex said with a huff.

The DA gave an eye roll. "I have to say I was none too pleased to be pulled out of bed. Fortunately, Ms. Vayden has been very forthcoming. She has given me quite a lot of information. I've agreed we have enough for warrants on Yuri Makarov, Reynaldo Reyes, Carlton Briggs. Judge Garrison should be signing them as we speak. He wasn't too happy to be awakened, either." She shrugged. "So what. It's his job."

"So, Zoe," he said, turning to face his ex, "what are your father and his partners up to?"

"I don't want to talk to you." She crossed her arms and averted her gaze. "I've already spilled my guts to the DA. She can tell you."

"Let me guess." He placed his palms on the table and leaned forward. "Your father, along with the financial support of his partners, was trying to buy up the majority of the businesses in town to use for money laundering, at least, until the casino gets rolling. Protection rackets and extortion were his methods of choice."

"On the nose," DA Gannon said. "Furthermore, Reyes was to funnel drugs and weapons while Makarov would handle sex trafficking. Ms. Vayden has admitted she's responsible for setting the Mercantile on fire and for throwing a brick through the front door of the Yellow Rose Inn. She will go into witness protection until her father and his fellow conspirators are brought to trial. If at that point, she does not testify, her plea deal will be invalid, and she will be charged with arson in the first degree and felony vandalism."

"Good luck finding Reyes and Makarov. Reyes has probably skipped over the border by now and Makarov is reportedly on his way back to Houston."

DA Gannon picked up her briefcase with a smile. "I'm sure the Texas Rangers won't have any problems pulling in Makarov and his cohorts." She stood making ready to leave. "What about your kidnap victim?"

"Safe and sound. According to Ms. Wheaton, Yuri Makarov was at the airfield giving his men directions after her abduction. We barely caught them in time. She was already on a plane headed who knows where."

"And charges to be laid?"

"None for the two who kidnapped her. They're deceased. The pilot was rounded up at the airfield and is already in a cell."

"Good work. Maybe we can get him to turn."

"That's my plan. He can cool his heels a while. In the meantime, I'm going to serve those warrants and haul Brigg's ass in here."

"Enjoy yourself," DA Gannon said with a wry smile.

"You better believe it!" But first, it was past time to update Major Innes.

Determined not to do anymore snooping, Beth set the file back on the desk. Still edgy, she stood and paced the small office. Then the phone caught her eye. It was past time to let Lola know she was all right. Indeed, if she ended up in a safe house, then she wouldn't be able to contact Lola at all. Best call her now while she could.

She reached for the phone and dialed her sister's cell. "Lola, It's me. I'm fine." No point in telling her about the black eye. Time enough for that later.

"Thank heaven, I've been so worried."

"Long story, but I'm at the Sheriff's Department right now. Ben said something about placing me in a safe house, but I just want to come home and sleep in my own bed."

"Duh! Your bed is burned up, and all you have here is an air mattress."

"True." Beth's stomach growled, reminding her she hadn't eaten. "Did you save me any pizza?"

Lola broke out in a peal of laughter. "Only you would be thinking of your stomach at a time like this."

"I'm starving. My kidnappers weren't interested in serving dinner."

"Tell me what happened. Who kidnapped you in the first place? Where did they take you? How did Ben find you?"

"Slow down. One question at a time." Beth spent the next few minutes giving her sister the gory details finishing with, "Ben was hit, but it was just a flesh wound."

Lola gave a gasp. "Is Will all right? Please tell me he's not hurt."

"He's fine. Don't you worry your pretty head."

Lola let out an audible sigh. "You know, it's kind of creepy here out here, even with Darby here."

"Why don't you come down to the Sheriff's Department with me? We can go to the safe house together. You shouldn't be alone either."

"Sounds like a plan. See you in a few." Lola hung up.

Standing at the office door, she could see the deputies running back and forth. They all seemed to know what they were doing. Organized chaos. If only there were something she could do instead of just pacing back and forth like a long-tailed cat in a roomful of rocking chairs.

She opened the door just a fraction and waved at Kelly. "Do you have a minute? I need to tell you something. "I called Lola. I hope that's all right? She wants to come down here. She's feeling kind of antsy."

Kelly nodded. "No problem. I'd rather have you both in one place."

Beth nodded and reached for the phone.

"What now?" Lola questioned breathlessly. "We were on our way out the door."

"Wait." She opened the office door a crack. "Something's going on."

"What?"

"I don't know, but Ben and Kelly just scooped up four deputies and ran for the door. Gotta go." She hit the disconnect button. What now? Dang it. She didn't get to tell Ben how much Matt Freeman resembled this Reyes guy. That would have to wait.

Accompanied by Deputy Longworth, Lola rushed into the office, tossed a pizza box onto the desk, and then threw her arms around Beth. "OMG! Now, I can really see that you're okay. "

Beth untangled her sister's arms. "I really am."

"Darby said on the ride down here that they'll probably keep us together since we could both be targets."

"Someone's looking for you." Beth nodded toward the bullpen. "Will keeps glancing over here."

Lola shook her head. "He's busy. I don't want to bother him."

"You could say hello."

Turning away, Lola said, "No. It's bad enough we're taking up his office."

"I'm pretty sure he doesn't mind."

"Take it from me, you'll never catch your man if you

stay so freaking remote and reserved."

"Like you've caught yours, have you?" Lola scoffed.

Beth bit her lips, then smiled. "I have."

"What?" Lola gave a squeal. "Spill. Tell me everything, or so help me, I will eat the rest of the pizza."

"You wouldn't dare!" Beth snatched the box from the desk, flipped the lid back, and grabbed a piece of pepperoni pizza. After she'd inhaled it, she gave a moan of pleasure. "So good. And I'll tell you one thing only. His kiss is even better than this pizza."

"He *kissed* you?" Lola placed her hand over her chest. "Be still my heart."

"Boy-howdy did he ever." She gave her sister a smile.

"And...?"

"Wonderful is all I can say." She licked a dollop of pizza sauce from her lip.

After downing another slice of pizza, Beth closed the box. "I think I'll live now." She reached for the Reyes folder, opened it, and tapped Reyes's photo. "See this guy. Who do you think he looks like?"

Lola's eyes widened into pools of blue. "Your favorite security salesman?"

"Damn straight, he does. They could be father and son."

"Do you think Ben has noticed the resemblance?"

Beth sighed. "I was going to mention it, but he ran out of here before I could."

"That was hours ago. Text him."

"He might be busy." She reached for her phone. "I'll text Kelly instead. That's not to say she's not as busy as Ben, but she might be more inclined to check her phone."

Lola nodded. "Right."

***

Ben slammed the cargo door shut. "That ought to be sufficient proof Briggs and his partners were up to no good." He walked around to the passenger side of Kelly's truck, opened the door, and climbed inside. Briggs was already on his way to jail, courtesy of the deputies. "That's quite a haul. Reyes may have hopped back over the border, but he left behind a semi-truck full of weapons. Or maybe the mayor was planning on starting his own army."

"We'll get Reyes sooner or later, boss," Kelly said, settling behind the wheel.

Kelly reached to turn the ignition when her phone beeped with a text message. She glanced down at it. "It's from Beth. Seems she did a little snooping. She wants to know if Matt Freeman and Reynaldo Reyes could be related?"

So, Beth had done some snooping. He held back a smile. "Damned if I know. Come to think of it. Freeman did remind me of someone."

"Let's find out!"

They drove to the hospital where Donovan reluctantly handed Ben her keys. "Careful now. You've already wrecked two vehicles. I'm kind of fond of this baby." She patted the armrest and got out.

"Don't forget I'm your boss, Donovan. I have the power of life and death over your career," he said with a smile.

"Yes, *boss*."

"According to the doctor's last report, Freeman is awake and alert. Question him about who might've shot him, and then bring up his resemblance to Reyes. He has a troubling gap in his resume. I want to know what he was up to during that time. Plus, the DEA doesn't claim him as one of theirs."

"Yes, boss." She grinned, then saluted him sharply.

***

By the time Ben drove back to the Sheriff's Department, he found Beth asleep with her head on the desk and Lola stretched out on a bench. "Any progress on finding a safe house for these two?" He asked the Dispatcher.

"Not yet," he replied with a wide yawn.

Ben glanced at his phone. Four in the morning. He called the only place he could guarantee safe at four AM—the ranch.

His father answered, "Yup?"

"I need a couple of beds for the Wheaton sisters. Tell you more when I see you."

"Bring 'em on."

Before he could end the call, he heard his father wake his mother, "Adela. Company coming."

"Thanks, Pop."

He left the keys to Kelly's truck with the Dispatcher, then walked back into the bullpen. "Deputy Longworth, I'm leaving Donovan's truck here for her when she gets back from the hospital. So, if you don't mind, I'm borrowing your truck to take Beth and her sister out to my folks' place. You're to ride along. You can keep an eye out until we can get them situated and I can tie things up in town."

She responded with a quick nod. "Sure thing." She cast a questioning glance at Will. "Boss?"

Will nodded his approval.

He walked over to Beth's sleeping form where he resisted the strong urge to waken her with a kiss. "Beth," he said gently, touching her shoulder.

She jumped. "What?"

"We're taking you and Lola out to the ranch. Deputy Longworth's coming along. She'll be on the lookout for trouble."

Still half asleep, she nodded. "Okay."

She rose. "What about your parents? Won't we be putting them in danger?"

"It's just for a while until we can get you into a safe house. The Rangers in Houston are hauling in Makarov and his mob as we speak. Once they have that situation under control, you might not even need a safe house."

She nodded slowly. "Okay."

"You're dead on your feet."

"Better than being plain dead," she said with a quick chuckle.

Ben smiled. This was his Beth, always able to see the positive of a situation. "You'll like mom's breakfast."

Her eyelids at half-mast, Beth smiled up at him and stifled a yawn. "She has that reputation."

"You and Lola can sleep late, and then she'll feed you good. That's a promise."

"I'm counting on it."

"Let's go, darlin'." He slid his arm around her waist, more to steady her than a desire for closeness. Heck. No point in lying to himself. He wanted—no, needed—her close.

Together they left the office and walked into the bullpen. Lola was sitting up and rubbing her eyes. She gave a wide yawn. "Okay, I'm awake."

"We'll go out the back where the deputy's truck is parked." No point in advertising where they were taking Beth and her sister.

Beth woke when the truck stopped. "Are we there?"

"You're home." He gave a chuckle. "I mean to say you're at my folks' ranch."

"If there's a bed, I'll sleep anywhere, the porch, the

stable?"

"We can do better than that."

The front door opened. Ben's mother stepped out, carrying a twelve-gauge shotgun. Beth gave a chuckle. "I see you brought me to the right place." Adela was a tall, raw-boned Texas-born-and-bred woman with a friendly face and welcoming smile. Her iron-gray hair was cropped in a no-nonsense cut as if she'd cut it herself.

"You'll be safe."

She gazed into his sky-blue eyes and sighed. "You're not staying, are you?"

"'Fraid I have a lot of loose ends to tie up."

She nodded. "I understand."

His mother set the shotgun aside and opened her arms wide. "Come on, girls. Let's get you into some PJs and into bed."

A swarm sensation flooded through her body. Home indeed.

Ben walked into the kitchen and gulped down the hot coffee his mom had thoughtfully provided. "Thanks, Mom," he said aloud, but his mom was upstairs getting Beth and her sister bedded down.

He needed to head back to town, but one thing he needed more. He had to see Beth one more time to say goodnight. Gingerly, he climbed the steps to the second floor. His mom emerged from his old bedroom. "Beth?" he asked.

"Hm." His mom gave him a long piercing look. "Yes, she's in your old room. Something to tell me, son?"

"In time."

"All I need to know." She gave him a pleased little smile

and walked on down the hall.

He tapped on the door. "Beth?"

He waited for a response. None. Slowly, he opened the door. And smiled. She'd already fallen asleep before even pulling up the covers. He tiptoed across the room. Her fair hair spilled across the pillow in a tangle of curls. He leaned over and secured the light blanket across her shoulders, then placed a tender kiss on her cheek. He turned and left her, hopefully, to a dreamless sleep. His chest filled with a tenderness he'd never felt before. His woman. A woman to protect. The woman he would love for the rest of his life.

Early Wednesday afternoon

After a full country breakfast with ham, scrambled eggs, hash browns, and fluffy biscuits, Beth felt as if she could finally take a deep breath without looking over her shoulder. Carrying a cup of coffee, she walked outside onto the porch.

Darby nodded at Beth's approach. "I'm on lookout. Don't worry."

From the Darby's slumped shoulders and heavy eyelids, Beth could tell the young deputy was slowly wearing down. "You look beyond tired."

She gave a casual shrug. "I'll catch up on sleep tonight. Donovan will take the night shift. I just have to stay awake until six," she said with a smile. "I'm good."

"It's not fair. Lola and I had a good five hours of sleep before Adela woke us and fed us with that enormous breakfast. I'm sure she fed you as well."

"Mm." Darby smiled and rubbed her stomach. "Most definitely. And all the coffee I can drink, but that breakfast really hit the spot. It reminded me of my mom's breakfasts. She always sent my brothers and me off to school with full tummies."

Darby's phone trilled.

Beth could only hear one side of the conversation, but it didn't seem to be good news. "What's happened?" she asked after Darby ended the call.

"Just as we figured, Reyes definitely crossed the border late last night. But while the Rangers have picked up a majority of Makarov's gang, they haven't located him or the men he had with him."

Beth gasped. "Meaning they could still be in the area?" Her heart rate pounded in her ears. Her hands went to her head. She took a ragged breath. "What else could it mean?"

"It could mean they've fled the country along with Reyes, but I wouldn't bet on it." Darby squared her shoulders. "Rangers Rasmussen and Stirling are on their way here. The rest of the Sheriff's Department will be combing the county for any sign of Makarov and his men."

Lola walked onto the front porch and pointed at the cloud of dust at the far end of the drive. "They must've hurried."

Beth turned. Her stomach lurched. "That's the limo."

"Back in the house," Darby ordered.

Chapter Sixteen

As Beth raced back inside, she heard the sound of Darby racking her shotgun. What good was one bleary-eyed deputy armed with a shotgun against Makarov and his men who were undoubtedly heavily armed?

"Mrs. Rasmussen," Beth called out. "Men are coming. Heavily armed men."

"It's Adela," Ben's mother said with a nervous smile as she shoved a twelve-gauge and a box of shells into Beth's hands. "Know how to use this? It's already loaded."

Beth nodded and took the gun, even though her hands shook.

"Got another?" Lola asked and pulled a small revolver from her boot. "This won't do much."

Adela pulled a key from her jeans pocket and ran to the gun safe. She unlocked it and opened the heavy steel door. "Take your pick." Then she grabbed another shotgun and ran out the back door. The furious sound of the dinner bell broke the peace of a quiet morning. That would alert the rest of the men on the ranch there was trouble.

Beth prayed the sound would carry to wherever the Rasmussen men were working.

Darby came in from the front porch. "I texted the Rangers. They'll be here soon." She crouched in front of an open window.

Beth and Lola copied the deputy's actions. The limo had stopped a mere twenty feet or so from the front porch. One man emerged, then another, and another. Then she saw Makarov climb out. With the driver, that made five in all.

Four women to hold off five men.

Makarov planted his feet apart. How arrogant could the man be? "We're coming in, and you can't stop us."

Darby fired first at Makarov's feet.

With a frown, he stepped aside sharply. "Nice shooting. But now I'll have to have my shoes cleaned."

"Just a warning shot," Darby yelled. "The next one will dirty more than your shoes."

"Let me have the little blonde, and we'll go away. Leave you in peace."

"Don't know what blonde you're talking about, Makarov. No blondes here," Darby bluffed.

Did Makarov really think they would just hand her over? Did he really think they were stupid enough to believe he'd actually leave them alone afterward? "I'm not going anywhere with you," Beth called out.

"So, she *is* here. Thank you for verifying."

Damn. Why couldn't she have just kept her mouth shut?

Hurry, Ben. Please hurry.

Makarov gestured and his men began to spread out. They were heavily armed all right. Each man held a machine gun.

She turned to Darby. "If we fire on them, won't they spray the house with gunfire?"

"Not if we aim carefully."

Aim to kill? Beth's mouth grew dry as sand. She turned to Lola. Her sister's eyes grew wide. "Can we do this?" she whispered.

Lola gave a slow nod. "No choice."

"If we can hit three, that'll leave two."

Across the room, Adela crouched beside Darby. "Make that four leaves one."

"I'm aiming for Makarov," Beth said, taking a deep

breath and slowly letting it out. *Teach him a lesson. This woman fights back.*

The four women took aim.

After receiving Longworth's text, Ben radioed Will. "All units converge. Makarov sighted at Rasmussen ranch. Repeat. All units converge. Rasmussen ranch."

Stirling sped along the road as if he were on a familiar racetrack, fence posts and trees whipping past in a blur.

Ben warned, "The turnoff to the ranch is half a mile on the left."

"Noted," Stirling said. "Check the rearview. We've got some company."

Ben glanced over his shoulder. "That's my brother's vehicle."

Stirling slowed just enough to keep from flipping his truck and whipped into the tree-lined lane leading to the ranch house.

Ben's heart sank. "I hear automatic gunfire." Images of Beth's body riddled with bullets came to mind. No. She had to be all right. Or he would tear Makarov limb from limb and worry about the consequences later.

The mobsters advanced toward the house fast. Beth held her breath and fired. The buckshot went wide and nicked his ear. "Crap!" She reloaded. Hitting a moving target—not so easy.

The other women fired simultaneously. Two of Makarov's men went down, leaving three who scrambled for cover. One disappeared around the side of the house.

She held her hands to her ears. So damn loud.

Then, bold as brass, one of the men stood and sprayed the house with automatic gunfire.

Beth flattened to the floor. What were they thinking? They must've been insane to think they could hold off men with automatic weapons.

Adela gave a low grunt. "I'm hit."

Ben's mom. No! Beth set the shotgun aside. Keeping her head low, she scooted over to Adela's side where blood was streaming from her upper arm.

"It's not so bad, but it hurts like a son—" Ben's mother frowned and clenched her teeth.

"I'm *so* sorry."

Darby got another shot off, but it missed. "Just trying to keep them at bay," she explained. The back door burst open. She sprang to her feet. "Cover me."

Lola nodded and fired another round toward the two men out front.

Beth watched over her shoulder as she tried to care for Adela's wound. She looked around. What could she use? Whatever... She ripped off her T-shirt and folded it, then applied the makeshift bandage to Adela's wound. "I'm so sorry. But I have to press hard to stop the bleeding." Not to mention she was half-naked. She'd just have to worry about that later.

"Uh—"

At the sound of Darby's voice, Beth looked up.

The deputy was backing into the living room. One of Makarov's men had his gun shoved under her chin.

"Enough bullshit," he growled. "Put down guns." Keeping his weapon aimed at the women, he collected their guns and leaned them in the far corner of the room. He then walked to the front door and opened it. "Okay," he called to his cohorts. "Situation under control."

Makarov and his remaining goon strode inside the

house.

Frowning, the mobster shook his head at the women huddled together. "Four women. So much trouble. I should kill you all."

"Yeah? Five big bad men with big automatic guns," Beth sneered. "And four brave women with old-fashioned shotguns. We took out two of yours. All you did was hit one of us, who by the way—" Her voice rose to a shout. "—needs a doctor!"

Stirling tromped the gas pedal speeding up the lane, then stopped about ten yards from the limo.

Crouching low, they climbed from the vehicle. Ben motioned for Stirling to go left while he swung to the right.

In the distance, he heard the sound of rifle fire. Had to be his father and brothers. Normally, they carried rifles while they worked the ranch. He kept low, moving stealthily until he could see around the limo. Two men lay on the ground. One moving. One not.

He ducked and ran for the far end of the house.

From the corner of his eye, he spotted the barrel of an automatic weapon. He rolled and flattened his body into the tall grass. A spray of automatic fire zipped over his head, so close he felt the heat of the rounds. He scrabbled through the grass and inched forward in order to get around the side of the house.

As for returning fire, he couldn't risk it. He had no way of knowing the location of the four women who were inside. Or the extent of their injuries. From the sound of rifle fire, he judged his father and brothers were located somewhere behind the house. But for now, they too were quiet. No doubt carefully choosing their shots.

Over his shoulder, he saw Will and his deputies had arrived and set up a cordon using their vehicles.

Makarov wasn't getting away this time. No way.

Inside the house, Beth knelt beside Adela and glared up at Makarov. "Are you deaf? She needs a doctor!"

"Too bad. Your aim was lousy." He held a handkerchief to his ear which bled profusely onto his silk suit.

"Don't I know it. I wish I'd shot your head off instead of your ear lobe."

He leered down at her. "Little girls shouldn't play with guns."

Beth remembered that Lola still had a small revolver in her boot. Would she have an opportunity to use it, or would her attempt result in more bloodshed?

She tried to staunch Adela's blood flow, but the T-shirt was already saturated. Hopefully, this was one of those wounds often described as *worse than it looks*.

At least it wasn't spurting. Thank heaven for that. But the older woman's skin was pale. "She's losing too much blood."

"Shut your mouth, or I'll see to it her bleeding stops for good."

Beth sucked in a breath and held it, then said quietly to keep from antagonizing the big man with the big gun, "You won't get away. The rangers and the deputies are already here."

"Gregori, keep an eye outback," Makarov ordered.

Outside, Ben scrambled through the grass, until he

made it around the corner of the house. Wondering where his father and brothers were hidden, he spotted movement in his mother's vegetable garden. The tasseled corn swayed, then stilled. And not a breeze to be had. He retrieved a rock from the border and lobbed it at the back of the house, then he ducked behind a lawn chair.

As he'd hoped, one of Makarov's men came to check out the noise.

Come on. Come outside. See what the noise is. Come on.

Makarov's goon opened the back door slowly

Come on.

The goon tentatively stepped down onto the patio. He glanced to his left then his right.

That's it. A little closer.

Ben's brother Brock materialized from behind a redwood bench. Ben tossed another rock to distract the mobster, then he stood. "You looking for me?"

The goon raised his gun to fire, but Ben was quicker.

Brock rushed forward and pounced on the thug before he could hit the dirt. Together they dragged him out of sight.

At the sound of a gunshot, Beth's heart felt as if it dropped to her knees. She swallowed to keep the panic from her voice. "You need to put an end to this. You're surrounded. The sheriff and his deputies aren't going to let you leave. You have nowhere to go."

From the corner of her eye, she saw Lola glance at her boot. Beth gave the tiniest shake of her head. Not yet.

If the hood who went outside had been taken down, there were still two inside. *And please, let it not be Ben who was shot. Please. Be careful.*

"Alexei, go see what's going on. But stay *inside*," Makarov ordered in his guttural rasping voice.

Makarov's goon returned shaking his head. "Nothing to see. Gregori's gone."

"Dammit." Makarov fisted his hands while he paced.

"You might as well be smart, Makarov. There's no way out."

"All I need—" He grabbed Beth's wrist and jerked her to her feet. "—is this one."

"Lola..." She nodded toward Adela. Lola sprang to take Beth's place at Adela's side.

"One valuable hostage." With one of his meaty arms around her neck and a semi-automatic pistol at her head, Beth was afraid to breathe, much less piss him off any further.

He dragged her to the front door and opened it. "I'm taking the limo," he shouted. "I have a hostage. If anyone tries to stop me, I'll kill her."

Ben heard Makarov's threats. Dollars to donuts, the Russian mobster had Beth in his grasp again.

Easing around to the front of the house, his worst fear was confirmed. Makarov held a half-naked Beth in a chokehold and a gun to her head. What had they done to her? Blind fury raged through him. Then he heard the pop of small arms fire from inside.

The mob boss heard it too. When he turned his head, his grip on Beth loosened. She went limp and collapsed on the front porch, leaving Ben the split-second he needed to fire center mass.

Makarov's eyes widened in surprise. His hands clasped his chest. He dropped.

Ben ran forward and kicked the gangster's Glock out of reach. He crouched beside him and checked for a pulse. "He's still alive." He examined mobster again. No blood. Bastard was wearing Kevlar. "Ambulance!"

Makarov began to moan and rub his chest. "You shot me."

Ben quickly cuffed the mob boss. "I should've gone for the head."

Beth got to her feet and stumbled into his arms. He jerked off his shirt and covered her shoulders. "Did they hurt you?"

Shaking her head, she slid her arms into his shirt and tied it at the waist. "No, but your mother was hit. She needs—"

His mom? His breath came in ragged gasps. He kicked Makarov. "You shot my mother? Bastard!" He kicked him again. "Call an ambulance! Civilian casualties," he shouted." Grabbing Beth's hand, he ran inside the house fearing the worst.

Instead, Lola was holding a weapon on the remaining thug who was bleeding from a shoulder wound. "He tried to keep me from tending to your mom," she said with a shrug.

"Bitch," the bleeding goon muttered.

He flew to his mother's side where Darby had taken over tending to her wound. "How is she?"

"She's lost a good bit of blood, but it's a through and through."

Ben knelt beside his mother, the one constant in his life. The woman who never failed to support his choices, not counting his marriage to Zoe, and she'd been right about that. "Mom, there's an ambulance on the way. You're going to be all right."

She struggled to sit up. "Of course, I am. You act like you think I'm dying, and I'm here to tell you I'm not. I just didn't duck fast enough. Slower reflexes when you get to be my age. Remember that, son. You're no spring chicken."

He chuckled. A disturbance arose from the back of the house. He glanced up to see his father and two younger brothers come trooping into the living room.

His father's face paled when he saw the blood. "Adela." He knelt beside her, gently taking her hands in his.

"I'm all right. What took you so long?"

Ben's father nodded. "She's all right. She's her usual feisty self."

Beth stood back and watched the ambulances as they came and went. The coroner's van did the same. Ben's father Byron took off with the first ambulance. His brothers jumped into a pickup and followed.

Ben handed his weapon over to Will who seemed pretty shaken from seeing their mother injured, but he had to remain on scene. "You sure she's going to be all right?"

"Yeah, quit worrying," Ben told him. "She'll be fine."

"And Lola, she's the one who shot—"

"Alexei," Lola supplied. "His name is Alexei."

Will pulled a blue bandana from his pocket and mopped his brow. "You took a big chance." It seemed as if he couldn't take his eyes off Lola, who seemed to be doing her best imitation of casual.

"He pissed me off. I was trying to take care of your mom."

Will hooked his thumbs in his belt loops. "Well, now, do you have a permit for that handgun?"

Lola squared her shoulders and raised her chin a notch. "You're asking me a question like that? Now? When I used it to defend your own mama?" She gave a haughty jerk and looked away.

Will's mouth twitched with a grin. "Well," he drawled, "since you put it like that." Using his forefinger, he touched her chin and brought it around. "I'm mighty glad you're all right. I'd really hate to see anything happen to you."

Smiling, Beth looked up at Ben and winked. Even Ben, who was usually clueless when it came to sensing the sexual tension between his brother and her sister, winked back. Clearly, his brother was ready to move on from his loss. And Lola was going to get her Rasmussen brother, after all.

Ben leaned down and whispered in Beth's ear. "Let's give these two some privacy." He took her hand and drew her outside onto the brick-paved patio. "Have a seat," he said, then sat beside her on the bench. "I hope you know what I'm about to say and can help me fill in the blanks. I'm not too good at this emotional stuff. But I honestly thought I was goin' to die when I saw Makarov holding that gun to your head." He took her hands in his.

Trying not to give away her nervousness, Beth smiled. No way was she going to make this easy. He had to say the words. "You're doing pretty good so far."

His blue eyes shone with a never seen before warmth. "I don't want to live in a world if you're not there by my side. You know what I mean?"

She let out a long sigh. This was almost as hard on her as it was on him. "Maybe. But you're going to have to spit it out."

"But you know I love you."

She nodded. "I'm pretty sure that's the case since you managed to get those words out at least once in the last few days."

"I love you, Beth, with everything that I am."

"That's better," she said with a nod to encourage him. "You're doing just fine, but you need to keep going." *Come on. Just say the damn words.*

"Do I have to—uh, get down—?"

Finally. "Yes, you do." Her heart rate kicked into overdrive.

He gave a little groan then knelt before her. "Now, I know you might prefer something flowery and poetic, but I'm damned if I can come up with anything like that on the spur of a moment." He wiped his mouth with his hand. "Here goes. Beth Wheaton, would you do me the honor of becoming my wife?"

"Hallelujah!" she squealed and threw her arms around his neck.

He gazed up at her, his confusion only too apparent. "Is that a yes?"

"You better believe it's a 'yes.'"

"Yahoo!" He got to his feet, picked her up, and swung her around. "I don't have a ring yet, but there will be one."

"Oh, you better believe there'll be a ring," she said beaming, her heart racing with excitement.

Longworth poked her head out the back door. "Congratulations, you two! About damn time." She turned to go back inside, then stopped. "By the way, Briscoes has been calling all over town for you, Beth. Something about a furniture delivery?"

Beth grabbed her head with her hands. "Right! I completely forgot." She gazed into Ben's eyes. "Sorry. I have to go."

His handsome face was wreathed with a wide smile. "Go on. Now that I know you'll be safe, I can let you out of my sight for a few minutes. We have the rest of our lives to be together."

Her heart swelled with love and desire for this one man, so much she could barely breathe for loving him. "I love you, Ben Rasmussen."

"Ditto." He angled his head forward and kissed her.

Man, did he ever kiss her! A long swoony kiss. Her toes curled inside her running shoes and her knees weakened. She staggered. Only his strong arm around her waist kept her from falling.

While Beth ran over to the condo to deal with the furniture delivery, Ben drove Longworth and her truck back to the Sheriff's Department. He found Donovan sitting at his desk with a wide smile on her face. She jumped up. "Boss, have I got news for you."

He reclaimed his seat and leaned back. "Okay. What did you find out?"

"Once Freeman started talking, he couldn't seem to shut up. Like we sort of guessed, he's the son of Reynaldo Reyes by an American doctoral student who, when she found out that Reyes's bad boy persona wasn't just a persona, fled Mexico and relocated to her hometown. Those missing years after grad school, he spent in Mexico under his father's watchful eye. As for who might've shot him, he figures your ex, or more likely, her father ordered the hit."

"Why? What does he have to do with either of them?"

"He was blackmailing Zoe. He had the footage of her setting the fire to Beth's store, and he kept an eye on her and witnessed Zoe throwing the brick through the Yellow Rose Inn. He called her, set up a meet, and that's when he was shot. He's demanding witness protection. Says he knows everything about his father's business, and he's willing to tell all. He tried to make it clear that he wasn't in town at his father's behest, but I didn't buy it. Too big of a coincidence. I inveigled an arrest warrant from Judge Garrison, and I arrested Freeman. There's a deputy guarding him while we speak."

"You have been busy. Good job." Donovan would go far. She'd used her initiative, and she'd gotten the information he needed to make a case.

"Sounds as if you were rather busy, too."

"Makarov's in custody. Two of his men are in the morgue and two others in the hospital under guard."

"And..." She smiled expectantly.

"What?"

"I hear congratulations are in order."

"Oh, that." He couldn't wipe the smile from his face. "Yeah. Beth and I are going to get married."

"Excellent," Kelly said. "Took you long enough."

Small towns. Everybody knew everybody's business. "It has been hectic around here."

"Now that Makarov, Briggs, and his daughter are in custody, things should settle down."

"For a while."

Hopefully, long enough for a wedding and a honeymoon.

Chapter Seventeen

Beth spent the next hour tweaking the furniture arrangement. Given that it was a standard three-bedroom condo, there wasn't much leeway in where the sofa and chairs should go. Ditto the bedroom furniture. Her hands on her hips, she stood back and surveyed the adjustments. Perfect.

Her phone trilled. She pulled it from her pocket and answered.

"This is Sara." Sara Billingsley and her husband rented the Wheaton family home on Spring Street. "I'm afraid I have a huge favor to ask."

"Ask away. I'll do what I can. As you can imagine, I'm pretty stressed for time at the moment."

"I know. And I really hate to do this, but we have to think about what's good for our family. Kenton Valley just isn't what it used to be what with the drug cartels and the mob and fires. I'm asking you if I can break my lease?"

What luck. The solution handed to her—on a silver platter, no less—to where she and Ben could live. "Of course. And don't worry about the penalty. I understand completely. You must do whatever you think best." Her parents still owned the house, but she was sure they would be willing to sell if it was to a family member.

"The thing is I felt so bad about asking, and I've put it off until the last minute. Actually, the movers are here now," Sara finished with a rush.

"So, you're moving out today? Don't worry. It's fine." Even better. Now, she could inspect the house right away and see what needed to be done. "I wish you and your family the best, Sara."

"Thank you so much. I really, really appreciate you being so nice about it."

"Not a problem. Take care."

After Sara rang off, Beth called Ben. "Can you meet me at my parents' house? The tenants are moving out today, and I thought maybe, just maybe, we could buy it from my folks. Just a thought. No pressure."

"Very Interesting," he said. The sound of his familiar baritone warmed her heart. "Just a few things to tie up with the DA. Say around six-thirty?"

"Perfect. "I'm going over to inspect it, and I'll see you there."

Beth smiled. Everything was working out as if it were meant to be. Had to be a sign of good things to come.

Ben put down the phone. So, Beth wanted to buy her folks' house? He and Beth had only been engaged a couple of hours. Not long enough to stop and think about where they might want to live. But now he must. His work was based in Waco, a two-hour commute from Kenton Valley. As co-owner of the Merc with her sister, Beth had strong ties to the Valley. What if she didn't want to move? What if she had second thoughts about getting married?

Better they talk now than argue later.

But for now, Major Innes was due an update. No doubt he'd be pleased with how things turned out.

The urgent discussion with Beth continued to weigh on his mind. Were they about to have their first argument? An argument that could derail their entire future.

But before he called the Major, it was past time to check

on his mother and his injured ranger, Jeff Ocala.

First to check in on his mom. Ben stopped by the information desk to ask her room number.

"Adela Rasmussen?" the clerk said. "No one admitted to the hospital by that name."

"She has to be here. She was brought in earlier this afternoon by ambulance with a gunshot wound."

The clerk frowned. "What I meant to say was she was seen by the ER doctor, treated, and then discharged home. She's not here *now*."

"Thank you." He turned to leave. Dang it. Dollars to donuts, he bet his mother insisted on going home. Nothing kept her down long, not even a gunshot wound.

Dragging his cell phone from his pocket, he called the ranch. His father answered and assured Ben his mother was busy hiring a catering service in order to feed them all and to stick around for the big weekend barbeque.

"Thanks, Dad. Tell her I stopped by the hospital, and I'm glad she's doing so well. I'll see you all later."

After his dad assured his messages would be delivered, Ben headed for Ocala's room.

Not quite sure of how he'd be received, he hesitated before knocking on Ocala's door. Other than immediately after he'd been hospitalized with burns from the hotel explosion, Ben hadn't had time to check on the newbie ranger's condition. Yes, he felt guilty. More to the point, how would Ocala react?

Might as well suck it up. Ocala was due an apology. Ben tapped lightly.

"Come in."

He certainly sounded strong. Ben opened the door and

eased inside. Ocala was scooping up a cup of lime Jello with a plastic spoon. His hands were still bandaged, but the facial dressings were gone leaving the ranger with, at worst, a bad sunburn.

"Hey, boss." Ocala set aside the tiny container of gelatin and grinned.

"Ocala—Jeff, man, I owe you an apology. I've been here, but things have gotten crazy since you were burned." He removed his hat and ran a hand back through his hair. "I was here right after they brought you in, but..."

"Not a problem. I know you've had a lot going on." Ocala shot him a brave smile. "I hear you arrested a few bad guys. Wish I could've been more help."

"You heard about that, have you?" Ben nodded. Kelly had kept her partner informed. Good for her.

"Kelly..." Ocala shifted uneasily in his hospital bed.

"No problem. I'm aware you're close." He gazed down at Ocala's gauze-wrapped hands. "What does the doctor say?"

"The doc says I'm lucky. I won't need any grafts." He held up his hands. "No scarring or contractures to limit function. They're wrapped mainly to keep them from getting infected. Doc says I might need a bit of P.T. once the burns heal."

Ben let out a sigh of relief. "That's good to know. That was a real concern."

"Don't worry, boss. Before you know it, I'll be back in the saddle."

"Again, sorry, I haven't been by before now." Ben nodded, then added with a grin. "I'll let you get back to your dessert."

All things considered, his visit with Ocala had gone better than expected. The fact there would be no permanent damage was the best news. And Major Innes would be more than pleased.

Ben walked out to the parking lot. Before he could climb into the truck, his phone signaled a text. He glanced down. The text was from Will telling him Eva Johnson's funeral would be held tomorrow. Will figured Beth would want to know.

Yep, she'd want to know all right.

Beth ran up the steps to the old Victorian. She loved every curlicue and every piece of gingerbread scrollwork. The wide veranda swept around three-quarters of the house. She envisioned a new swing, a ceiling fan, and pots of ferns. The song of two wrens drifted through the air. Heavenly.

The siding would need painting next spring, but for now, it was okay. She unlocked the front door and walked into the hall. Since Sara waited until the last minute to break the lease, Beth expected to find a mess. Instead, the house was empty and cleared, not so much as a box of trash had been left behind.

She scanned the hall and then walked into the living room. Okay, the woodwork needed a good wash and fresh wall paint was in order. She moseyed into the dining room which opened into the kitchen. Maybe time for new cabinets and appliances, otherwise it was spacious, and, in spite of being over a hundred years old, the work triangle was decent. A half bath on the first floor wouldn't go amiss. Maybe there was room to tuck one under the stairway.

Now for the bedrooms. She ran upstairs. More fresh paint. And the windows could certainly do with a wash.

They'd left the bathroom clean—thank heavens. The old clawfoot tub had seen better days but it was functional. Maybe time for an update?

She checked the largest bedroom, hoping against hope that the antique chifforobe her father had inherited along with the house hadn't been moved out with the rest of the Billingsley's furniture. And it hadn't. Seven-feet tall of heavily carved solid oak, it was a monster to move, but so lovely. She opened one of the doors and pulled out a stack of folded quilts.

Giving an approving nod, she smiled. They just might come in handy.

"Beth!" Ben's voice jolted her from her reverie.

"Upstairs," she called back. His heavy footsteps came pounding up the stairs. "Here." She beckoned from the largest of the bedrooms.

"Evenin', beautiful." His smile was broad and welcoming.

Trembling, Beth gazed up into his sky-blue eyes. They were alone. After so much waiting, they were finally going to make love. And for once, no one was trying to kill either one of them.

Ben's hand brushed aside the spaghetti strap from her shoulder. He placed a tender kiss on her tanned skin.

The gentle sensation of his lips on her bare skin sent a jolt through her entire body. "Finally," she whispered.

He smiled. "You're so impatient."

"You're *too* patient."

"Patience is a virtue, so I'm told."

"Never put off 'til tomorrow what you can do today."

Ben laughed. "So, it's *today*."

"Yes. Yes, it is."

"Speaking of not putting off things..." He removed his cowboy hat and turned it around using the brim.

Was he nervous? Surely not about making love. "What?"

"We need to talk."

Had he changed his mind? "About?" Stepping back, she readjusted her strap. It seemed as if talking, not loving, was on her man's mind. Her stomach gave a nervous quiver.

His expression solemn, he began, "Two things. Eva Johnson's funeral is tomorrow. Will just texted me. He knew you'd want to know."

She sucked in a quick breath. Eva's funeral. How could she have forgotten even for a moment? "I'll have to go. Lola too. I should let her know." She reached into the pocket of her cutoffs for her phone.

Ben stayed her hand. "I have a feeling my brother will take care of telling your sister."

"Yeah. I guess you're right about that. You said, 'two things.'" She set her hands on her hips and frowned.

"Right," he said in a level tone. "Now, you said no pressure."

Beth held back the panic that threatened to consume her. "You don't want to buy this house?" How could she have been so mistaken? "Okay, I guess we can live anywhere as long as we're together." Hopefully, he wouldn't pick up on her uncertainty. But moving away from the Valley had never been on her bucket list.

"Hold on a dang minute." He took her hand in his. "We have to be logical. You know I'm assigned to Company F in Waco. That's where my job is. If we live in the Valley, that's a two-hour-plus commute."

Beth stepped back. "I never thought about that. I was just so excited by the idea of our getting married, and then the house was suddenly free..." She sank down on the stack of quilts, folding her legs. "I can't run the store from Waco. That would be a two-hour commute for me as well. What'll we do? I guess I could sell Lola my share of the store. Granted it's a burned-out shell now, but we have plans to rebuild. I'd planned on being close by for all that." She rubbed her forehead. "I was just so excited about the house." She gazed into his blue eyes. "Are we about to have our first fight?"

"No," he said quietly and sat down beside her. "Fortunately, there's a better solution. When I debriefed with the major, he said he was pretty sure I'd be offered a field lieutenant position at HQ. Austin is only a forty-five-minute drive—give or take."

"Forty-five isn't bad. But is that what you want? You'd want us to live in Austin?" Leave the Valley? Even with everything that had happened, she'd never wanted to leave her hometown.

He plopped down on the quilts beside her. "No, darlin', if it's offered, I'll take the position in HQ, and then I'll commute to the Valley. If your parents agree to sell us the house, then we should buy it."

Twisting around to face him, she threw her arms around his neck. "So, you thought you'd torture me a little bit before telling me? You're so mean! But I love you anyway. And the house, it won't take much to fix it up. Paint, a little elbow grease. And new appliances in the kitchen. Um, maybe new cabinets."

"Slow down, cowgirl. One thing at a time." He slipped the spaghetti strap down again. And then the other followed. A hard thrill ran through her body centering in her core. He kissed her neck, his breath warm gentle puffs against her skin.

A moan escaped her lips without her volition.

"Too many clothes, darlin'." He pulled up her top and tossed it aside. Reaching around he unfastened, then tossed her strapless bra.

She was so ready for this. His hands caressing her breasts, tweaking her nipples until they ached. His lips on hers. She opened and he deepened the kiss until she was dizzy. She fell back onto the folded quilts. "You're right. Help me."

"Anything to oblige," he said with a beaming smile. He tugged off her running shorts and skimmed the panties down her hips. Still holding her lace panties, he brought them to his nose and inhaled. "Pure heaven."

In spite of herself, she let out a giggle. "Really? I never took you for a panty sniffer."

"Never know what drives a man wild. And that would be *everything* about you drives me wild."

"You want wild?" She reached his shirt and ripped it open, then busied her hands on his belt buckle.

"Wild is good. Let me help." He got to his knees, shucked his jeans down, then sat and yanked them off. He toed off his boots.

"Now who's impatient?"

He gazed down at her, his blue eyes glittering with desire. "I've wanted you for a long time. Longer than you know."

"I can beat that." She splayed her hands down his muscled chest. She could feel the pounding of his heart. "I've wanted you since before I ever knew what 'wanted' meant. Eighth grade. You saved me from that bully. Remember?"

"Of course, I do. You were just too sweet and young to be tormented."

"My hero."

"You talk too much." He stopped any further attempts at conversation by kissing her and slipping his hand between her thighs.

She opened to his probing fingers. "Yes," she said to

encourage him. His every touch was magic setting her nerves afire. "Just like that," she said with a long sigh.

Moving over her, he thrust deeply inside her core. Again and again, he thrust, filling her completely. She arched to meet him stroke for stroke until the intensity grew and exploded sending them both over the edge. A kaleidoscope of color burst before her eyes. She gasped his name.

Afterward, she lay cuddled in his arms, his broad chest warming her back. "So, how do you like the house now?"

He chuckled. "Given we've already christened it, it's our duty to buy it. Agree?"

"I definitely agree." She squirmed around to face him. "Are you sure we christened it sufficiently?"

"Darlin', if there's any doubt, let's make sure." He pulled her on top of him and eased her down over his growing erection.

Her body welcomed him again. Home was where her lover was. She began to move with his hands cupping her breasts.

He bucked. "Ride, cowgirl, ride."

Chapter Eighteen

Thursday

Morning dawned bright and clear. She opened her eyes to a strange room and a strange bed. Sitting upright, she smiled. Right. The first night she'd spent in the condo. The first overnight with Ben. She glanced over at his sleeping form. Waking up in his arms—now, that she could definitely get used to.

He stirred, then yawned. "Mm." His strong arms pulled her close. "Do I smell coffee?"

"Um, maybe. Lola must be up."

He levered up onto one elbow and smiled, his blue eyes sparkling with mischief. "Did I make a big mistake? Am I sleeping with the wrong sister?"

"Doofus!" She gave him a playful whack on his broad shoulder. "I know how to make coffee, and I have other skills as well."

"Mm." His rumbling low baritone sent a thrill through her body. "I can vouch for that."

"I need a shower." She stirred, anxious to get what would be a difficult day over with. "Eva's funeral is at ten." She sighed. "I really dread seeing Sophie. I don't want to upset her, but I have to show my respect and express my condolences, no matter what."

He nuzzled her neck. "I'm going as well. I'll sit with the rest of law enforcement. But I'll be there if you need me."

She caressed his tanned cheek, relishing the slight stubble along his jaw. "Lola and I will go together. But just knowing you're there—that helps a lot."

"I love you. Where else would I be?"

Her arms snaked around his neck. She dropped a peck on his mouth. "Shower. Coffee. And in that order."

"Conserve water?"

"You betcha." She laughed, sprang from the bed, and raced to the bathroom. He caught up with her and held her tight. Heat pooled in her belly.

"You better slow down, or our long hot shower might have to be a quick cold one."

He laughed, hearty and long. Reaching inside the shower, he turned on the water, then gave her bottom a slap. "You first."

She stepped into the just-right warm spray, and he followed.

After dressing for the funeral in a charcoal gray suit and white silk blouse, Beth flew down the stairs, carrying her stilettos.

Her sister stood at the stove, scrambling eggs. "Coffee's ready." She nodded at the coffeemaker. "Where's Ben?"

Beth sat at the table and bent over to tug on her high heels. "Still getting dressed. If you can believe he takes longer than I do." Beth shrugged. "Who knew?"

A peal of laughter erupted from her sister. "I can believe it."

"I didn't expect you to cook breakfast, but I'm so glad you did."

"I figured you might need some extra sustenance...after last night."

Beth's cheeks heated. She hid her face in her hands. "Did we—?" She broke off, unable to continue.

"Luckily, the bathrooms separate our two bedrooms."

Lola eyeballed Beth. "So, how was it?"

Beth zipped her lip. "I don't kiss and tell."

"From the wide smile, I'd say pretty good."

"Wonderful," Beth said, barely breathing the word.

"I figured."

Sounds of Ben's heavy tread coming downstairs reached her. He entered carrying his cowboy hat. He set it on the counter away from the food. "Something sure smells good."

"Have a seat, Ranger." Lola ladled a heaping of eggs onto two plates.

"Aren't you eating?" Beth asked her sister.

Lola shook her head. "I had a cup of coffee. Not really hungry this morning. I just want this today to be over."

Beth nodded. "I know what you mean."

Ben reached over and covered her hand with his." Tears welled in her eyes. His silent gesture beyond touching.

The beautiful day certainly brought out the mourners in droves, Beth mused. Not surprising given that nearly everyone in town had eaten Eva's delicious cooking at one time or another. The fact she'd been murdered had only added to the swelling crowd of mourners. Beth and Lola waited until they were among the last to leave.

Beth sucked in a deep breath, hesitating. Given how angry Sophie had been right after Eva's death had been discovered, how would she react?

Causing a scene at Eva's funeral was the last thing Beth ever wanted to do. But she had to offer her condolences. Even as a formality, it had to be done.

"Come on," Lola said, grabbing her hand. "You braved being kidnapped. You braved a Russian mobster. We can do this."

At their approach, Sophie glanced up, her lips tight, her dark eyes fierce.

"I'm so sorry for your loss," Beth murmured, determined not to make a commotion.

"We miss her so much, Sophie. We loved her too," Lola said, her stern expression daring Sophie to make a fuss.

"Thank you," Sophie said, through gritted teeth.

Lola nudged Beth to move on. "She doesn't want a scene either. That's the best we can hope for."

Away from the mourners, Beth said, "Sophie has a right to be angry. Her mother never would've been killed if she hadn't worked for us."

Lola elbowed Beth. "Look. There's Ben and Will. I'm glad they came."

"Most of the local law enforcement officers came. A real tribute."

Ben walked toward her; his solemn expression lightened the closer he came. "How'd it go?" He reached for her hand. "Are you all right?"

Beth gave a sniff. "All right is relative. I still feel responsible. I won't get over that anytime soon."

"Darlin', would Eva want to you to remember her like this?"

"Eva didn't *want* to be killed by a freaking mob assassin. Will we ever know who killed her? I mean, I figure Mayor Briggs was the one who gave the order, but the actual gunman?"

"We're confident her shooter was pulled in with the rest of the Russian mob in Houston. DNA tests are pending on a sample he left behind, but it's a match to Freeman's shooter too. It's only a matter of time until we get the one who pulled the trigger."

She looked at him sharply. "I didn't know you found any

DNA at Eva's."

He leaned forward close to her ear. "Shh. We don't tell everything we know to just anyone."

She smiled. "Does that make me special?"

"It does." He gave her a hug. "Now, come on. You're invited to dinner at the Rasmussen Ranch."

"But your mother was just shot. Surely, she's not ready for company."

Ben's tan face darkened with a blush. "Didn't I tell you?"

"No."

"Must've had something else on my mind. Here's the official story: treated and released. She's home. According to dad, she's hired caterers, and she's bossing them around like an army general. They're sticking around to cook for the family's big barbeque picnic this weekend. Not the barbeque part. My dad and brothers will handle the meat."

Beth shivered. "I never would've forgiven myself if your mom had been more seriously injured."

Ben chuckled. "Now, we know it takes more than a bullet wound to keep my mom down."

"Just sayin'. I'm responsible for all this."

Aiming an elbow into Beth's ribs, Lola huffed. "Snap out of it. You're not any more responsible than I am. At the very least, it's fifty-fifty, but we all know who's responsible for the crap that came down."

"She's right," Ben said, his blush fading.

"Logically, I know you're both right. But today, of all days, when Eva is being buried, I accept that I—no, *we* played a part in her death."

***

Saturday

The Rasmussen Ranch barbeque was in full force by the time Ben and Beth arrived. Over the last few nights, he'd stayed with Beth at the condo. Nights that were full of lovemaking. Nights that assured him he hadn't made a mistake like he had last time. Nights that washed away the bad memories of a certain blonde.

Beth was everything warm and loving. And she had enough passion for three women. He never tired of her, and she couldn't seem to get enough of him.

He smiled contentedly. This was the way being in love should be. "Ready?" he asked since they'd agreed the picnic was the perfect occasion for making their big announcement. The Rasmussen barbeque was a tradition and had been for the last decade. And everyone in the county was invited. That was part of the tradition too.

She nodded. "I am if you are."

Taking her hand in his, he walked up onto the small stage where the musicians were tuning up for another song. In the audience, he was pleased to see Vince was again wearing his badge, and Abbie was by his side, glowing with her pregnancy. The case against Vince had been quickly dismissed after ex-Deputy Powell had confessed to falsifying evidence. After the mayor's arrest, Bradley, the mayor's head of Security, had skipped town so Vince was again running unopposed.

Ben tapped on the mic. "Just want to say a few words here. First, welcome. I guess my dad has already taken care of that before I got here. I have—I should say we—have an announcement to make." He took Beth's hand and pulled her close to his side. "For those who haven't already figured it out, the beautiful and brilliant Bethany Wheaton has accepted my humble hand in marriage, and y'all are invited to the wedding. That's it."

A burst of applause broke out. "How 'bout the bride-to-be, doesn't she get to say anything?" his brother Jack heckled from the sideline.

"I figured this was my only chance to get a word in first," he quipped. He smiled down at her. "Just kidding."

Ben reached for the mic and adjusted it for Beth. "There's not much else can I say," she said. "I snagged the bravest Texas Ranger in the state..." She paused then continued, "...as well as the handsomest." She returned his smile. "He's a great kisser too."

What else could he do but kiss his darlin'? Their friends and neighbors sounded their approval with thunderous applause.

He leaned down and whispered in her ear. "This is the life. Our life, darlin'."

"And I wouldn't have it any other way." She squeezed his hand, happiness shining from her chocolate brown eyes.

More reassurance that he'd made the right decision this time. This blonde was a keeper.

Epilogue

Six months later, Beth and Ben stood in front of the newly rebuilt Mercantile and Bistro. With Ben's arm around her, happiness filled every cell in her body. Her baby bump wasn't visible yet, but it soon would be. "Are you happy?" she asked.

He gazed down at her with a warmth that set her heart to thrumming. "Happy beyond belief."

"I can't believe your mom has agreed to be our temporary cook." Indeed, Adela had even suggested the arrangement. "I could work from that morning coffee-break time until after lunch. Would it help?"

Would it help? Oh, heavens, yes, it would.

"I can't quite believe it either," Ben said. "She's never worked outside the home."

"She's adorable. She even came in and helped with stocking the shelves."

"That's because she thinks highly of the new daughter-in-law who's about to have her first grandchild."

Beth smiled. "That does give me an edge."

He smiled down at her, his blue eyes glimmering with love. "I like it when you're smug."

"Are you happy at Headquarters?"

A broad smile wreathed his face. "It's a win-win. Who could argue with a promotion to headquarters field lieutenant and a raise in pay? This way we can put down roots here in the same county where we grew up."

"Yes, this is what I've always wanted to raise our family here. Just imagine, a new generation of lawmen—or women," she added with a smile. "Just think, Vince and Abbie's little boy and our baby will grow up together." She rubbed her belly. "The only bad thing is the casino will still open three months from now. You hate that."

"True." He grimaced. "We've struck a hard blow against organized crime, but the casino means we'll have to stay on guard."

"I'd say you definitely struck a very hard blow at the heart of organized crime with the ex-mayor and the Makarovs in jail waiting for trial, along with the hitman who killed Eva and shot Matt Freeman as well. Thank God for DNA."

"Two out of three. Lots of room for improvement." Ben shook his head. "Reyes is still in Mexico."

"Pfft, let 'im stay there."

Ben smiled broadly. "But his son is incarcerated and singing like a canary."

"I never liked him."

"You could've fooled me." He pressed a kiss on her forehead. "Seriously, the casino and Reyes are the reason HQ has decided to open a Ranger office in the Valley. Dave Stirling will man it."

"Best of all, Zoe is out of our hair for the near and probably distant future."

Ben chuckled. "I wonder where she'll end up after she testifies? I hope Wit. Sec. moves her to the farthest corner of the country."

"Fargo, North Dakota would be nice." Beth a theatrical sigh. "How will she ever manage without her father's money and influence?"

"Like the rest of us. She'll have to work for a living."

Beth gazed up at her husband, her handsome, wonderful husband. "Let's go home. The Merc will be open for business tomorrow. I need a good night's sleep."

And *home* was the house where she'd grown up. As planned, she and Ben had purchased it from her parents with Lola's blessing. Now that the store had been rebuilt, along with the apartment above, Lola had the apartment to herself. She'd already decorated it in what she called cowgirl-chic—whatever that was.

"Bedtime it is then," he agreed with a twinkle in his sky-blue eyes. "Not sure how much sleep you'll get, though."

Her heart filled with love for this man. Every single time he kissed her or held her or made love to her, it was like the first time. "Then I'll enjoy losing sleep, as long as you're the one who's making me lose it."

The End

About Marie-Nicole Ryan

Marie-Nicole Ryan was born in a small western Kentucky town, but after college and marriage, she said "Goodbye" to small-town life. After spending three years as an army wife, she landed in Nashville, TN, where she spent several decades working as an R.N. and case manager. Finally, in 2002, she achieved her dream of becoming a published author.

She loves writing about lawmen and detectives and writes contemporary romantic suspense, as well as erotic historical western romance. TOO GOOD TO BE TRUE, won a 2008 EPPIE for erotic romantic suspense. In addition, her mystery/suspense novel, ONE TOO MANY, was a 2009 EPPIE Finalist.

She was an active member of RWA® for many years, as well as PAN, MCRW, and PASIC. Currently, she lives in western Kentucky. When she's not slaving away at her current work in progress, you might find her walking her dog Kelsea, a Sheltie rescue, or at the Y. But you won't ever find her in an airplane. No, not ever.